Volume 2

The Devil's Shield

Also by Leo Kessler and available from
Spellmount Publishers in
The Dogs of War Series

No 1   Forced March
No 3   SS Panzer Battalion
No 4   Claws of Steel

THE DOGS OF WAR SERIES VOLUME 2

THE DEVIL'S SHIELD

by

Leo Kessler

SPELLMOUNT
Staplehurst

British Library Cataloguing in Publication Data:
A catalogue record for this book is available
from the British Library

Copyright © Charles Whiting 1975, 1984, 2004

ISBN 1-86227-265-4

First published in the UK in 1975

This edition first published in the UK in 2004 by
Spellmount Limited
The Village Centre
Staplehurst
Kent TN12 0BJ

Tel: 01580 893730
Fax: 01580 893731
E-mail: enquiries@spellmount.com
Website: www.spellmount.com

1 3 5 7 9 8 6 4 2

The right of Charles Whiting to be identified
as the author of this work has been asserted by him
in accordance with the Copyright, Designs
and Patents Act 1988

Printed in Great Britain by
Bookmarque Ltd, Croydon, Surrey

Blow the bugle, beat the drum!
Clear the street, here comes the Wo-tan!
Steel is our weapon
To hew through bone.
Blood our purpose,
Wotan hold close.
For Death is our Destiny . . .'

Marching Song of SS Battle Group
Wotan, Autumn 1944.

In the grim autumn of 1944, the fifth year of the war, Colonel von Dodenburg's SS Battle Group Wotan had become the 'Führer's Fire Brigade', the elite unit of the German Wehrmacht, to be thrown into any battle as a last desperate measure to redress the balance. Its men, teenage veterans who had grown savage and brutal on the battlefields of half Europe, owed no loyalty to their nation, their Führer or their state. Their sole loyalty was to their comrades, their beloved commander and their very weapons.

Dedicated to death, knowing that their dreaded silver death's head cap badge condemned them as war criminals, they felt no fear, fighting savagely against overwhelming odds for a cause already long lost. Thus, in the grey September of that year, Colonel von Dodenburg's black-uniformed troopers came to Aachen, Germany's 'Holy City', with the Führer's order to hold it ringing in their ears. SS Battle Group Wotan was fighting on German soil at last!

Leo Kessler. Trier,
Germany, 1974.

ONE: THE HOLY CITY

'This goddam Catholic Aachen is Charlemagne's city – the heartland of Germany, *not* National Socialist Germany, *but* all Germany . . . Aachen must remain German!' *SS Police General 'Devil' Donner to Colonel von Dodenburg, September 1944.*

ONE

'FREEZE!'

Fearfully the little reconnaissance patrol dropped into the damp grass at the river's edge, weapons gripped tightly in suddenly sweating hands, and stared hard into the little valley beyond.

The September sun was going down now. Long black shadows were sliding into the valley from the east. The silence was thick and unnatural, heavy with menace. Even the persistent rumble of the artillery to the west seemed to have vanished.

Staff Sergeant Warner Holzinger, the patrol leader, who had rapped out the order, raised himself cautiously on one knee and stared at the wrecked bridge which led across the border river and into the valley. The Krauts had destroyed it only hours before. They had heard the thick crump of the explosion distinctly as they had felt their way carefully behind the retreating Krauts. That he knew for certain. What he didn't know was whether they were now hidden up on the darkening heights, waiting for his little patrol from the US 5th Armored Division to cross into their territory before beginning the slaughter.

'What do you think, Sarge?' Corporal Driver asked as he crouched next to him, grease-gun at the ready. 'That stream sure looks deep. Hell, the whole goddam place gives me the creeps! Shall we hightail it out of here?'

Sergeant Holzinger licked his scummed, cracked lips, 'Listen, fellers,' he whispered, 'You know the CO's screaming for info. He'll screw us real hard if we goof off now. We've got to check the place out. You know that, don't you?' He looked hopefully around the little patrol's worn unshaven faces. But his men avoided his eyes. Holzinger knew they were as scared as he was. Still they weren't noncoms. They didn't have to make the goddam decisions. He did.

'Okay then,' he commanded, raising his voice. 'This is the deal. I'm going to check the creek out. Frenchie,' he nodded to their French guide. 'You give me cover. Once we're across, the rest of you guys follow. And get the lead out of yer asses. I don't want the Krauts catching you in mid-stream with yer skivvies down. Get me?'

Raising his .30 carbine to his chest, the young American

8

sergeant stepped cautiously into the fast-flowing border stream. Slowly and carefully he started to wade into it, followed by a tense, half-crouched Frenchie. The icy water reached up to his knees. Then his thighs. He was half way across now. Still no sudden, high-pitched burst of mg fire from the other side. Nothing, just a faint icy wind heralding the night.

Holzinger struggled on, fighting the current and the slippery stones underfoot. The water began to recede. It fell to the level of his rubber-soled combat boots. With a last grunt, he tugged his right foot clear and stepped on to the muddy bank – 'a historic moment,' the *Stars and Stripes*[1] was going to call it later – carbine pressed tightly against his hip, ready for trouble. But still there was no sign of the Germans. Sergeant Holzinger wasted no further time. He spread the fingers of his hand out on the crown of his helmet – the infantry signal for 'rally on me' – and started up the steep slope, followed by a still tense Frenchie. Moments later the rest of the reccon patrol had joined him and, like the combat veterans they were, had spread out in the attack formation, advancing cautiously up the darkening hillside to what looked like a cluster of poor, rundown farm buildings.

But their caution was unnecessary. When they reached them, they found them empty, obviously hastily abandoned by the fleeing Germans only hours before. They found more too. They weren't farm buildings, but cunningly camouflaged bunkers, their walls behind the rotten wooden slats thick slabs of ferroconcrete.

'Jeez, sarge,' Driver breathed, running his flashlight around the dripping grey walls, unbroken save for the gun slits. 'You know what this place is?' Holzinger shook his head, as puzzled by his discovery as the rest of the reccon platoon.

'It's the Siegfried Line. We've gone and penetrated the goddam Kraut Siegfried Line!'

Holzinger's mouth dropped open as he absorbed the information. 'Brother,' he exclaimed suddenly, his face lighting up, 'I think you're goddam right! Wait till the CO hears this!'

In the cold gloom of the bunker, heavy with the stench of German soldiers' black tobacco and unwashed bodies, they grinned jubilantly at each other. But Holzinger knew there was no further time to be wasted. He pulled the walkie-talkie from Private Locke's shoulder and pressed the speech switch.

'Hello Sunray One,' he called urgently, 'Hello Sunray One.

1. GI newspaper.

Charlie One here . . . Do you read me? Sunray One, do you read me? Over.'

The little instrument crackled into life and the CO's voice came through distinctly from his forward CP on the Luxembourg side of the border. 'Hello Charlie One . . . hello Charlie One, reading you loud and clear. Over!'

Sergeant Holzinger hesitated, aware suddenly of the significance of the message he would now give through. He cleared his throat. 'Hello Sunray . . . hello Sunray. Charlie One speaking. Time eighteen zero fire hours, eleven September forty-four.' He coughed. 'Charlie Patrol has just crossed into Germany northeast of Stalzemburg. We have penetrated Objective A. No opposition. Positions abandoned by the enemy. Over!' For a long moment there was silence, broken only by the static and the tense breathing of the men crowded round Holzinger in the centre of the German bunker. Then the CO's voice came through loud and excited, radio procedure thrown to the wind.

'Holzinger, you goddam lucky sonuvabitch! You've just become the first goddam enemy soldier in history to cross into Kraut territory since the days of that frog Napoleon!' The CO gasped for breath. 'Now get your butts back on over here, while you've still gotten them in one piece. I want you to tell this particular bit of info to the commanding general *personally*! Hot shit, Holzinger, he's gonna be tickled pink that it was his division of the whole goddam Allied Army which was the first to penetrate into Kraut country. Now move it! Over and out.'

'Roger and out,' Holzinger snapped, thrusting the walkie-talkie into Locke's hands.

The sergeant needed no further urging to get out of the bunker and back to their White[1] hidden in some pines on the Luxembourg side of the Our.

'Okay guys,' he announced. 'Appears we've gone and made history or something. Now let's get the hell out of here – this place is colder than a well-digger's ass. And I just don't trust them Krauts . . .'

As the Amis scrambled down the hillside, slipping on the suddenly dew-soaked grass in their haste to get back to their White before the sinister little valley was completely dark, the little

1. White Scout Car, standard reconnaissance vehicle in US Army in World War II.

bespectacled signaller, who had stayed behind, rose from his hiding place. He breathed out hard with relief and wiped the sweat off his dirty, earth-stained brow with the sleeve of his tattered grey uniform jacket. He would have dearly loved to have had a smoke. But he knew there was no time and his hands were trembling like leaves as it was. He would not have been able to hold one of the Wehrmacht issue cancer-sticks. Besides he didn't have one. He had smoked his last one after Lieutenant Rausch had ordered him to stay behind and report while he withdrew the rest of their decimated, demoralised battalion. Trying to control his trembling, he whirled the handle of the field telephone.

Cupping his hand over the mouthpiece, as if he were afraid that the Amis now wading through the stream might hear him, he whispered, 'Can you hear me, sir?'

'Of course, I can hear, you four-eyed shithouse,' Lieutenant Rausch's familiar, schnapps-thickened voice answered. 'I might not be altogether right in the head for not getting out of the stubble-hoppers, but I'm not shitty well deaf. Get on with it, Meier, what have you to report?'

'Beg obediently to report,' the little signaller began, using the traditional Army formula for addressing an officer.

But Rausch cut him short with a, 'Go shit in the wind, man! What did you see?'

'Ami panzer troops, Lieutenant. Just one armoured car. But I could hear the noise of a lot of tracked vehicles on the other side of the river. They're out there in force, sir. Now can I come back?'

Rausch did not answer his plea for a moment. Instead the signaller, who had been with the officer ever since they had started the long, bloody, panic-stricken retreat from France at the beginning of August, heard his CO sigh heavily as if he were weighed down with the cares of the Führer himself.

Then Rausch said wearily 'Well, Meier, you pale-faced pineapple-shitter, you know what this means, don't you?'

Meier, who knew that the CO meant the expression to be regarded as a form of endearment, was not offended.

'No, sir, what does it mean?'

'It means, you horned ox, that tonight or tomorrow morning, those sodding Amis will start the attack on Aachen and that by tomorrow night you and I will be running for our precious lives once more.' The CO's voice dropped almost to a whisper. 'The dream's over, Meier. The glorious Greater German Wehrmacht is beaten at last.'

TWO

'Will you just take a look, sir, at those rotten currant-crappers,' Schulze groaned, as the line of infantry holding the heights broke finally and began to run. 'The whole shitty lot of stubble-hoppers are beating it.' He spat contemptuously and looked at his young blond CO perched next to him on the deck of the Royal Tiger. 'What the hell are we going to do with a bunch of wet sacks like that, sir? I ask you.'

Colonel von Dodenburg, the commander of SS Battle Group Wotan, drawn up in readiness in the thick, fragrant pine wood, five kilometres west of Aachen, took his eyes off the ragged line of panic-stricken infantry streaming across the plain towards them. An officer was unsuccessfully trying to hold them back. The guns of the US VII Corps were beginning to plaster them. Soon the enemy Jabos[1] would add weight to the softening up prior to an all-out Ami attack on the old Imperial City.

'Wet sacks, did I hear you say, Sergeant-Major Schulze?' he queried calmly, as if he were watching a movie and not the breakdown of the German line in front of Aachen. 'I'm a little surprised at you – a senior NCO in the Armed SS's most elite formation – saying such a thing.'

The big-shouldered, ex-Hamburg docker, who had served with von Dodenburg on every European front since the Wotan's earliest days, made an obscene gesture, thrusting his thumb between his two big fingers.

'That's what I think of those African warthogs out there, sir,' he said contemptuously.

The handsome, aristocratic colonel, clad in a black leather jacket, devoid of any decoration save the gleaming black and white enamel of the Knight's Cross of the Iron Cross with palms and jewels, smiled. But there was no answering warmth in his hard blue eyes. 'Those – er – African warthogs as you describe them, my dear Schulze, are German soldiers. The same men who marched to Moscow, conquered half of Europe, are fighting against a world in arms. All they are doing is what I believe our

1. Fighter planes used as dive-bombers.

12

leaders call so delicately, a "correction of the front". Tut, tut, Schulze, how can you say such things about the Führer's beloved stubble-hoppers?'

'And if I may humbly make the observation, Colonel – the Colonel is a cynic, sir.'

Von Dodenburg's reply was drowned by the screech of the Ami Jabos streaking in at 500 kilometres per hour. Angry purple lights crackled along the length of their wings. The fleeing stubble-hoppers scattered wildly. The vicious red and white tracer sliced yawning cavities in their ranks. Men went down everywhere, arms flailing, screaming as the Ami Lightnings swooped high into the grey September sky, twisting and turning exuberantly at the success of their sudden strike.

Still the rest of the retreating stubble-hoppers came on, stamping over the bodies of their dead and dying comrades, pressing them deeper into the mud, ignoring their fervent pleas in their frantic attempt to escape.

'Stand by!' Colonel von Dodenburg yelled, swinging round to check that the black-clad crews with the gleaming SS runes and death's head on their collars were alert and ready.

Lightly he dropped off the tank's deck and pushed his way through the bushes into the open. Feet spread apart, hands clasped on his hips, apparently oblivious to the Ami artillery barrage, he waited for the fugitives to reach their positions.

'Great crap on the Christmas Tree,' Schulze groaned. 'Here we fucking well go again!'

Nevertheless he followed his CO into the open, signalling the crews of the leading Tigers to join him. Now they formed a long silent line, machine-pistols unslung and at the ready, as the first of the stubble-hoppers came running towards them, chests heaving violently, helmets and rifles gone, one thought uppermost in their panic-numbed minds – escape! A boy drew level with them. His eyes were wide with fear, his hair tousled and disordered, his breath coming in short, leaden-lunged gasps.

'*Stop!*' von Dodenburg commanded.

The boy did not hear him. He blundered on, hands stretched in front of him like a blind man.

'Schulze!' von Dodenburg bellowed without turning round.

The big Hamburger thrust out his foot. The boy stumbled over it and fell full length. Schulze kicked him in the side of the head. He sprawled unconscious on the ground. Now the fugitives were everywhere, trying to break through the line of grim-faced, black-clad SS men.

'The Amis,' they gasped and wheezed. 'The Amis – they're coming . . . on the other side of the hill . . .'

'Stop them!' von Dodenburg thundered, still not taking his eyes off the heights over which the first Amis were expected at any moment.

The black-clad SS men raised their butts and drove them into the faces and bodies of the panic-stricken stubble-hoppers.

'Hey, give over,' a fat-faced stubble-hopper with grey hair shouted. 'We're German just like—' The words died abruptly in a mouthful of hot blood and shattered teeth. He staggered back, clutching his ruined mouth, his eyes wide and damp-gleaming with shocked outrage and pain. A young SS soldier slammed his nailed boot into the man's crotch. The SS man did not even look down. He stepped over the fallen stubble-hopper, writhing in agony in the mud, and crashed his butt into the next one's face.

In a matter of moments the rout had been stopped and the surviving stubble-hoppers were standing there, crestfallen, their bleeding, battered faces staring down at their comrades lying moaning in the mud.

As the first Ami Shermans breasted the hill with the infantry crowded behind them in tight frightened tails, Schulze bellowed: 'All right, you perverted banana suckers, get in that ditch! And don't a one of you dare to stir out of it till I tell you to.' He raised his hamlike right fist. 'Because if you do, you're gonna get a knuckle sandwich which will keep you from getting hungry for a month of Sundays. Now come on, you jam-shitting stubble-hoppers – *move it*!'

They needed no urging. Like a pack of frightened mice they scurried for the cover of the rain-filled drainage ditch, blocked by the bloated body of a dead cow, lying there with its legs sticking upwards like a tethered balloon. The SS men followed, running to their sixty-ton steel monsters. The long hooded cannon swung round. Hatch covers were dropped. The twin air-cooled machine guns focused on the Ami infantry.

The enemy barrage covering the advancing Shermans crept closer and closer. Two hundred metres. One fifty. One hundred metres!

'Stand fast!' von Dodenburg rapped over the command tank's mike. 'Here it comes!'

As the stubble-hoppers pressed themselves ever deeper into the mud of the stinking drainage ditch, the enemy barrage descended upon the wood in which the Wotan tanks were hidden with an elemental roar. Tree bursts, von Dodenburg noted automatically. The Amis thought they were faced only by infantry. He smiled coldly in spite of the earth-shaking thunder crack and howl of red-hot slivers of steel striking against the Tiger's metal sides. The Amis were soon going to be in for an unpleasant surprise.

In the drainage ditch, the stubble-hoppers screamed, sobbed and sweated with fear as the shrapnel whizzed over their heads. Meier felt his bowels open. Hot liquid ran down his legs. The air was filled with a disgusting stench.

'Holy God in heaven,' he screamed, 'let it end . . . *please*.' The next instant, his wish was granted. A hunk of gleaming metal sliced his head off neatly, sending it rolling to the bottom of the ditch, complete with issue glasses.

Next to him Rausch felt the hot vomit well up into his mouth. While the severed head seemed to watch him with unruffled calm through the glasses, Lieutenant Rausch retched violently.

And then the barrage had moved on, leaving the wood full of fallen branches hanging from the pines like newly severed limbs. The Amis had not spotted them after all. Colonel von Dodenburg did not hesitate. The Amis were completely out in the open.

'What a sight for the gods, Schulze,' he cried enthusiastically, 'a whole Ami battalion lined up as if they were on parade and not a bit of cover within the nearest two hundred metres!' Thrusting back the hatch-cover, sending the shrapnel lying on it flying, he drew out the Very pistol and fired in the same instant.

The red signal flare hissed into the morning sky and hung there for what seemed an age, bathing the battlefield in its unreal, flickering light. Then it started to sink down to earth again. It was the signal that the thirty gunners of Battle Group Wotan had been waiting for ever since they had taken up their positions two hours before. The great 88 mm cannon crashed into action as one. The first Ami company advancing down the slope ran right into the salvo. They disappeared, as if they had been brushed aside by a gigantic hand. Still the tanks came on, attempting vainly to steer their way through the sudden holes and the great piles of khaki-clad dead.

Von Dodenburg, standing upright on the turret of the Royal Tiger, glasses focused on the slaughter, fired the second flare with his free hand. The wood was bathed a sickly green. The gunners reacted at once. They thrust home the AP shells which the signal demanded.

The 88s thundered again. The white blobs sped towards the Shermans, curving slightly and growing faster at every moment. Suddenly the Ami tank-drivers realised they had run into a trap. Desperately they tried to avoid the armour-piercing shells, but in vain. A couple of Shermans smashed into each other as their drivers panicked. Another swung round in a cloud of mud and pebbles and ploughed into the following infantry, cutting a great swathe through the screaming GIs.

Metal struck metal with a hollow boom. The first Sherman came to an abrupt halt. Its 75-mm gun sank suddenly like the falling head of a dying animal. Another rocked as if in a great storm as it was struck too, and thick white smoke started to pour from its engine. Evil little flames licked the paint off its metal sides. With a roar, the Sherman disappeared in a blinding yellow light. When the SS men looked again, the Ami tank had vanished completely save for one lonely boogie wheel sailing slowly through the air.

But they had no time for the uncanny sights of the battlefield. Most of the cover Shermans had been hit and were burning fiercely now as their terrified crews made frantic attempts to get out of the escape hatches before their 'ronsons' exploded for good.[1] They turned their attention to the infantry.

The 7.62 twin machine guns started to chatter. A stream of green and white tracer winged its way towards the Amis. Some threw themselves on to the ground and von Dodenburg could see the bullets striking their defenceless bodies over and over again. Others tried to run and were caught in mid-stride, throwing up their arms in extravagant gestures, spines arched in exquisite agony before they were thrown into the mud by the remorseless stream of lead. But mostly they just cowered there behind the burning Shermans, allowing themselves to be slaughtered.

Then from the other side of the height came the soft plops, followed seconds later by the howl of the Ami 3-inch mortars.

1. i.e. Ronson lighter. Because the 30-ton Sherman was easily set on fire, it was nicknamed the 'ronson' by its disgusted crews.

Bombs exploded everywhere in front of the trapped infantry, pouring thick grey smoke, masking the Amis from the German gunners. One by one the machine-guns ceased their deadly chatter. Finally von Dodenburg fired his last flare – the signal for ceasefire.

He grabbed the plug-in mike at the side of command tank's turret and cried urgently, 'To all gunners – cease fire. Do you read me – cease fire now! We've got a long war in front of us, boys, and we'll need all the ammo we can lay our shitty fingers on!'

Standing beside him on the turret, his face blackened by cannonfire, Schulze laughed. 'You can say that again, sir! We'll still be fighting this war when we've all been long in hell.'

Von Dodenburg laughed bitterly. 'Hell, Schulze? Why hell is too good a place for the men of Wotan!'

Half an hour later, the Amis had retreated over the height back into Belgium; the only sign that they had ever dared to approach German soil were the still burning Shermans on the hillside and the muddy field littered with their khaki-clad dead. Swiftly von Dodenburg re-organised the shattered stubble-hoppers into the semblance of a defence force. Arming them with whatever weapons they could pick up from the Amis and allowing them to loot the dead for Hershey bars, Camel cigarettes and all the other luxuries with which the Amis always seemed equipped, he ordered them back to their original positions on the height. But he knew they would break again under the next US attack unless they were more frightened of him than of the enemy. An example had to be made.

'One which will frighten them shitless, Schulze,' he explained to the Wotan's senior NCO, 'so that they'd rather allow the Amis to shoot their eggs off than face me for running away.'

He ordered that the stubble-hoppers' CO be brought to him, a senior lieutenant with one arm and his dirty mud-stained tunic covered with the 'tin' of five years of war.

'You've been around, I see,' the SS officer said. 'Narvik Medal, the Frozen Flesh Order,[1] Wound Medal in Silver, Bronze Combat Badge, Sevastopol Medal. Hm. But why didn't you try to stop your men running away?'

Rausch stared blankly at the handsome, black-clad SS

1. Award given to German soldiers who had taken part in the terrible Russian winter campaign of 41–42.

colonel, who looked as if he had just stepped out of one of those Armed SS recruiting posters which one saw everywhere in the battered Third Reich these days.

Patiently, von Dodenburg repeated his question. Still the infantry officer did not answer. His mind was full of Meier's headless body and the bespectacled head staring up at him from the bloody rainwater at the bottom of the ditch. Von Dodenburg drew back his hand and slapped the infantry man squarely across the face. It wasn't a hard blow, but it had the desired effect. The stubble-hopper shook his head, as if he were just coming out of a trance.

'What did you say?' he asked thickly through vomit-caked dry lips.

'I asked you why you didn't try to stop your men from running away?'

The stubble-hopper shrugged.

Von Dodenburg hit him again. This time harder. A thin trickle of blood flowed from his right nostril and his eyes were suddenly liquid with pain. 'I can see that this is the only method of talking with you, Lieutenant. I asked you a question – please be good enough to answer it. Why?'

'Why? Everyone knows why, Colonel. Just look around you.' He waved a dirty hand at the survivors of his battalion. 'Old men from the stomach battalions and young kids from the Hitler Youth who are still wet behind the spoons. You can't fight with such material.' He pressed his worn face closer to von Dodenburg. 'Believe me, you can't fight a war with that kind of man. The army's finished and the war's over for Germany—' He broke off abruptly, as von Dodenburg swung round, leaving him standing there.

'Schwarz,' he bellowed. 'Major Schwarz, to me at once!'

His adjutant, a one-armed dark-haired major with burning, crazy eyes pushed his way through the crowd of gaping SS troopers watching their CO 'making a sow' of this pig of a stubble-hopper.

'Sir,' he snapped, coming to attention as if he were back on the parade ground of the SS Officer Academy at Bad Toelz. 'At your command!'

'Get a detail with a rope, Schwarz, and take care of this matter. The officer in question has been found guilty of cowardice under fire, defeatism and lack of moral fibre. The sentence is death by hanging. You will execute it immediately.'

'Sir!'

There was a gasp of horror from the stubble-hoppers. But there was no expression on Rausch's face. He accepted his fate, as if he had been expecting it all along.

Five minutes later, Rausch was hanging from the nearest tree, his tongue protruding from his purple lips, his eyes bulging from their sockets, his worn grey breeches wet where he had evacuated his bladder with the intense pain. A rough-and-ready placard hung from his neck, reading: 'I was a defeatist and coward. I have suffered a just fate. Let this be a warning to all defeatists and cowards.' Now he swung back and forth gently in the morning wind, while the stubble-hoppers stared up at their former CO in wide-eyed horror. Von Dodenburg took a last look at them. He was satisfied that they would hold now, whatever the Amis cared to throw at them. But still one couldn't be too sure.

'Just to make certain that your patriotic fervour will not diminish during my absence elsewhere,' he said, 'Officer-Cadet Krause here will have orders to shoot the culprit out of hand.' He pointed to the skinny cadet, whose black tunic was already adorned with the Iron Cross and the Wound Medal in Silver, despite his seventeen years.

Krause grinned cheekily and toyed with his Walther pistol significantly.

'But,' von Dodenburg added, 'I'm quite sure now that you have all seen the errors of your previous conduct and will never again allow the Amis to set foot on the sacred soil of the Reich.' He swung round to his hard-faced, waiting veterans. 'Mount up!' he yelled at the top of his voice.

With the skill acquired in months and years of practice, the black-clad men of Wotan clambered easily on to their vehicles and swung into their positions.

'Start up!' von Dodenburg waved his arm in a great circle.

Schulze passed him his goggles. Hurriedly he pulled them down over his eyes, as all along the edge of the shattered wood, the great 360-hp engines burst into crazy life, sending metre-long streams of purple flame from their twin exhausts. The air was suddenly full of the acrid stench of diesel.

'Move off!' von Dodenburg yelled and grabbed the turret ring as his own Royal Tiger started to rattle forward.

Behind him the rest of the sixty-ton monsters began to follow suit. The stubble-hoppers scattered out of the way as the broad steel tracks showered them with mud and pebbles. But Colonel von Dodenburg had no further eyes for them. His hard, embittered gaze was fixed on the round gleaming tower of the church in the far distance. Aachen's cathedral, in which the bones of the great Charlemagne, the father of Germany's glory, were housed: the bones of the Frankish warrior who had made the border city, which now stood squarely in the path of the Ami armies, a holy place for all Germans. Suddenly that old fervent belief in the righteousness of Germany's cause swept over von Dodenburg. He thought it had been destroyed in him completely by his knowledge of the corruption and defeatism of some of the powerful men who ran the Third Reich in this fifth year of war. But now he felt as he had in those heady victorious days of 1940, as a young lieutenant, when it had seemed that nothing could stop a reborn, revitalised Germany from conquering Europe and, with its bright new National Socialist creed, give a new lease of life to a tired old continent.

As his eager young veterans of Battle Group Wotan in their great tanks swung into line behind him and began to rattle towards the city to which the Führer himself had ordered them, Colonel Kuno von Dodenburg promised himself grimly that no enemy soldier would ever set foot in Holy Aachen.

THREE

'*Heil Hitler!*'

The tall, emaciated man standing at the shattered window of the Aachen Battle HQ, dressed in the black uniform of an SS Police General, did not react to the new 'Hitler Greeting,' which everyone in the Wehrmacht had been forced to use instead of the traditional salute since the abortive July Putsch.[1]

Colonel von Dodenburg looked inquiringly at Schwarz to his right and then at Schulze to his left. Schulze tapped his right temple in silence, as if the Police General's silence was yet another symptom of Donner's well-known craziness.

'So you too think I haven't got all my cups in the cupboard, Sergeant-Major?' General Donner asked tonelessly, still not turning round to face the three Wotan men. He laughed,

1. The attempt on Hitler's life by the Werhsmacht generals in July 1944. (Transl.).

humourlessly. 'Do not feel embarrassed. You are in a goodly company, including that of the greatest captain of all times.[1] Who else but a crazy man would take over the command of the defence of a place like Aachen! It's a one-way ticket to heaven, isn't it – or, perhaps better, hell?'

Then von Dodenburg realised how the General had seen Schulze's disrespectful gesture. A small mirror was attached to the window in front of him.

'Ah, my dear Colonel, you've spotted it – my little trick eh? Very necessary in the Third Reich in this year of 1944, believe you me. It is a wise person who knows what is going on behind his back and takes precautions accordingly. Like this!' Donner's foot shot out. He pressed a brass button let into the floor. The next instant a great opaque sheet of what looked like glass crashed down from the ceiling and formed a barrier between the three soldiers and the man at the window. 'Bullet-proof glass, gentlemen,' Donner said, amused at the shock on their faces. 'A little trick of mine, which usually impresses my visitors. And it does take the edge off the initial impact of this handsome mug of mine.'

In that same instant he turned and von Dodenburg gasped with horror. The General was a mutilated monster. Half his face had been shot away, a glass eye fixed for ever in a stiff unwinking stare in the livid pink hole. His mouth was a thin mauve line without lips in which the great false teeth were visible right to their bright red plastic gums. With a shell-shattered arm from which the hand hung like a withered black talon, Donner gestured towards his ruined face. 'The Ukraine in forty-two, gentlemen. Partisan attack. Forty thousand Ivans had gone up the chimney that year.[2] The cost? Very low. I was made into a monster whose own wife has screaming fits when her husband feels one of those nasty male urges and is forced to remind her of her marital obligations.'

Colonel von Dodenburg pulled himself together with difficulty. 'Colonel von Dodenburg reporting obediently for duty,' he snapped, using the traditional address. 'Battle Group Wotan under command. Fifteen hundred effectives. Thirty Tigers presently in position. The panzer grenadier element following on foot from Dueren. *Sir!*'

General Donner waved him to stand at ease and sized the

1. Satirical reference to Hitler.
2. Chimney – SS slang for concentration camp ovens.

handsome young SS officer up for a few moments before speaking. 'I have heard a great deal of the Wotan. Even we rear-echelon stallions sometimes take a little interest in the activities of you front swine. The capture of Eben Emael in forty – now I'm afraid in Ami hands, if my Intelligence is not mistaken. The surprise crossing of the River Bug in forty-one at the beginning of Barbarossa.[1] Russia and then Cassino this year. An impressive record. No wonder they call the Wotan the Führer's Fire Brigade, sent wherever there is a blaze.'

'We are no different from the rest of the formation, sir,' von Dodenburg said while Schwarz nodded his agreement. 'We share the same spirit. It is just that my men are more experienced than those in other SS units.'

Donner swung round on him stiffly and von Dodenburg could see that his ruined body was supported by some kind of metal corset underneath the immaculate black uniform. 'My dear Colonel, I hear a lot of rubbish talked about the spirit of the SS. I shit on the spirit of the SS!'

Schwarz, the fanatical Nazi, who had been turned nearly crazy by the discovery that he was half Jew, looked shocked. But the Police General went on.

'They are as good or as bad, as corrupt or as loyal, as the rest of our nation is in this fifth year of war.'

'Corrupt, sir?' von Dodenburg queried, avoiding Donner's glassy stare.

'Don't try to fool me, Colonel! I may be a little crazy, but I'm not that crazy. You know and I know that our system is rotten. Since July everybody can't help but notice it. Even in the ranks of black élite there are those who are paid to betray their corps, their folk comrades, their very nation to save their precious skins or positions.' The bitter tone went out of his metallic voice which, like his face and body, seemed yet another artificial product of the military surgeons in Berlin. 'That is why I asked the Reich Main Security Office[2] for your formation, von Dodenburg. My dear Colonel I have not been a police officer for most of my life for nothing, you know.' He tapped the withered black claw on the sheaf of papers lying on his desk and at the same moment pressed the button which sent his safety device shooting back into the ceiling. 'I have all I need to know about you and your men in these documents.'

1. Operational name for the invasion of Russia.
2. Berlin HQ of the SS.

'And that is, sir?'

'That your men are trained killers, men who have no loyalty to anyone but their comrades and their regiment – the Wotan.' He looked at von Dodenburg keenly. 'There is only one gap in my information. To whom do you owe your loyalty?'

Schulze caught his breath and tightened his grip on the Schmeisser machine-pistol which hung from his neck. Ever since the July Plot he had appointed himself the CO's unofficial body-guard, a necessary precaution in a Germany lousy with informers and Gestapo spies. They could make a simple wet fart into a statement of disloyalty to the Führer, and that could mean being garrotted to death by chicken wire in some stinking Gestapo cellar. Would his handsome young CO put his foot in it with this monstrous-looking policeman?

'To whom do I owe my loyalty?' von Dodenburg echoed. 'Why, I owe it to the men of Wotan in the first place and then to Germany.'

Donner's thin mauve line of a mouth puckered into the sem-blance of a smile. 'Good, von Dodenburg. This is exactly what I wanted to hear from you. Excellent. It is for that reason that I have volunteered for this command. This goddam Catholic Aachen is Charlemagne's city — the heartland of Germany, not National Socialist Germany, but *all* Germany. If it falls to the Amis, the rest will not be long in following. For two reasons – the door to the Reich will be opened for good and the psycho-logical effect will kill the man in the street's will to resist. Aachen must remain German.' He pointed the withered claw at von Dodenburg and the young officer felt the blond hairs rise at the nape of his neck. 'And you and your Wotan will help me to ensure that it does. Now let us get down to business.'

As they grouped themselves around the big wall map and tried to forget the roar and thunder of the Ami barrage which was already pounding the town's suburbs, the Police General briefed them on the situation.

'Aachen stands directly in the path of the US First Army. At present its commander, the Ami Hodges, is grouping his three corps on the Reich's frontier with Belgium and Holland, here and here.' He placed the blackened claw on the map. 'But it is more likely that he will try to break into the Aachen Gap with this corps here – the Seventh – commanded by an Ami named Collins. Lightning Joe, I believe they call him. With the kind of enemy the good General Collins will find opposing him in and around Aachen, it will not be too difficult to justify such a nickname.'

He drew breath and they could hear the air wheeze through his ravaged lungs. 'In essence, I have one good division to defend Aachen – von Schwerin's 116th Panzer out in the forest area to the east. You may ask what an armoured division is doing out in the woods. The answer is simple. Von Schwerin has exactly ten tanks left from the débâcle in France, but his men are well trained and skilled. That is more than can be said for my force in the west. There I've got three stomach battalions, one ear-and-nose and four fortress battalions.[1] Cannon-fodder, in other words. But they'll hold out well enough as long as they've got a metre of ferro-concrete bunker in front of them, and,' he smiled, 'a company of chain-dogs[2] behind them ready to string them up at the nearest tree in case they lose their patriotic fervour'.

He took his eyes off the map and turned to the three SS men. 'Now, von Dodenburg, I want to keep your Battle Group as a mobile reserve, at least till your panzer grenadiers arrive. You will bolster up any section of the Aachen front which comes under undue pressure. Once the Amis launch their full-scale attack, the front will begin to spring leaks everywhere, believe me. But we will have to worry about that eventuality when it occurs. For the time being, I want you to take up positions in the city and carry out certain special tasks I have in mind for you.'

'And they are, sir?'

Donner did not answer for a moment. Instead he reached up with his forefinger and thumb and squeezed out the glass eye. Behind it was a deep cavity filled with red mucus. Von Dodenburg barely repressed a sound of disgust as Donner began to wipe the glass eye with an immaculate silk handkerchief.

'Blood and scum,' the Police General explained easily, 'it collects there. I have to clean it regularly. There are other, more unpleasant chores that I have to carry out in the privacy of my own quarters. Apparently the product of a surgeon's knife is not as efficient in ridding itself of its waste products as nature is.'

Casually he replaced the glass eye. Von Dodenburg thought he

1. Second-class troops grouped in special battalions according to their physical disabilities. (Transl.).

2. i.e. Military policemen, who were given the name because of their silver chains of office which they wore round their necks.

could now understand the reason for the unpleasant odour of the crippled Police General.

'Now where was I, von Dodenburg?'

'Certain special tasks?' he prompted thickly, imagining what Donner's body must look like under the immaculate black uniform, and feeling the vomit rise in his throat.

'Yes. I want you to tidy up the city.'

'Tidy up, sir?'

'Yes, there is a bloody awful situation here at the moment. As you probably know Aachen is nearly one hundred per cent black [1] and now those damn warm brothers of popes are encouraging their flock to stay behind in the city.'

'But I thought the Führer himself had ordered the evacuation of the civilian population, sir?'

'Yes, he did. So who do you think evacuated the city first, leaving the population and those mealy-mouthed masturbating priests to do exactly as they liked? No other than our brave folk-comrades of the SA, who were supposed to be in charge of the evacuation, including their courageous leader County Leader Schmeer, who is now safely lodged fifty kilometres away in Cologne. But by God, not for long!'

Schulze guffawed suddenly. 'Typical golden pheasants,' he snorted, using the soldiers' contemptuous name for the gold-braided SA leaders, 'it's the migratory season for them – they always fly away at the slightest sign of danger, General.'

Donner nodded stiffly, as if his scarred neck were worked by steel springs. 'Quite right, Sergeant-Major, but it is not too advisable to go about risking a big lip like you do. Someone might sew it up for you one day for good!'

Schulze's big grin vanished. Donner was not a man to be fooled around with.

'As a result the remaining population of Aachen – some twenty thousand – has buried itself in the ruins and cellars of the old city to wait for the Amis – those teatime soldiers – to come. Then those damned black crows will pause from fingering their genitals to use their flock as a means of putting pressure on me to declare Catholic Aachen an open city. Well, von Dodenburg, they are not going to pull that kind of trick on General Degenhardt Donner! So your first task will be to clear the old city of the civilian population. They are only useless mouths to feed.'

'And if they won't go, sir?'

1. SS expression for Catholic.

25

Donner's mouth twisted in a horrible parody of a smile. '*Won't*, the word does not exist in my vocabulary, my dear Colonel. The answer to your problem is simple.' He pulled an imaginary trigger with his forefinger. 'This is, after all, total war, if we are to believe our own little poison dwarf.[1] We shot the useless mouths in the Ukraine. What is to stop us doing the same thing in Holy Aachen?'

'Nothing, sir' von Dodenburg answered weakly.

'Fine. Then that is all for the present. Get to it, Colonel von Dodenburg.'

The dèbris-littered, shattered street, still smoking from the morning's artillery bombardment, was deserted save for two old women in rusty black looting an abandoned coal stock.

Schulze pushed his cap to the back of his big head and breathed, 'By the great whore of Buxtehude – if you'll forgive my German, gentlemen, that man in there looks like the shitty devil himself!'

Colonel von Dodenburg nodded thoughtfully. His eyes were fixed on the wall sign which had appeared everywhere these last few weeks, '*Hush, the enemy is listening*,' accompanied by the sketch of a listening Ami spy, but he was remembering Donner's horribly mutilated face.

'You might be right, Schulze,' he said at last. 'A devil – but a devil whom I think I can follow.' His voice rose with growing confidence. 'For if General Donner is a devil, I wish Germany today were full of such fighting devils.' He shouldered his Schmeisser machine pistol more comfortably. 'Come on, gentlemen, let's see if we can't sort out those shitty civilians now.'

FOUR

Aachen was dying. The two hundred Flying Fortresses, which had carried out the afternoon raid with such cold, majestic detachment, were flying back to their bases in England, as von Dodenburg's 'hunting commandos' started to penetrate the shattered old city to root out the civilians. As the smoke started to drift away, Aachen appeared before them in stark, macabre

1. Wartime nickname for the dwarflike vicious Minister of Propaganda, Goebbels.

horror. Whole blocks had been replaced by wastelands of rubble, pockmarked by hundreds of craters and laced by the grotesquely twisted, reddened girders of ruined buildings. But it was not the gutted, windowless, roofless buildings nor the mountains of rubble that caught the 'hunting commandos'' eyes as they paced the cobbled, littered streets, handkerchiefs tied round their mouths against the soot and ash still raining down from the houses set afire somewhere in the suburbs; it was the dead. They were everywhere.

'Holy straw sack,' Schulze exclaimed, as he led his own group through the piles of human débris,' the place looks like a sodding butcher's shop!'

'Serves the black pigs right,' his second-in-command, one-legged Sergeant Matz grunted, 'the bastards should have got out when they were ordered to!' With his good foot he took a hefty swing at a head still encased in a white-painted civilian helmet. It bounced away like a football and rolled into a bomb-crater.

A short thundering roar like that of a great wave breaking drowned his next words. It was followed by a long-drawn-out hiss, as a wall directly in front of them crumbled and came crashing to the ground in a cloud of thick grey choking dust. Bricks bounced across the road towards them and the 'hunting commandos' ducked instinctively. It was fortunate that they did so. For at that same moment, a vicious high-pitched burst of machine-pistol fire cut the air just above their heads.

Schulze reacted immediately. He lobbed a potato masher blindly into the general direction from which the sudden fire had come and sent his men running to left and right, firing from the hip.

'Amis,' he yelled, 'Amis have penetrated the old city!'

But Sergeant-Major Schulze was wrong; their assailant turned out to be a German. A small heavy-jowled man, with bulging eyes like glass marbles and long dangling hands which reached down below his knees, dressed in the brown uniform of a SA major, his fat chest heavy with the 'tin' of the old war.

Matz punched him in the face and threw him in front of a surprised Schulze. 'A jam-shitting golden pheasant,' he exclaimed. 'He was hiding out over there behind that jam-shitting chimney-stack ready to take another pot-shot at us.' Matz hit him again with his clenched fist. The man's fat lips burst. His false teeth bulged out of his mouth and blood began to trickle from one corner.

'All right, Matz, leave him alone,' Schulze commanded. 'Give him a chance to speak. Now then, you shitty golden pheasant, what are you doing here and why did you fire on us?'

'I mistook you for civilians,' the heavy-jowled SA man stammered. 'A nervous reaction.' He wiped the blood from his mouth. 'Why should I fire on our own brave boys? You see those civilians would like to take it from me?'

'Take what?' Schulze snapped.

The SA man was suddenly hesitant. Schulze nodded to Matz. The one-legged NCO brought his hand down smartly in a brutal chop against the SA man's nose. Something snapped like a twig. The SA man staggered back, tears streaming from his eyes and mingling with the thick red blood which poured from his shattered nose.

'Now, you piece of ape-turd, let's have it or you'll be looking at the potatoes from below in five minutes flat!' Schulze threatened.

In spite of his pain, the SA man hurried to explain. 'I didn't go with the rest when Scheer ordered the evacuation. I had too many interests in Aachen . . . and I couldn't leave my girls behind. There wasn't enough room for them in the convoy—'

'What did you say?' Schulze broke in. '*Girls*.' He threw a significant look at the suddenly attentive patrol. 'Girls with tits and legs right up to their arses?'

The fat SA man nodded.

'Well, where, man – *where*?' Schulze exploded.

Schmees pointed a blood-stained finger at the heap of rubble of the newly collapsed wall, his face miserable. 'Below that – it used to be the old SA headquarters . . . I fixed it up myself for me and the girls so that we—'

'Come on, lads, let's not waste time,' Schulze interrupted excitedly, his eyes gleaming with anticipation. 'I'm already beginning to limp at the thought of those dames! Let's go and have a look at this bastard's passion parlour.'

But Battle Group Wotan's attempts to evacuate Aachen's remaining civilian population was not having the same pleasureable results everywhere. Von Dodenburg was driving Donner carefully through the littered smoking streets in the VW jeep when he heard the sound which told him that something had gone wrong with the evacuation plan. At first it was not much more than a subdued murmur, a distant monotone without pitch or form.

'What's that?' Donner snapped.

'I don't know, General, but we'll soon find out.'

With difficulty he turned the VW round in the narrow, rubble-littered street and headed slowly towards the sound, now beginning to form itself into three words, chanted over and over again by hundreds of hoarse throats:

'STOP THE EVACUATION!'

The VW jeep swung round the corner and came to a sudden halt. Drawn up in front of them, Schwarz and Officer-Cadet Krause plus two 'hunting commandos' were facing a mob of screaming women: fat housewives in dark ugly clothes; plain immature girls, undernourished and pale-faced, their budding unfettered breasts pushing gently through the thin washed-out material of their dresses; nuns in great sweeping white head-dresses – 'white swans', von Dodenburg remembered having called them in his youth; grandmothers in rusty black coats; female auxiliaries – 'field mattresses', the troops nicknamed them – in sloppy grey uniforms, all of them screaming hysterically at the top of their voices.

Von Dodenburg sprang from the jeep and ran across to Major Schwarz. 'What's going on, Schwarz?'

Schwarz swung round and shouted above the row: 'They won't let us move any farther. I tried to clear the street, but they wouldn't allow me to get far.' He turned his face to emphasise his point. His right cheek was clawed and bleeding from cheek to jaw. 'One of the bitches did this to me!'

Suddenly the hysterical chant stopped. The women had spotted Donner. Someone gasped with horror at his face. Another cried: 'There he is, Monseigneur – that devil Donner! He's here himself!'

The front rank of the sweating, flushed women parted and a fat unshaven priest wearing the soutane and shovel hat of a monseigneur stepped into the space between the apprehensive young SS men and the women who had called him. He fumbled with his gold-rimmed pince-nez and cleared his throat.

Donner beat him to it. 'What do you want, you damned black crow?'

'Don't you talk to the monseigneur like that, you God-forsaken devil!' a woman in widow's black in the front rank cried angrily.

The fat priest raised his plump soft hand to silence her. He looked up at the tall SS General. 'Excuse my children, General,' he said humbly. 'But all they want is to be left in peace. Left in their homes or what is left of them.'

Donner did not deign to look at the priest. His glassy gaze was fixed on some far horizon high above his head. 'Firstly they are not your children. They are German folk comrades, albeit female, who must obey the laws of the Reich like any other good National Socialist. Secondly they are useless mouths, which must be removed from the city, at once.'

'But sir,' the priest pleaded and raised his sweating hands in supplication, moving forward as if he were about to throw himself at the SS General's gleaming jackboots and plead for mercy.

Donner pushed him away with the tip of his riding crop. 'Keep your damn distance, Pope!'

'But I must insist, General. You can't do this terrible thing to my people—'

'Schwarz,' Donner cried, ignoring him, 'arrest this damned black crow, will you! He's beginning to bore me.'

'Sir!'

The Jewish SS Major, whose hatred of the clergy was as fanatical as his hatred of his own race, stepped forward. His face empty of emotion, he raised his black-gloved artificial hand and swung it against the priest's face. The priest staggered back, his glasses falling to the ground. Schwarz ground his iron-shod heel on them and snapped: 'Officer-Cadet Krause, arrest this man at once!'

A roar of anger went up from the women. They surged forward. Donner backed away:

'Stop them, von Dodenburg,' he cried, alarmed by the naked hate in the women's faces. 'Order your men to fire!'

'But General, they are women and they are German,' he protested. Then it was too late.

Their eyes shining crazily, cursing and spitting, they fell on the handful of troops. The street became a confused mess of twisting, snarling men and women, clawing and grabbing at each other. Krause dodged the low kick launched at his crotch by a field mattress and grabbed at her grey blouse. It ripped. The screaming snarling woman's great bare breasts, released from the official-issue bra, fell out.

Krause's grin vanished. 'What tits!' he breathed in awe, just as another woman sprang on his back and clutching her skinny arm round his neck began to strangle him, shouting at the top of her voice.

An elderly woman tried to hit Schwarz with her umbrella. He ducked and a blow landed on his helmet with a hollow boom. The next instant he had punched her in her fat belly with his wooden hand. She gasped and went down like a deflated balloon.

A pretty girl with long bright red hair ripped her nails across von Dodenburg's face. He winced with pain. 'You sow!' he grunted and attempted to grab her hand, the blood dripping down her fingers. He missed. She swung at him again. He ducked and flung his arms round her. Suddenly he felt her body, warm and nubile, pressed close to him and sensed the heady scent of her flaming hair just under his nose.

'Let go, you SS swine,' she screamed, wriggling desperately to break his hold, her green eyes looking up at him, burning with rage, her soft stomach pressed provocatively into his loins as she tried to do so.

He felt his excitement grow. Suddenly she realised that the handsome blond colonel in the black uniform was aroused. Her struggling ceased. She tried to withdraw her body from the importuning loins. But he wouldn't let her.

'Come on, you bitch, don't let go now,' he said hoarsely.

'You swine – you absolute swine,' she whispered, looking up at him, the anger suddenly gone out of the green eyes, 'Have you no shame?'

But his answer was drowned by the shot from Donner's pistol and the scream of the woman in the black widow's weeds, who slowly began to sink to the ground, her black-stockinged legs buckling under her.

'Heaven, arse and twine,' Schulze breathed as he looked around the great underground room, piled high with supplies, with the drunken whores sprawled out on the cushions listening to the ancient horn gramophone, 'it's like ladies' night in a Turkish bath.' He gulped and, pushing back his helmet, took in the seven or eight whores, dressed in gaudy underwear, champagne glasses in hand, listening to Johannes Heesters singing *'Gern' hab' ich die Frauen gekuesst!'*

'Oh, my holy Christ,' Matz standing next to him said. 'Have you ever seen so much meat and so few potatoes in all your life, Sergeant-Major? I'd like to fill their teeth – one by one – and slowly.'

31

Suddenly the girls became aware of their presence. A big blonde whore in transparent black underwear tripped drunkenly towards Schulze, arms outstretched.

'Men,' she breathed, her eyes half closed, 'real men – with tails.'

Gently Schulze avoided her grasp. 'Later, darling, later.' He turned to the fat squat SA man. 'You mean you've been living with this lot?' he asked incredulously. 'No wonder you've got such round shoulders.'

'It wasn't easy,' the SA man answered, trying to stem the flow of blood from his broken nose. 'I had to take a lot of rest.'

'The pig,' the blonde whore sniffed. 'At it all day like a fiddler's elbow. Nothing in his head, but plenty between the legs, that one.'

'I should have such troubles,' Matz breathed, putting his arm around a dark-haired whore in a frilly negligee and sheer black silk stockings. 'I'd have died a happy man.'

'Hold yer water,' Schulze snapped. 'Can't you see that I'm shitting well thinking?'

'Oh, I thought you were suffering from wind, Sergeant-Major,' Matz answered, giving the dark-haired whore's mighty right breast a powerful squeeze.

Schulze ignored him. 'All right, you golden pheasant,' he answered, 'I'm not going to turn you and your little bees in. You can stay here.'

The SA man's face lit up despite his pain, while the excited half-naked girls crowded around the soldiers, giggling and laughing. 'Thank you, sir, thank you from the bottom of my heart.'

'Shut up,' Schulze said brutally. 'There are conditions. You've got to keep your hairy paws off them. From now onwards, your little bees belong to us and to us exclusively. Get it?'

'Of course, of course,' he agreed.

'You've got plenty of chow and booze here. And when you run out, we'll supply you with more. All we want is that when we're off duty, your bees' pearly gates are open, ready and waiting.'

'Don't worry, soldier,' the big blonde said, lighting a thin black cigar, 'we're all ready for a little bit of fresh meat, aren't we girls?'

'Yes,' they chorused enthusiastically. 'We have had enough of that pig. If you only knew what the fat bastard made us do these last few days.'

Matz laughed throatily and began fumbling with his flies. 'You ain't seen nothing yet, ladies.'

Schulze gave him a rough push. 'Knock that off! There's no time for that now. You'll have to wait till tonight when the colonel stands us down.'

'Not even a quickie, Sergeant-Major? I won't even bother to take my wooden leg off.'

'I'll take off yer stupid head, if you don't shut up,' Schulze threatened. 'We're supposed to be on patrol. You can't go screwing around when you're on duty. All right, all of you outside – on the shitting double. And you, my little fat golden pheasant,' he brought his big face close to that of the SA man's threateningly, 'I'm making you responsible for seeing that your bees are ready for us tonight!' Gallantly Schulze raised his helmet. 'Then, ladies, I must bid you adieu till later.' He beamed at them. 'I trust you will have a pleasant day, and can stand the long wait till your prince returns.'

The whores giggled uproariously. At the door to the cellar he turned and gave them one long hand-kiss as did Johannes Heesters in the movies.

'Till tonight, my fair ones.'

But Sergeant-Major Schulze and his 'hunting commando' were doomed to disappointment. They had hardly recommenced their patrol when Colonel von Dodenburg's VW jeep came bouncing up and down the pitted road, its horn sounding an urgent signal. The colonel pulled up with a squeal of brakes.

Schulze looked at the CO in surprise. He was helmetless, his face flushed and scratched, and a red-haired beauty was slumped sulkily in the back seat, her pale oval face stained with drying tears. But von Dodenburg did not give him time to dwell on the situation.

'Matz, you take over the platoon and get back to HQ at the double. You Schulze, get in the front next to me. I need you urgently.'

'What's up, sir?'

Colonel von Dodenburg rammed home first gear while Matz rapped out his orders to the platoon. 'Everything's up. We've just put down a shitty riot – women and a priest. And now the balloon's really gone up.'

As the jeep shot forward, throwing Schulze violently against the hard seat and nearly tossing the redhead from her perch, von Dodenburg snapped through gritted teeth, 'The damn Amis have broken through in force in the Aachen State Forest. We're in trouble, real trouble, Schulze!'

FIVE

The little red lamp inside the lumbering Royal Tiger blinked on and off evilly. It signified that the tank's 88 mm and twin mgs were ready for action. Schulze, squatting in the gunner's seat next to von Dodenburg, did not need the warning light, however, to tell him that they were heading for trouble. He felt it in his bones.

Now they had left the ruined suburbs and were advancing in an attack V across rough undulating country. The landscape ahead had that tense, empty look that always signified a coming battlefield. It was as though the very earth itself were dreading the slaughter to come.

'Driver straight along the embankment,' von Dodenburg intoned. 'Schulze – six hundred. Traverse left.' With the easy efficiency of years of practice, Schulze swung the fourteen-ton turret round and set the range at the same time. They were getting close to the thick pine wood in which the Amis had dug in. Soon the trouble would start and he might get his stupid turnip blown off without even having had a chance to sample the delights of his private brothel.

'Shitting war,' he grumbled to himself and pressed his eye to the rubber-shod eye-piece. 'Can't even get a piece of tail in peace?'

'Did you say something, Schulze?' von Dodenburg queried, busy with his twin periscopes.

'Yessir,' Schulze snapped. 'I said – I'm going to rip 'em to pieces today. I feel just in the right mood.'

'Hm,' his CO answered. 'I'll believe you, but thousands wouldn't.'

The tanks rumbled on across the open fields. The woods came closer and closer. Five hundred metres, four hundred. Three hundred and fifty.

'Stand by, Schulze,' von Dodenburg ordered. 'Driver reduce speed now.'

With a deafening roar the driver crashed through half a dozen of the sixty-ton monster's thirty-odd gears to bring down the Tiger's speed. At the same time, Schulze pressed his shoulder against the 88's leatherbound grip so that he could move the great hooded gun with the slightest movement. His hand gripped the trigger handle tightly. Now the crosswires inside the glass circle of the sight were aligned perfectly with the wood. A few seconds more and the CO would give the order to fire; he would send the first HE[1] shell screaming into the wood. The rest of the Wotan would follow suit and then they would sit back to wait for the panic-stricken Ami stubble-hoppers to come running out to be massacred by the waiting machine-gunners. It was a simple plan – a risky one if faced by well-dug-in, trained infantry armed with bazookas. But von Dodenburg, like most SS officers, was contemptuous of the Ami's fighting ability. He was prepared to take chances he would never have taken with the Tommies and Ivans.

Von Dodenburg's attack did not develop as he had anticipated. Suddenly an open truck, filled with troops, came flashing from behind the wood, travelling across the field at high speed, its occupants bouncing up and down like toy soldiers.

'Amis!' the driver gasped. 'Amis at twelve o'clock, sir.'

'I'm not blind,' von Dodenburg commented coldly.

Even before he could rap out the order, Schulze had swung the 88 round.

'FIRE!'

There was stomach-jerking spasm of the recoil. The turret flooded with acrid yellow smoke. The gleaming shell-case clattered smoking to the metal deck, as the shell itself screamed towards its target. It struck the Ami deuce-and-half[2] just above the engine. With a roar it exploded, ripping apart metal, canvas, human flesh.

As the force of the shock wave struck him in the face, von Dodenburg grabbed the turrret mg. The force of the explosion had thrown some of the Amis from the shattered, now burning truck. Frantically the survivors were trying to pelt for the wood. Von Dodenburg pressed the trigger. 7-mm slugs tore through the the air at 800 rounds a minute. A man caught in mid-stride seemed suspended there like a statue of a runner. Then he flopped down, his body hiccupping convulsively. Another fell, throwing up his arms with wild pain so that his grease-gun rose

1. High explosive. (Transl.).
2. Standard two-and-half-ton US trucks.

high into the air. Others were felled, as if their legs had been sawn off at the knees.

Von Dodenburg lowered the gun. With a last burst he swept the grass so that even those feigning death would not escape. In thirty seconds it was all over and they were rattling past the smashed truck leaning on its side on burst tyres, the flames licking up about its cargo of dead Amis. Their great tracks churned over the bodies and were turned red with their blood.

'Ami tanks!' the driver yelled frantically.

As the first Sherman burst out of the bushes, trying desperately to protect the threatened infantry of the 'Big Red One',[1] Schulze pulled the firing lever. The Royal Tiger shuddered. They hit the Sherman just below the turret at point-blank range. The tank was flung high into the air. It descended with a bomblike whine and buried its gun deep into the soft earth.

'Two o'clock – Ami!' von Dodenburg screamed, automatically pressing the fume-extractor to clear the acrid yellow smoke now blinding them.

A Sherman armed with the new British seventeen-pounder gun was trying to approach them from the flank, knowing that the Tiger's half-metre-thick glacis plate[2] was virtually impregnable. But from the side the seventeen-pounder might be able to penetrate the base of the turret-ring or knock off a boogie wheel and cripple the massive German tank.

Using all his strength, Schulze flung the gun round. The Sherman slid into the glass circle of his lenses. The cross-wires sliced it in half. He snatched at the lever. The gun erupted. For a fleeting instant his vision was obscured by the yellow-red burst of the shell. Then the Sherman rocked from side to side, as if in a high wind. Oily black smoke and red sparks welled from its open turret. The tank commander was fighting his way out of the hatch but the flames were already licking at his body. He slumped over the turret. The flames leapt up, eating his uniform. They caught his hair, sprang to the face and the slow-moving, ever-weakening hands that tried in vain to beat them out. Before Schulze's eyes, the tank commander's face began to turn into a charred grinning death's head.

But there was no time for such horrors. An American self-propelled gun was lumbering out of the forest, followed by another – and another. And the Ami SPs were armed with a

1. Nickname of the First US Infantry Division.
2. The thickly armoured front plate of a tank.

36

105 mm which was a match even for the 88. This time the Amis scored first. A 105 mm roared with a tremendous fury. One of the Tigers on the right flank shuddered to a halt, a broken track flapping in front of it like a severed limb. The Ami SPs saw their advantage. In an instant they had turned their massive guns on the stricken German tank. Red and white balls of flame, AP shells, hurtled through the grey sky towards the Tiger. Time and again it heeled back and forth struck by each new shell. Its crew began to panic.

'Stay there! For Christ sake, stay there!' von Dodenburg yelled desperately over the radio.

But even the veterans of Wotan could not stand up to such cruel, concentrated fire. They bailed out from the turret and escape hatches and began to pelt madly for cover. From the cover of the woods came a vicious burst of US BAR-fire. One after another, the black-clad tankers flung up their arms in wild abandon and fell to the ground as the hot lead buried into their defenceless flesh.

'Lights!' von Dodenburg commanded urgently. 'Driver, flick off your lights quickly — and on again!'

The expected reaction came. The M-40s swung round their long cannon and started to concentrate their fire on the command tank. For some reason which von Dodenburg had still not been able to work out, the sight of the lights always angered or attracted enemy tank fire. A shell scored its way along the outside of the tank turret. Fascinated, he watched as the impact traced a white-hot line around the inside of the turret. It would only take one fragment to penetrate the armour somewhere or other and they would all be dead or maimed within seconds; for the fragment would fly from side to side until it found a victim inside the tight confines of the turret.

'Concentrate at nine!' he cried through the mike as his own gun erupted again. Swiftly he flung a look through the periscope at his nearest neighbour, Matz's tank.

Matz was way out. '*Nine*, I said, you whoreson,' he yelled. 'Not *eleven*! Turn seven minus thirty-six. *Fire!*'

A moment later Matz's gun joined in. Together he and Matz tried to pin the Amis down, backing them against the wood with their concentrated fire so that they would not be able to manoeuvre. But they hadn't reckoned with the commander of the first enemy SP. The tank was lumbering towards them at top speed. Desperately Schulze spun the turret round. The triangles

37

met in the sighting mechanism. He fired too late. The great shell missed the Ami by a dozen metres. The SP's bulk blacked out the whole lenses. It seemed as if the Tiger were about to capsize. It rocked on its base. Screams rang out from the driver's compartment, drowned by the grinding crash of metal meeting metal at speed.

Von Dodenburg was flung against the breech of the cannon. Fortunately he still had his helmet on. But his vision was obscured by violent, moving red lights. Schulze clung grimly to the leather grip, the blood pouring from his nostrils with the impact, and waited for the rocking motion to cease. Frantically he ripped off his earphones. Thrusting back the hatch cover, he raised his head into the air.

The crew of the M-40 was sprawled out in the SP's open deck like a bunch of drunks, paralysed momentarily by the shock of the impact. In a few moments, they would come out of it and begin to react. But Schulze did not give them time to do so. He grabbed a phosphorous grenade attached to the inside of the turret. He pulled the china-ring pin and lobbed it neatly into the centre of the sprawled-out men. It exploded at once, shooting fiery pellets of burning phosporus everywhere, burning whitely as they descended on to their human victims. He followed it by a normal potato masher. The scorching, screaming bodies rose and fell heavily onto the deck. Hastily he dropped back into his seat and pulled shut the hatch cover. The driver rumbled forward again.

The Ami SPs did not have a chance. Fifteen Tigers and Royal Tigers concentrated their fire upon them, as they backed into the wood, trying to scuttle for cover and finding that even their weight and power could not force a path through the thick pines. The Tigers rolled forward, intent on the kill, churning earth and mud. Shell after shell ripped through the burning, trembling air. One by one the crippled M-40s, rocked from side to side by the German fire, abandoned the fight, their crews bolting for the woods and finding that the enemy gunners were waiting for them to do exactly that. A last Sherman appeared and tried to give the fleeing crews some sort of cover. The Ami tank did not get too far. A blood-lust had overcome the sweating, smoke-blackened gunners. A direct hit knocked off the tank's turret and flung it high into the air. The gunners could see right into its guts where the lower part of the commander's body was still squatting in his seat. The gunner was crouched beside him over his gun-sight. But his gun and his hands were gone, and the blood dripped from his shattered wrists.

Moments later the last Ami resistance was over and the SS men had jumped out of their vehicles, eyes red with blood, faces black with smoke, to loot the enemy tanks for cigarettes and the highly prized Ami canned rations. But von Dodenburg knew that there were still Ami infantry in the wood and it would soon be dusk. Once it was dark, even the Amis might feel brave enough to tackle the Tigers with their excellent bazookas and Hawkins grenades.

'Schulze,' he bellowed above the crackle of the flames and the exuberant yells of the young SS troopers. 'Get those shitty wet tails out of these tanks, will you?'

'Yessir,' Schulze neatly pocketed two packets of C-rations, far superior to their own issue cans of 'Old Man', which was reputedly made of old men salvaged from the workhouses. 'I'll get right on to it. All right,' his voice rose above the noise. 'Get those leaden tails back into your vehicles before I have the eggs off'n yer with a blunt razor blade! *MOUNT UP!*'

It was a massacre. Swinging out to left and right of the wood, ignoring the wobbling clumsy bombs of the Ami bazookas with their trail of fiery sparks, and the patter of machine-gun fire against their thick armoured sides, the Tigers took up their positions and ground to a halt.

Von Dodenburg stood upright in the turret. He could imagine what must be going through the terrified Amis' heads now. They were trapped, and they knew it. From a small group of foxholes at the edge of the pines, a handful of desperate stubble-hoppers opened a wild fire at his tank.

Unhurried, almost casually, he spoke into his throat mike. 'Matz, clear up that mess at the edge of the wood, will you, before we start?'

The one-legged NCO, who had lost his leg with Wotan at Cassino, after lying out in the open for three days with gangrene, needed no urging. 'Yessir,' he barked and ordered his tank forward.

The Tiger rattled straight towards the dug-in Amis. Ignoring the terrified bursts of white tracer bouncing off its glacis like harmless golf balls, Matz ran over the first of the foxholes. Through his glasses, von Dodenburg could see the horrified GIs duck before their white blobs of faces were blocked out by the sixty-ton bulk of the Tiger. But Matz was too old a hand to allow the Amis to escape by cowering in the bottom of their little holes. Deliberately, he started to swing the Tiger back and forth, clouds of blue smoke pouring from its twin exhausts. The sides of the holes started to crumble. The Tiger sagged as one side of the pit gave way. If there were screams, von Dodenburg could not hear them, but he could imagine the crushed bloody pulp now filling the bottom of the foxhole.

Its track churned up flesh and earth as Matz rumbled on to the next foxhole and repeated the performance. Once von Dodenburg caught a glimpse of what looked a human arm swinging back and forth with the tracks, but it vanished as soon as Matz's Tiger rolled on to the next hole.

'All right, Matz,' he cried in the end, sickened in spite of himself. 'You've had your litre of blood for today. Come on back into line.'

'I'd sooner have a bit of the other any day, sir,' Matz replied, his excitement noticeable even over the crackling tank radio. But he pulled away obediently, leaving the bloody remains of the GIs squashed to pulp at the bottom of the graves into which they had unwittingly dug themselves.

Von Dodenburg did not waste any further time. The black clouds were coming in rapidly now from the east and he did not want to be caught out in the dark without the protection of his panzer grenadier infantry.

'HE five rounds,' he yelled over the mike,' commence firing!'

The twenty-nine cannon roared. The immense barrage crashed into the wood at two hundred metres range. Pines smashed like matchsticks. Within seconds the wood had ceased to exist. But von Dodenburg wanted to make sure that none of the Ami stubble-hoppers survived.

'Cease fire,' he cried into the throat mike. Then. 'Two rounds of incendiary!'

Rapidly the sweating gunners ejected the great heavy round of HE and replaced it by incendiary. Time was pressing. It was really getting dark now. They must get away. 'FIRE,' he bellowed.

The incendiary shells hissed through the darkening sky and smashed into the shattered wood at point-blank range, transforming it into a white-hot inferno. As the shelling ceased, the men of Wotan could hear the shrieks and screams of the Americans through the high curtain of leaping flame. Here and there, a GI, his uniform alive with fire, tried to crawl out of the inferno or came bursting panic-stricken into the open, burning arms held aloft in a frantic token of surrender.

But the SS troopers mowed the Amis down where they stood, until von Dodenburg yelled at last, 'Cease firing, we're pulling back. Follow me – convoy distance! And remember, you heroes, that there might be some Ami lurking out there with a bazooka. So keep a weather eye open.'

But as they swung into line, leaving the burning scene of the massacre behind them, the Amis had vanished from the bitter, war-torn landscape. Two hours later they rumbled back into a pitch-black, deserted Aachen without having been fired upon once. The swift intervention of SS Battle Group Wotan had temporarily brought 'Lightning Joe's' attempt to capture the Holy City to an abrupt and bloody halt.

SIX

'Gentlemen, our first attack on Aachen was a complete snafu.' General Collins, at forty-eight, the youngest corps commander in the US First Army, stared aggressively at his two infantry generals and let the words sink in.

Outside, the mud-stained ambulances were rattling in and out of the Corps HQ's cobbled courtyard, bringing in the critically wounded casualties of the massacre in the woods. In a nearby office a clerk was singing, '*I'm Going to Buy a Paper Doll that I Can Call My Own*', over and over again in poor imitation of Bing Crosby.

Collins frowned and told himself he would have a word with that damned chief clerk after the conference. 'I repeat, gentlemen, a complete goddam snafu.'

General Huebner, the gross, sallow-faced commander of the US Army's most experienced infantry division 'the Big Red One', opened his mouth.

Collins, blond, handsome and looking rather like an older Andy Hardy[1] the all-American boy, held up his hand to stop his words. 'It's okay, Clarence. I don't want any justifications, excuses, apologies. I take full responsibility for the failure of our

1. Popular film series in the USA in late thirties and early forties, which starred Mickey Rooney as 'Andy Hardy, the all-American boy.'

41

first attack. In Seven Corps, the buck stops here.' He jerked a thumb at his own broad chest. 'Get it?'

Huebner and General Hobbs, the heavy-set commander of the 30th Infantry Division – 'Roosevelt's Butchers' as they liked to call themselves, nodded their heads in appreciation. Most of the Corps Commanders in the ETO[1] were prepared to pass the buck when operations failed.

Outside a hoarse, beery voice was shouting. '*Mass!* Anyone of you lugs going to goddam mass? If you are, get goddam fell out!' There was the sound of weary feet shuffling over the cobbles to form up and be marched off to the 'church' improvised in the barn behind the latrines.

'All right, then,' Collins went on. 'So I made a mistake. I thought the Kraut had had it and I could bounce my way into goddam Aachen. I was wrong. Now what do we do?'

'Perhaps, General,' Huebner ventured, 'we shouldn't bother. We've got all the roads we need for the advance to the Rhine. Why get ourselves bogged down in Aachen? We could seal it off and leave the Kraut to sweat it out while we barrel for the Rhine. Believe me, General,' he added urgently, 'the capture of Aachen is going to cost us a helluva lot of doughs.'

Collins nodded. 'I agree, Clarence. The place has little military value. Its railroads are shot and the engineers tell me it'll take weeks before we can use them again for our own supplies for the advance past.' He paused and drew a deep breath, his handsome face set and worried. 'But there are other factors we have to take into consideration. Aachen will be the first major German city the US Army has captured in its two hundred-year-old history – a prestige objective in a way. Ike[1] is very keen on that. More important, Hitler has prophesied that his empire will last a goddam thousand years, just like Charlemagne's Holy Roman Empire. Thus, if we strike at Aachen, we are striking not just at a military objective, but at a shrine which is of tremendous significance for the Nazi faithful. When Aachen goes, the intelligence boys tell me, so does the man in the street's belief in the National Socialist creed. And that, gentlemen, is worth the lives of your doughs, I think.'

'All right, you fish eaters – over there,' the beery Nomcom's voice snarled, 'Gefillte fisch and bagels – over here . . . The good

1. European Theater of Operations.

2. i.e. General Dwight D. Eisenhower, the Supreme Commander of Allied forces in Europe.

guys, next to me.' With a lot of shuffling of combat boots, the various sections of the church parade began to sort themselves out.

'Aachen will have to be captured by a systematic attack,' Collins continued, rising and walking over to the large map which decorated one wall of his office in the old Belgian château that he had taken over for his HQ during the Battle of Aachen. 'Just as the Corps did at Utah Beach and Cherbourg. No more piecemeal attacks in other words, gentlemen, going in at half cock. Okay?'

The two infantry commanders nodded.

'All right, Clarence, let's do this in a democratic fashion. What would you do, if you were me?'

'Thank God I'm not,' the commander of the Big Red One thought, but he said, 'The squeeze, General, the squeeze'. He thrust out his big powerful hand and pressed the broad fingers together. 'Cut the Krauts off from their supplies, reinforcements etc. Then, when that's done, go in for the kill.'

'You, Leland?'

Hobbs, who was not given to talk, but preferred to express himself on paper with phrases full of bombast and appeals to the soldierly patriotism of his troops, grunted, 'I concur, General – decidedly the squeeze before attempting to eliminate the enemy.'

'Good, that is exactly my own idea. The question now is – where? Leland, I want you to get your doughs in positions around here.' He tapped the little town of Herzogenrath on the Dutch-German border on the map. 'That will be your start-line. How long would it take you to get into position?'

Hobbs shrugged. 'Two days – three at the most. My losses have been high in Holland. I'll need replacements.'

'You've got them, Leland,' Collins snapped. 'The First Army's ripple-dipples[1] have already been alerted to give you what you want in the way of bodies. Okay, let's say three days.' He turned to Huebner. 'Now Clarence, your people are already in position. All I want you to do is tidy up your line, as Monty would say, and then when we're ready to kick off the offensive, push a feint south-eastwards into the city itself, but making your main effort a drive for Verlautenheide. You and Leland will link up at this feature here – Height 239. We'll commence the offensive two October.' His voice hardened momentarily. 'And I'll expect you gentlemen to link up there eight days later. Get it?'

1. US Army slang for reinforcement centres.

43

Somehow the young Corps Commander's confident tone irritated the much older Huebner. 'Lightning Joe' did not seem to understand the difficulties of fighting in industrial areas like Aachen. It was nothing like the swift gallops across France where even infantry divisions could cover twenty miles a day. The grimy industrial settlements around Aachen could swallow up infantry by the battalion: before you knew it, a whole division might be engaged in fighting for some third-rate objective.

'Hill 239,' he said reflectively. 'Do you know what the GIs call it, General?'

Collins, already preoccupied with the next problem, shook his head.

'Well, you know it's surmounted by a large wooden cross. You know what the folks are around here – one hundred per cent Catholic—'

'Get on with it, Clarence,' Collins snapped with a sudden bite in his voice.

'Well, sir, the forward artillery observers have spread the word about the hill dominating the whole area and about the cross. So the GIs have made up their own name for it.' Huebner allowed himself a faint smile of triumph. 'Crucifixion Hill, General . . . Crucifixion Hill . . .'

Lightning Joe Collins sat thoughtfully at his desk until he heard the doors of their sedans being slammed closed in the courtyard below and the voice of the MP sergeant bellowing: 'Guard – guard – attenshun!' Smoothly the olive green Packards that contained his infantry generals drew away. 'Crucifixion Hill!' he snorted to himself and pressed the brass bell on the desk in front of him.

His bespectacled chief clerk came in almost immediately.

'Tell Colonel Porter I'm ready for him now,' he commanded. 'And listen, Jones, get a grip on that damned crooner in your office, will you! *I'm gonna get a baby doll to call my own* doesn't exactly go with a high-level military conference. Savvy?'

'Yessir, General,' a flustered Jones said.

A few minutes later Colonel Porter of the First Army's OSS section appeared and gave the Corps Commander another of his sloppy civilian sixty-day-wonder salutes.[1]

Collins sniffed. A typical cloak-and-dagger soldier. No wonder

1. Officers who had taken the wartime sixty-day officer training course.

45

that the Washington cocktail circuit sneered that the top-secret organisation's initial – OSS – meant the 'Office of Shush, Shush', or 'oh, so secret'.

'Well?' he inquired.

Porter, a big florid ex-Boston lawyer, whose total experience of war had been a day at Château Thierry during the 1918 'champagne campaign' in France, answered: 'The kikes are ready, if you want to look them over, General.'

Collins rose. 'Okay, let's go and see.'

A few minutes later they passed the guard of white-helmeted MPs, armed with grease-guns, into the big castle hall which housed the volunteers. They sprawled out on the linoleum floor, drinking steaming hot coffee from metal canteen cups, their leggings undone, fatigue caps at the backs of their cropped dark heads, but as soon as they spotted the commanding general they sprang to their feet. Collins took a long look at them. They were from all arms of the service-infantry, supply, engineers – there were even a couple from a laundry unit. But in spite of their different insignia and uniforms, they had one thing in common, a rigidity of stance which Collins could not remember even seeing in the old pre-war Regular Army.

'All right, men,' he said at last. 'At ease . . . you may smoke again if you wish.'

There was hasty fumbling in pockets. Camels and Luckies reappeared while he waited, again noting that there was something foreign about the way the volunteers lit their cigarettes. The average GI could flip a cigarette out of the hole at the top of the pack and light it in one easy movement; these men made two separate movements out of it.

'Now listen,' he said energetically. 'The Seventh Corps will be going over to the offensive on the Aachen front again in the near future. Intelligence tells us that the Krauts – er Germans – will have little to oppose us with, except for one elite outfit, which really fouled up the Big Red One's attack yesterday.'

Again he mustered them with his keen eyes and wondered for a moment what must be going through their minds, now that they were back where they had originated, spent their youth, gone to school, made friends before being driven into exile so cruelly only a few years before.

'Now all of you men have volunteered for a special assignment. All of you are of German origin, speak the language fluently and are trained soldiers – a combination which is essential to

46

the success of your mission.' He paused. 'Any questions so far?'

A tall skinny lieutenant, whose chest bore the combat infantryman's badge and the dark ribbon of the Purple Heart, said with little trace of an accent. 'Sir, we don't want you to pull any punches. Can we have it straight? What's our assignment?'

'Lieutenant Wertheim,' Colonel Porter explained hurriedly, flashing the Jewish lieutenant an angry look. 'Damn, big-mouthed kike,' he told himself.

'Well, Wertheim, if that's the way you want it, I'll give it to you straight. You're going to kill someone. But I'd better leave the details to Colonel Porter here. I just wanted to have a look at you – see what kind of fellers you were. All right, Porter, you can carry on now.'

'Attenshun!' Porter yelled.

They sprang to attention. Touching his hand to his blond hair, Collins walked out while Porter grinned behind his back. Typical West Pointer, he told himself maliciously. As hard as nails, aggressive to an extreme, ready to walk over dead bodies to further his military career, as all the guys from the Point were. All the same his regular soldier's code-of-conduct forbade him to involve himself more than necessary in the little scheme OSS in Grosvenor Square had cooked up – a scheme that might well produce more important results than one of his regular infantry regiments could. No, that kind of dirty work would have to be left to amateur soldiers like himself.

'All right,' he said when the door had been closed after the Corps Commander and the hard-faced MPs had taken up their positions again. 'Relax and get a load of this. Wertheim, you want it straight from the shoulder. Well, here it it. The OSS wants you to sneak behind the Kraut lines in German uniform. You know what that means?'

Wertheim spat drily. 'You don't need to spell it out, Colonel. We know. A short walk of an early morning if we're captured, and the firing squad.' He looked challengingly at the fat ex-lawyer. 'What we want to know is why. Don't we, guys?'

The men all around him, their dark faces set and intent, nodded.

'Okay,' Porter shrugged. 'It's no skin off my nose, Lieutenant. The only opposition in Aachen which is capable of stopping our doughs is an outfit called Battle Group Wotan – it's an SS unit. We want you guys to kill its commanding officer.' He consulted the piece of paper he held concealed in the palm of his hand. 'He's a Kraut called von Dodenburg. Colonel von Dodenburg. Some kind of crummy Kraut aristocrat or other.

You guys are going to be the Joes who will ensure that if the Kraut has a son, that kid will succeed to the family title real smartish. Get me?' The challenging look gave way to a fat smile. 'Yesterday, you see, you all volunteered to become professional killers.'

TWO: THE DEATH SQUAD

'Do you know what we talk about all day in the cellars, Kuno? . . . We talk about death, the various ways that one can die – that in Catholic Aachen.' *Elke Simons to Colonel von Dodenburg.*

ONE

As the third week of September 1944 passed and the Americans
still did not attack, the defenders of the City of Aachen settled
down to the routine of a siege. Supplies were now coming
through regularly from Juelich, but although Police General
Donner knew that there were some twenty thousand civilians
hiding out in the ruins of the old city, he abandoned all attempt to feed them.

As he told von Dodenburg, 'If they want to live in their
cellars like rats, then they must learn to scavenge for themselves like rats!'

Now and then the Americans blocked the supply routes with
their bombing and the Luftwaffe was called in to make air-
drops. But the slow-moving, three-engined. 'Auntie Jus', as the
troops called the Junkers 52s, rarely supplied them with anything worthwhile: Cellophane covers for grenades, but no grenades; boxes of official forms; great five-kilo cans of dehydrated
animal fodder when they had no animals; and once over four
million contraceptives, type 'Volcano'.

As Donner exclaimed angrily to von Dodenburg: 'What does
that fat fool Goering think we're doing out here – fighting or
fornicating?'

For the most part, enemy action was limited to Ami propaganda companies, armed with nothing more lethal than powerful radio transmitters, who played the same old popular song,
'After Every December, There is Always a May', over and over
again until the bored front-line troops would cry, 'Can't you
bastards play anything else?' This would usually result in a
powerfully magnified voice, crying in a thick Berlin accent:
'Give yourself up, German soldiers. We Americans will treat our
prisoners-of-war fairly!'

'*We Americans!*' the Wotan men would jeer cynically, 'Why
don't you give yourselves up and we'll shorten your German-
Jewish tails a little bit more for you than the Rabbi did!'

But, despite the overall quiet, there were signs that the Americans were preparing for an all-out attack on Aachen. In that third
week, highly trained, aggressive Ami snipers started to appear
in the suburbs nearest the lines of the First American Infantry

Division – 'the Big Red One' – as von Dodenburg knew it was called from prisoners. Systematically they wormed their way into the ruins, feeling out the German strong points, testing the strength of the long line and taking a heavy toll of the SS troopers, who had grown contemptuous of the Ami's ability to fight.

In the end, Diedenhofen, Wotan's fat, bald chief medical officer, went to von Dodenburg to complain bitterly of the activities of the snipers on the First Division's sector of the front.

'Thirty in three days, sir,' he snorted, drinking the fiery clear glass of *Korn* von Dodenburg had offered him in one angry gulp. 'Do you realise what that means? The bullet passes through the helmet, scalp, skull, small blood-vessels' membranes into the soft sponginess of the brain substance in the occipital lobe of the cerebral hemisphere.'

Von Dodenburg offered him another *Korn*. He drained it automatically. 'Then you're either paralysed or you're blind, or you can't smell anything or your memory is gone or you can't talk or you're only bleeding,' he paused for breath, 'or you're dead! It all depends on how your goddam turnip is carved when that piece of lead hits you.'

Von Dodenburg poured the angry surgeon another drink.

'Colonel,' he concluded, 'I'm heartily sick of picking out flattened slugs from young men's heads, tying up the tricky blood vessels, covering up the hole in the skull with a tantalum metal plate, knowing all the time that I'm burdening the Homeland with a human vegetable, who will have to learn how to walk, talk – even goddam smell again. Sir, you've got to do something about those snipers, or I'll be ending up in the nuthouse myself!'

Von Dodenburg smiled at the surgeon's rage. In spite of his toughness and chronic drinking, Diedenhofen cared deeply about his 'young blackguards', as he called the Wotan men; the tragic cost in human suffering was really affecting him.

The first clue to the fact that they were faced by a really expert sniper came in the shape of a captured copy of the US Army paper *Stars and Stripes*. Under the banner headline, '*New Volkssturm*[1] *on Aachen front made up of old men, stomach cases, cripples with glass eyes and wooden legs*', there was a small paragraph, concluding the account of the fighting on the Aachen front, detailing the activities of a Master-Sergeant Smart, 'a latterday Alvin Yorke from the backwoods of Kentucky', who could

1. German Home Guard.

'thread a piece of lead through the eye of a needle at fifty paces', and who boasted that he had already 'rid the world of twenty Krauts in the last three days alone'.

Thus while both sides prepared for the great battle to come, Colonel von Dodenburg, supported by Major Schwarz, both armed with sniper's rifles, set out on a little private war. Together they intended to outsmart Sergeant Smart!

For two days the First Division was quiet. Then on the third, two young SS men who had grown careless again in the lull, were neatly drilled through the head. They were both dead by the time Diedenhofen reached them.

On the fourth day, Schwarz and von Dodenburg sneaked out just before dawn into the shell-pocked waste of brick rubble which was no-man's land and started to study the ground carefully at a time when they guessed that Sergeant Smart from the backwoods of Kentucky would not be his usually alert self, and there would be no sun glinting on their binoculars to betray their position. Together they swept the battlefield. A reddened, burnt-out Sherman.

'Too obvious,' von Dodenburg whispered. 'Our Mr Smart wouldn't be that foolish.'

Schwarz nodded. 'The pillbox to the left of the Sherman?'

Hastily von Dodenburg focused his glasses. But that was not the Ami sniper's hiding place either. 'The slit's been blocked up, Schwarz. He's not in there.'

The glasses continued their sweep of the area. They passed over a rusty sheet of corrugated iron that might have once been used to roof some farmer's shed, a pile of brick rubble, and on to a series of surburban gardens or fields in which the spring-sown cabbages now rotted. Nothing!

Von Dodenburg cursed bitterly. 'Where the hell is the Ami arsehole hiding, Schwarz?'

Schwarz's black eyes narrowed. 'Sir, he can't be in the cabbages. There's no cover. The tank and pillbox are out. So?'

'Of course – the sheet of corrugated iron!'

The two officers focused their glasses on the innocuous pile of rubble surmounted by the rusty metal sheet. Nothing stirred. Everything seemed to be perfectly in order. But von Dodenburg knew that Schwarz was right. The place was the only hiding place available to the sniper.

He bit his bottom lip in irritation and bewilderment. 'I'm sure the bastard's in there, Schwarz. But how are we to find out?'

Schwarz did not hesitate. Slowly, but deliberately, he raised his artificial hand, encased in its black leather glove. Von Dodenburg peered through his glasses. A white fast-moving blur. The harsh dry crack of a high-velocity rifle. Schwarz swore and withdrew his hand hurriedly. There was a neat hole drilled through the centre of the black leather.

'Christ on a crutch,' von Dodenburg cursed excitedly, 'We've got him!'

Screaming convincingly to lull Smart's suspicions, the two of them scurried away half an hour later and started planning how they would kill the deadly Ami sniper.

In the end they decided that they had to place him at the greatest possible disadvantage by finding a spot where his position would be bathed in the maximum amount of sunlight. They found it and prayed that the September sun would do them the favour of appearing the next afternoon once they were in position.

Fortunately it did, and after firing a blind shot to attract the Ami's attention, the two officers settled in beneath their shell-crippled oak tree to wait. By late afternoon they had Smart at a disadvantage. Von Dodenburg, concealed now in the shade while Smart's position was bright with sunlight, focused his telescopic sight on the rusty sheet of corrugated iron. Suddenly something glinted. Glass! Smart's own telescopic sight.

'Schwarz,' he hissed, 'Mr Smart's showing himself!'

Schwarz wiped the sweat off his brow. Drawing a deep breath, he took off his camouflaged helmet and raised it carefully over the edge of their hiding place. Smart's rifle cracked. The slug whanged loudly against the helmet. The force of the impact flung it from Schwarz's hand. It clattered to the ground. For a moment, a surprised Schwarz did not react.

Von Dodenburg dug him in the ribs angrily. *'Scream, Schwarz – scream, Schwarz!'* he hissed.

Schwarz wet his lips and screamed, throwing his head back to do so, giving it all his energy, as if he were suffering the agony of death throes. Von Dodenburg waited. He could feel the icy cold drops of sweat trickling down the small of his back. His heart was racing madly and he had to fight back the urge to blink.

Sensing victory, Smart raised his head slightly from beneath the sheet to see his thirty-third victim. It was the last thing he did. Von Dodenburg squeezed his trigger gently. The sniper's rifle slapped against his shoulder hard. The high-velocity 9-mm slug sped through the September sunshine, and buried itself in Sergeant Smart's skull. When, after a suitable pause, they crawled out cautiously to check their victim, they found Smart sprawled on his back in the rubble, his red, leathery face relaxed in death, a neat hole between his eyes. Schwarz hawked and spat into his face.

Thereafter sniping stopped on the Aachen. The Amis returned to their saturation bombing; it was safer, it seemed.

Now as the autumn nights closed in, the besieged city took on a deserted look. Stretched out in the pale September moonlight, its ruins bathed a ghostly silver, it offered a submissive, clear target for the night enemy – and a chance for Colonel von Dodenburg to meet the beautiful, pale-faced redhead who had so excited him at the demonstration a few days before. For although the city might look deserted from the air, it was alive with civilians at night, in spite of the bombs and Donner's chain-dogs who seemel everywhere. Like neolithic cave dwellers, confined to their holes during the day, the Aacheners emerged from their cellars and basements into the ruins to scavenge for fuel, to loot abandoned food stores and above all to find sufficient water for the next day.

Kuno von Dodenburg and Elke Simons met for the first time during a raid. With the flak slamming burning red balls into the sky and the searchlights stabbing icy white fingers around the darkness, searching for the Ami Fortresses, they looked at each other in silence, until finally he asked: 'Where to, Elke?'

'I don't know.'

'We have to go somewhere,' he reminded her gently.

She laughed and pressed her hand on his black leather sleeve. 'I know, Colonel. You don't want to be seen with me – what would General Donner think? And I can't be seen with you. My fellow citizens would not be too gentle with me. What a mess, eh?'

He bent down and kissed her soft cheek. 'Home?'

'The cellar?' She shrugged. 'All right then, the cellar. It's the only home I've got left – all of us have got left.'

They walked swiftly down the dark street, the shadows of her fellow Aacheners scuttling around in the ruins, more sensed than seen. He held her tight to him. Now the sky in the east was ablaze yet once again.

'Bloody war,' he cursed softly, as the fiery white 'Christmas trees'[1] began to descend slowly, indicating that Aachen was in for a full-scale attack.

'Yes, bloody war,' she echoed sadly.

In the candle-lit cellar, with the walls heaving from the first 500-pound bombs, he put his arms around her and kissed her passionately, almost brutally. She responded wildly, with an abandon he had not expected from her, pressing her slim, rounded stomach against his. Gasping crazily, they fell on to the ancient bed, the room's sole furniture save for a chair and a crucifix.

His eager tongue burrowed deep into her open mouth. His hard hand followed the soft silken line of her stocking till his greedy fingers, striving fingers, found the wet softness they sought. The ruined city outside, Wotan, the war, the death all around him were forgotten as they writhed back and forth on the squeaking wooden bed.

Once a 1,000-pound bomb landed close by and sent the whole cellar shivering with the shock, showering their sweating naked bodies with tiny flakes of plaster. They did not even notice. Their shadows, gigantically magnified by the yellow, wildly-flickering light of the single candle, continued their frantic dance. Their fevered desire consumed them; it was as if there had never been another lovemaking against the background of a world gone mad.

But the world outside could not be forgotten for ever. Lying side by side on the little bed, their bodies lathered in sweat, hands under their heads, staring at the shadows flickering on the ceiling, scarred by the week-long shellfire, she asked softly: 'Why Kuno?'

'Why what?'

'You know. Why continue fighting? We can't beat the Amis – they'll win in the end.'

He shrugged, but still stared at the ceiling. 'Probably,' he said without emotion. 'But we must still fight on.'

She sat up, leaning on one elbow, her long red hair hanging over her face, her left breast dangling just above his mouth temptingly. 'But why?' she persisted.

'Because, my little cheetah,' he said, stroking her gleaming fire-red hair, 'there is nothing left for me and my men to do but to fight on.'

She was silent for what seemed a long time. Outside the flak

1. Massed flares.

thundered and the bombs howled down with stomach-churning regularity. But she did not move from her position, nor take her sad eyes from his worn, handsome face. He tried once to caress her nipple. But she shook her head.

'Do you know what we talk about all day in the cellars, Kuno?'

'Food?' he ventured.

'No, not food any more. That was at first, at the beginning of the siege. But no longer. We talk about death, the various ways that one can die – that in Catholic Aachen!' She licked her suddenly dry lips. Looking at her, von Dodenburg thought how beautiful, how fragilely innocent she was. 'Some advocate poison, others drugs or gas – but there is no gas any more.' She turned suddenly and slid her thin hand under the pillow, pulling out an old-fashioned cut-throat razor. 'My father's,' she announced simply. 'Before he was killed in the big 1942 raid.'

He sat up, alarmed. 'What the devil do you need that for?'

She flicked open the blade and stared at it, fascinated as it gleamed in the faltering yellow light of the candle.

'I asked you a question, Elke. I said, what do you need it for – that razor?'

She tucked the razor under her pillow again. 'Well, not to shave my legs with, as I hear the Ami women do. Now,' her cold little hand slid along his hard stomach down to his thighs, 'I want to make love again. Can I excite you?'

He did not see the tears in her eyes, as his greedy hand sought and found her nipple.

But the clandestine night life of the dying city was not all sadness. At least Schulze and his one-legged companion, Sergeant Matz, did not think so. Night after night, they staggered through the blacked-out streets, avoiding Donner's chain-dogs, or if they could not avoid them, slugging them swiftly before clattering off into the shadows in their great heavy dice-beakers, laughing uproariously.

Blundering drunkenly through the blackout curtain into the SA man's cellar, they would usually smash him in the face to send him flying into the nearest fire bucket – 'just in case he starts getting too big for his boots' – ripping off their jackets in the same instant and announcing their presence to the giggling whores by raising their left legs and venting two enormous farts.

The whores loved them. Schulze and Matz could do no wrong, even when they were blind drunk, which happened frequently in

56

that last week of September, after a 'hunting commando' had discovered an abandoned schnapps distillery and every platoon in Wotan had its own fifty-litre carboy of fiery liquor at hand. As soon as Schulze would bellow; 'All right, my ladies, I'm going to dance a mattress polka this night! Get those rags off at the double!' they would respond with alacrity, ripping off their underwear like virgin brides on the wedding night.

Even when Matz, as drunk as his senior NCO, would insist on taking off his artificial leg, 'so that I can get on the job better', the whores were not offended. They would tolerate the undersized sergeant's peculiarities, as he hopped towards them, completely naked, on one leg, big hands outstretched to grab the nearest whore's breasts, crying: 'Stand fast, girls! Hold on to something quick! Because this piece of meat is going to hit you worse than a 88 mm shell at close range!'

As an exhausted Schulze commented one night, his head nestled in the big blonde's breasts, while a brunette wiped the sweat off his naked chest and stomach, 'Matz, you cunning, one-legged fart-cannon, this is a dream come true.' He threw out a big hand to draw in the roomful of drunken naked women, being served by the downcast little SA man, who had now added a black eye to his swollen, green-coloured nose. 'Who would have believed it, eh, you puffed-up pineapple-shitter!' He shook his head in disbelief. 'My own private whore house! Matz, old cock, at this moment, I could die happy . . .'

And while the men of Wotan enjoyed their time out of war, Lieutenant Wertheim's men, their faces blackened, their bodies clad in the hated uniform of the German Wehrmacht, slipped out into the cold autumn darkness, night after night, to train for their mission.

TWO

The sound was unlike anything the Aacheners had heard before. It started in the distance as the sun slid up over the ruin-jagged horizon and they prepared to return to their hideouts with the loot of the night, a dull groaning noise unlike any of the other terrible noises of war they had heard in these last few years. Twice it sounded. Bright pink flashes sparkled to the west. For a moment the shabby night creatures seemed mesmerised. Then the low roar became a scream a baleful, angry scream – its fury elemental, but man-made and precise. They scattered, pelting madly down the ruined streets for the safety of their cellars. The enemy artillery shells, the first to strike the old city, burst with a mighty antiphonal crash. Dismembered bodies flew everywhere, the ruins splashed red with the blood of the victims. Men and women lay writhing in agony in the gutters. As the Amis settled down to the dawn bombardment, the sun revealed itself in its full frightening beauty, hanging in the pale blue sky like a blood-red ball. It was seven thirty on the morning of October 1st, 1944. Aachen itself had now become the front line.

Vicious purple tongues of flame leaped up from shattered rooftops all over the city. Weakened buildings collapsed everywhere. Military vehicles parked in the streets were up-ended or flung high in the air by direct hits. A convoy of horse-drawn goulash cannons[1] trotting down the Komphausstrasse received a direct hit. The drivers, their mates, their tired skinny nags and four hundred litres of 'giddiup soup' disappeared in an instant. Shells ploughed into the cupola of Charlemagne's Cathedral. Huge chunks of masonry started to fall on the terrified men and women sheltering below. They ran terrified into the Jakobsstrasse to be mown down by the red-hot, fist-large pieces of shrapnel. A military stable at the end of the little street was hit and the piteous whinnying of the horses mingled with the cries and shouts of the dying humans. Some of the horses stampeded out of the sudden inferno. Manes and tails blazing a fiery red, brown eyes wide with terror, they clattered down the street scattering all before them.

The merciless shelling seemed to have no pattern. It was aimless and incessant. Its razor-sharp, deadly shrapnel scythed down everything in front of it. In their foxholes the Wotan men huddled close together and cowered in abject misery as the earth shuddered and shook, thanking a God they no longer believed in that they were being spared – at least temporarily – while the civvies took the merciless pounding of the Ami guns.

And still the enemy artillery kept firing. The screams of their shells had now merged into one continuous cyclonic roar. Ami mortars joined in, dropping their 3-inch bombs into the centre of the city with obscene plops, the blasts of their explosions tearing out the lungs of the civilians cowering in the rubble. The new enemy rocket batteries followed with a fluttering chromatic

1. SS name for field kitchen.

whine, showering Aachen with the fiery, spark-trailing canisters, which exploded with such force that the dark red blood spurted from the civilians' ears and noses. As the sun's rays, growing warmer every minute, cleared away the dawn mist, the city was wreathed in thick yellow, choking acrid fumes and a fine cloying dust.

And then, as suddenly as it had started, the initial barrage ended, leaving behind it an echoing silence. Awed, white-eyed with shock, shaking their dust-covered heads to clear away the ringing noise, the shabby civilians rose slowly to their feet and stared at the new shape of their ancient city.

Aachen had stood in the path of many invaders in its two-thousand-year history. Once the Amis began to push into the city, there would be no leaving the refuge of their cellars at night; and SS Police General Donner – *Devil Donner*, as they were beginning secretly to call the hideous battle commander – would not waste precious supplies of food on them. They would have to fend for themselves.

The looting started almost immediately. Goods trains lined up outside the Hauptbahnhof were broken into by a mass of screaming, almost hysterical women. They grabbed cases of tinned fruits and the standard Wehrmacht ration meat cans – the notorious 'Old Man'. A patrol of chain-dogs tried to stop them. The women tore them to pieces. When they had finished looting the trains, the four MPs were found, trampled to death and naked on the platform. In one case, the crazied women had thrust the MPs' crescent-shaped, silver-metal badge deep into the dead, blood-covered man's anus,

A rumour flashed through the crowd that one of city's great department stores was being looted. Dragging their stolen tins of fruit and meat behind them in little handcarts, they streamed towards the store, fighting their way in a mob through the doors or crunching across the shattered glass dèbris of the shell-blasted windows. An old, bald-headed man in the shabby, but well-brushed frock coat of another era and a 'father murderer'[1] tried to stop the invasion. An enraged housewife in a coat made from a dyed blanket knocked him to the ground.

And the looting began all over again. The women grabbed anything in sight. If they discovered a moment later an item was useless, they simply dropped it. Soon the floor of the food depart-ment, where Donner had used the refrigerators to keep the

1. Stiff, wing-collar.

supplies intended for Aachen's fighting men, was a centimetre-thick carpet of sticky, slippery mud, made up of flour, honey, syrup, jam and condensed milk, all dropped or overturned by the screaming mob of women. They swarmed back and forth, grabbing coats, dresses, shoes – anything that could be worn or sold on the flourishing night-time black market. Suddenly whistles started to blow.

'The head-hunters – Devil Donner's head-hunters are coming?' a fat woman with glasses screamed.

'Devil Donner's head-hunters!' a hundred hysterical voices took up the cry of alarm.

Panic-stricken the women streamed out of the store, carrying their loot with them. Outside the dèbris-littered square, hefty middle-aged Army MPs were dropping heavily on to the cobbles, weapons at the ready. They formed up rapidly into line, Schmeissers levelled at the frightened but determined women. Suddenly the senior NCO, a florid-faced sergeant with his chest covered in decorations from the old war, nodded to his men to lower their weapons.

'All right, let the bitches through. Hard times are coming, they might as well have their little bit of loot.'

The women streamed through the cordon, silent, subdued, eyes fixed demurely on the ground, as if ashamed of themselves.

They had just turned into the Grosskoelmstrasse when someone yelled, 'Horses, dead horses!'

Before them lay a long line of singed dead horses, shot a few minutes before by the chain-dogs. They lay sprawled out everywhere, their skinny ribs showing through their moth-eaten skins. Knives appeared, as if by magic.

'Fresh meat,' the woman in the dyed blanket coat cried in delight. 'Come on!' She flung herself on the nearest animal, plunging her knife into the soft flesh of its flank.

Like the furies themselves, the other women followed suit, their hands red to the wrists, cutting and slashing at the flesh in a desperate attempt to get a share of the precious meat before it was all gone.

'Animals – pure animals,' Donner murmured metallically, as he and von Dodenburg watched from above. The Police General fixed von Dodenburg with his glassy-eyed hideous stare. 'That down there is just the beginning, von Dodenburg,' he said carefully. 'Just the beginning.' Devil Donner brought his terrible face closer to the younger man's. 'Soon all of Germany is going to be like that down there, a pack of whining undisciplined animals, snarling in the dirt of the gutter for the offal cast them by the victors, if we don't manage to stop the Amis here.' His crippled hand clenched tightly and his voice rose. 'Von Dodenburg, you must hold Aachen for me, whatever the cost!'

THREE

The three German half-tracks emerged from the farmyard into the eerie light of the false dawn. They seemed to make a deafening noise as they ground down the stony track, and the lean, dark-skinned lieutenant standing up in the first vehicle bit his lip, as if he feared that the noise would alert the enemy.

A sentry loomed up out of the coils of mist floating a metre above the fields and the curtain of vapour fogging the narrow beams of his half-track. 'Wotan?' he challenged, his machine pistol held at the ready, his body protected carefully by the ruined Sherman.

'Wagner,' the lieutenant answered promptly, with only a trace of a Viennese accent.

The sentry relaxed. 'Pass, friend.'

The lieutenant raised his hand in signal to the other two vehicles, a grey ghost in the bleak glow of their headlights. 'Any sign of the Amis, sir?' the young SS man inquired anxiously as the lieutenant's driver thrust home first gear.

'Not yet, soldier. We're just back from a recce. They must still be eating their Ami bacon and eggs – they never go to war on empty stomachs, they tell me.'

'Lucky sods,' the SS man replied. 'I've had nothing but a bowl of giddiup soup in the last twelve hours.'

'Tell the chaplain,' the lieutenant snapped unsympathetically, as the half-track jerked forward. 'Perhaps he'll give you a signed certificate for a sausage sandwich.'

'Kiss my shitty arse,' the sentry cursed. But the half-tracks were already vanishing into the thick dawn mist. He yawned and went back to his vigil, his stomach rolling persistently at the thought of the canteen of 'nigger's sweat' – black coffee and black bread – which would be his breakfast in another hour's time.

Steadily the big half-tracks, laden with panzer grenadiers,

rumbled towards Aachen, well behind German lines now, but still cautious as if every bend might conceal a platoon of infiltrators, heralding the all-out Ami attack which the defenders of the city had been expecting for nearly twenty-four hours now.

Suddenly the lead half-track came to a halt. The other two rumbled to a rusty-tracked stop behind it. While the panzer grenadiers gripped their weapons in sweaty palms, straining their eyes to penetrate the October morning mist, the lieutenant swung himself easily over the bullet-pocked metal side of his own vehicle. Dropping on to one knee behind the rear track, he waited tensely, feeling the morning dew soaking into his breeches.

The lights were getting closer now. His brain alert, his pulse racing, he counted the headlights. One . . . two . . . three . . . four. Four trucks heading towards them slowly. Tension built up inside him with an electric crackle. Would they turn off at the little muddy crossroads two hundred metres ahead, or would they continue on the side road and bump head-on the three half-tracks, their headlights now extinguished and engines turned off?

The four trucks came closer and closer. The lead driver began to decrease speed even more. The lieutenant, crouched in the grass, felt the sweat start to trickle coldly down the small of his back. He raised his machine-pistol. Had they spotted them? The lead truck braked. He could hear the squeal of the hard rubber tyres on the wet cobbles. He ducked swiftly. The thin blue beams swept by where his head had been. In the half tracks, the panzer grenadiers froze into fearful immobility. The lieutenant swallowed hard, but the first truck was turning off. It was taking the other fork, and its driver had not spotted them, for he was already gathering speed again. One by one the rest followed suit, while the frightened lieutenant prayed fervently that their drivers were as unobservant as the first one. Within a matter of minutes the sound of their motors was dying away in the distance and all was silence again save for the slow chattering of an Ami machine-gun a long way off in the west. The lieutenant breathed a sigh of relief and rose stiffly to his feet. His hands shaking slightly, he walked slowly back to his half-track.

'You can start up again,' he ordered the driver.

The lieutenant climbed aboard and slumped down wearily next to a man wearing the stars of a sergeant-major.

'Great crap on the Christmas Tree,' the swarthy NCO breathed in relief, 'I thought they had got us by the short hairs just then, Lieutenant!'

As the first half-track began to jolt its way up the little secondary road again, the officer nodded his agreement. 'Yes, Fein,' Lieutenant Wertheim answered in English, 'you ain't shitting!'

Wertheim checked his watch. Nearly ten and still the fog was holding as Porter's tame weather man had promised him it would. Thank God, although the fog cover had the disadvantage of making it damn difficult for them to find their base – the shattered farmhouse on the western outskirts, which Porter's man in Aachen had promised him was deserted and one hundred per cent safe.

By now his nerves were thoroughly keyed up. They had been behind Kraut lines for four hours, and his mind was oscillating crazily between two impulses – the need for caution on this last lap of their mission, and the need to get under cover before the fog lifted and they ran out of time.

The three half-tracks clattered through what appeared to be an abandoned hamlet. Their tracks made a hell of a row on the cobbles, Wertheim thought fearfully. He glanced at his men. They were as pale and tense as he was, eyeing the gaping glass windows of the grey stone houses, weapons at the ready, as if they expected the SS to appear at them at any moment. The lead vehicle, provided like the rest from First Army Ordnance's special park of captured enemy weapons, swung round a corner. There were GIs sprawled out everywhere in the extravagant postures of the dead. They were a gory, heart-moving sight, but they filled Wertheim with a sense of relief; for he knew that they were still the dead of the earlier offensive and indicated that no Krauts had been in this area during the period of lull. The Germans would have buried the corpses long ago.

'Lieutenant.' It was Fein.

'Yes?'

'There it is – Crucifixion Hill.'

Fein pointed a dirty forefinger at the hill which had suddenly appeared out of the grey gloom. 'That's the big wooden cross, Porter told us about in the briefing.'

Swiftly Wertheim focused his glasses. All round, the mist lay like thick grey pile carpet. But the height stood out clearly, its great cross an unmistakable landmark. They had made it, passing through the German lines from almost one end to the other. The

Kraut front, facing the Big Red One, would be up there near the hill, perhaps only a matter of a mile away. They were right on target. Their farm hideout couldn't be far away now.

'Okay, driver,' he whispered, lowering his voice instinctively, 'take the next right. That should lead you on to the dirt road, going up to the farm.'

Just as the yellow October sun started to burn away the last of the mist, the three half-tracks began to edge their way down a narrow bumpy dirt road in first gear, the disguised GIs holding their weapons at the ready.

But their caution was unnecessary. As they ground closer to the holed roof of the little farmhouse, they saw that fields on either side, churned up by shell-fire, were also filled with American dead from the previous attack. The Krauts had not been in this area for a long time either, just as Porter had promised them. In spite of his obvious Bostonian anti-semitism, he had at least planned the mission well.

Half an hour later they had the three half-tracks under cover, had eaten, using the special self-heating cans so that they would not have to betray their presence in the smelly, deserted farm to any curious Kraut with nothing better to do than to run his field glasses over the forlorn, battle-torn countryside. Then they settled down to sleep. But, despite his tiredness, Wertheim lay awake. Even though he told himself that Porter's contact man would not be arriving from Aachen for another two hours at least, his nerves were jangling like telephone wires from the benzedrine he had taken the night before. In the end he gave up and, rising stiffly to his feet, went outside to urinate against the farmhouse wall.

The sentry scurried into sight, alarmed by the noise of the hot urine gushing down the stones. When he saw the officer he was embarrassed, trying to salute and lower his rifle at the same time.

Wertheim grinned at the soldier's predicament. 'Do you really expect me to return your salute with my dong in my hand, Rosen?' he asked. 'It ain't exactly the textbook way of doing things, is it?'

Rosen was a twenty-year-old from Berlin whose father had been a captain in the Prussian Foot Guards Regiment Number Four in the old war and had died at Dachau despite his 'Blue

Max'[1] gained for bravery at Verdun in '16. Now he blushed furiously. 'I didn't know it was you, sir,' he said stupidly.

'Who did you think it was then – Betty Grable without her pants? I can't sleep. Too much dope. I'm going to have a look-see at that hill up there. Top-Kick Fein is in charge while I'm away. Kay?'

'Yessir,' Rosen snapped, standing to attention as if he were in the old Prussian Foot Guards himself or back in training at Fort Bliss, instead of deep behind enemy lines on a life-or-death mission.

Shouldering his grease-gun and checking that his two grenades were still attached to his webbing, Wertheim set off cautiously in the direction of the hill feature which dominated the area, hopping expertly from cover to cover as he did so. He had been a trained and experienced infantry officer before he had volunteered for this mission; that was after he had heard his sole surviving relative, his sister Rosie, had died of a 'heart attack' at Theresienstadt. That, at least, was the Swiss Red Cross's report. Rosie, who had been the star girl athlete of her high school in Vienna and the best amateur skier of her age and class in the whole of Upper Austria. That day something had snapped within him and afterwards he knew he would never be the same man again. Now the future no longer interested him. Survival neither. Not even the ordinary animal pleasures of his fellow soldiers – women, food, drink. The only thought present in his mind, save sorrow at Rosie's memory, was that of murder – how he could kill the maximum number of Krauts before they killed him.

Twenty minutes or so later he was sheltering behind a knocked-out civilian Opel truck and surveying the hill with his binoculars, shading the glass carefully with his free hand to prevent it glinting in the slanting rays of the cold October afternoon sun. But he could spot no activity on the crown below the great cross save for a thin trail of blue-grey smoke, which might be coming from some careless soldier's cooking fire.

In the end he gave up; Porter had told him that the hill would play an important role in what was to come, but he would only learn the full details from the fat OSS man's spy from the beleaguered city. Slipping away as carefully as he had approached, he made his way back to the farm, accompanied by the ever-increasing roar of the afternoon barrage that heralded the all-out attack of the morrow.

1. Highest imperial award for bravery in World War I.

He had almost reached their hideout, when a strange slithering sound made him drop to one knee, grease-gun at the ready, his heart thumping with apprehension. Someone was approaching stealthily through the long grass and bracken to the west of the farmhouse. He licked his suddenly dry lips and clicked off his safety catch. The intruder, whoever he might be, was only a matter of yards away now. He raised his grease-gun. Directly ahead, he could see the tops of the bushes waving slightly. He was in there.

Making himself breathe more calmly, knowing that his aim would be unsure if he were forced to open fire, he swallowed and called softly. 'The devil?'

For what seemed an age, nothing happened, except that the soft crawling sound ceased at once. Yet Wertheim sensed that someone was out there in the long grass, as tense and as frightened as he was himself.

He repeated the code word in German, curling his finger around the trigger of the grease-gun, ready to fire if he had made a mistake, 'The devil?'

Hesitantly, a scared voice answered only a score yards away, 'Devil's Shield.'

Wertheim clambered to his feet, his dark eyes shining with relief. 'Over here,' he called urgently.

For a moment nothing happened. Then a fat little man with a shining black eye, dressed in what Wertheim recalled with a shock of recognition was the uniform of the Nazi bully boys from the SA, popped up from the grass, his plump face gleaming with sweat in spite of the cold.

'It's me,' he said in a shaky voice. 'Colonel Porter's man from Aachen.'

FOUR

At nine o'clock precisely on the morning of October 2nd, 'Roosevelt's Butchers' attacked. The German defenders of the northern flank had been expecting the attack ever since the great artillery bombardment had started. Still they were caught off guard in their bunker line. No matter how long you sat and waited, an attack always took you by surprise.

A loud explosion. The first of the bunkers shuddered violently, like a ship in a high sea striking a trough. It was followed by a rapid series of explosions that plastered the whole line, held by second-class troops of one of Donner's 'stomach battalions'. Here and there the ashen-faced defenders panicked and tried to bolt outside. Their NCOs swiftly forced them back to their positions with curses and kicks.

The softening-up bombardment lasted twenty minutes. It stopped abruptly, leaving behind it a sinister and unnatural silence. The stomach battalion men held their breath tensely and wondered what new horrors were going to be sprung upon them. Peering through the observation slits, their officers and NCOs could see a grey-fogged lunar landscape, stark, ruined and desolate. The minutes ticked by in leaden foreboding.

Suddenly a heavy Ami machine-gun began to fire, hammering away like an angry-woodpecker. White tracer sailed through the air, slow at first, but growing faster with every instant. The first 50-mm slugs started to patter against the thick concrete walls of the bunkers. The observers ducked instinctively, atlhough they were safe enough. Everywhere now, other Ami heavy machine-guns joined in, aiming at the observation slits in an attempt to blind the bunker line.

'Stand by,' the NCOs barked. 'Here they come!'

The stomach battalion men sprang to their positions. In the command bunker, a choleric battalion commander who had lost half his stomach at Stalingrad whirled the handle of the field telephone and bellowed at the artillery commander dug in five hundred metres to the rear, 'Get those shitty Ami mgs for me, will you! *But quick!*'

Moments later the big howitzers crashed into action. Great half-metre-long shells hissed through the air, smashing into the Ami machine-gun battalion. One by one the machine-guns, easily located by their tracer, were knocked out. The Ami infantry, waiting in the long grass at the edge of the stream which fronted the bunker line, were without protection. But there was no stopping now.

Their officers rose to their feet. Whistles were blown. Red-faced irate noncoms bellowed orders and kicked those to their feet who were too slow.

'At the double,' the battalion commander roared.

Carrying the duckboards that were to provide dry paths across the stream, they lumbered heavily through the sodden fields of suger beat and turnips. A moving target is less easily hit than a stationary one, as their officers had drummed into them while they had been training for the great attack. Now they operated on that theory.

A young second lieutenant, with the build of a football player, doubled forward ahead of the rest, duckboard clutched tight to his chest. He splashed into the stream and slapped it into place.

'There's your goddam bridge!' he yelled at the men behind him.

A second later the first German bullet slammed into him and he fell face forward into the water, his helmet rolling on one side.

The German machine-gunners hissed into high-pitched action. The first wave of Amis was scythed down in a flash, turning the dirty water red with their blood. The second wave came on, using their fallen comrades as bridges, trampling pitilessly on their torn, bleeding bodies.

For a moment they were in blind ground. Then they came up over the far bank of the stream, screaming angrily. In their midst they had half a dozen soldiers with strange unwieldy packs on their shoulders, bouncing up and down rapidly as they doubled forward.

'Jesus, Mary, Joseph!' one of the stomach battalion men gasped. 'Flame-throwers!'

'Hold your stupid Bavarian trap!' an officer snapped angrily, not taking his eyes from the observation slit.

The first of the flame-throwers went into action. While the infantry men to his right and left poured a stream of covering fire at the nearest bunker, he doubled in from the side, safe now because the bunker was momentarily blinded. At ten-yard range, he pressed the trigger of his terrible weapon. A long tongue of blue-red flame, tinged with oily brown, blazed out and wrapped itself momentarily around the bunker. It disappeared in an instant, leaving a steaming blackened mark on the concrete. In front of the soldier the grass had vanished completely. He pressed the trigger again. The flame embraced the bunker greedily once more. Another soldier doubled forward, crouched low, an explosive charge tied loosely to the end of a ten-foot pole. Skilfully he poked it through the nearest slit. They heard a thick muffled crump and the sound of muted screaming. Heavy black smoke started to pour from the slit. The Amis waited.

Suddenly a blackened, bare-headed figure stumbled out of the bunker's rear entrance, his clothes in rags, his arms held high above his head.

68

'Comrade ... comrade,' he croaked weakly.

The man with the flame-thrower straightened up. He could tell from the Kraut's boots that he was an officer. He would have a Luger and a Luger would fetch a small fortune on the black market in Paris's Pig Alley.[1] He began to run heavily towards him to get his hands on the pistol before the rest, but in that instant the officer fired. The Ami fell without a sound.

'He killed Smitty!' a furious voice yelled. 'The son of a bitch shot Smitty!'

A good dozen men turned their weapons on the German officer. His body was whirled round by the impact of the concentrated fire. The GIs rushed and pumped the rest of their magazines into his twitching body. Still angry, they threw grenade after grenade into the bunker's rear entrance. After a while no more sound came from within.

The attack went on. By eleven o'clock the first bunker line had been taken. The stomach battalion was wiped out, the bunkers and their support trenches awash with blood. Mangled bodies, American and German, lay everywhere, locked together in death. And in the wraithlike smoke that covered the ground ahead, their commander staggered back to his own second line of defence, a bayonet thrust through his throat.

Donner's HQ at the Hotel Quellenhof on the outskirts of Aachen was in a state of acute alarm. Staff officers ran up and down the corridors, where genteel elderly guests had once walked to take the waters, maps clutched in their elegant hands. Dispatch-riders, their ankle-length leather coats splattered with mud from top to bottom, roared in and out of the courtyard. Black-clad SS NCOs bellowed orders to their men to form up, ready for instant action.

But von Dodenburg, who had experienced this kind of situation many times in the last five years of war, did not seem to share Donner's alarm.

'General,' he said firmly, tapping the big wall map. 'The breakthrough at Rimburg cannot be the main push. Look at the distance the Amis will have to cover before they are within striking range of the city itself.'

'But von Dodenburg,' Donner protested. 'They are pouring men into the gap they've forced there. Our observers are pretty shaken, I realise that, but they estimate that the Amis have passed through at least three battalions and a prisoner states that

1. GI slang for Pigalle.

69

the whole of the 30th Infantry Division is involved, plus support troops.'

Von Dodenburg nodded his agreement. 'I don't dispute that, General. But is Rimburg their *Schwerpunkt*?[1]' He answered his own question. 'Definitely not.' He tapped the area on the map held by General Huebner's First Division. 'This is where our main attack will come. After all, the Amis there are almost in Aachen's surburbs.'

'But they haven't made a move yet, von Dodenburg,' Donner protested, taking out his glass eye and polishing it. 'To the north, however, they must have already gained a kilometre since this morning. What are you going to do about it?'

Von Dodenburg took a deep breath. 'I'm going to take a calculated risk, General. If I commit Wotan there and the Amis attack on the southern flank, we are sunk. You could say goodbye to Aachen then. I haven't got enough men to stop an all-out drive on both fronts. Rimburg is the lesser evil for me.'

Donner sucked his yellow false teeth thoughtfully for a moment. 'All right, von Dodenburg, so be it. We'll wait with your Wotan until we see how the other flank develops. But what happens if you're wrong?'

Von Dodenburg forced a grin. 'Then, my dear General, we are definitely in the shit – very deep in the shit indeed.'

All afternoon 'Roosevelt's Butchers' continued their drive towards Rimburg, steadily punching holes in Donner's line and forcing his second-class troops to retreat to new positions. The fields were shell-pitted everywhere, grass torn and trampled. Abandoned, shattered farmhouses bore the signs of companies and battalions which no longer existed. The cobbled country roads were lined by trees, broken off half-way by the shellfire, the roads themselves littered with jagged shrapnel like the scabs of an ugly disease.

Now the 30th Infantry was taking serious casualties. Some of the reinforcements, culled from the Service of Supply and thrown into the line as riflemen after a mere three weeks' infantry course, were hit within five minutes of entering their first battle. Some survived the whole afternoon and found themselves as acting private first class, acting corporal, acting buck sergeant commanding platoons that had been reduced to five or six men.

But the casualties did not worry Hobbs. The big general con-

1. Untranslatable phrase. Roughly 'area of main concentration'.

fidently told his attentive staff, 'My doughs have got their feet over the dashboard. We're nearly there. The Krauts are bugging out. They'll be creaming their skivvies by night-fall.' Privately he started to compose the divisional communiqué for the morrow, full of resounding bombastic phrases about, 'living up to the glorious traditions of the 30th US Infantry Division . . . never in the history of land warfare . . . unparalleled in the annals of the United States Army'. He had just arrived at 'and so I say to you, officers and men of the 30th US Infantry Division, that this day all America is watching you', when he was called to the phone by one of his aides. It was Colonel Sutherland of the 119th Infantry Regiment.

Sutherland did not pull his punches. 'General,' he gasped urgently, 'the Kraut has got us by the short and curlies up here at Rimburg.'

'What happened?'

'My point bumped into half a dozen flak wagons.[1] Now they've got the whole lead battalion pinned down in an area of five hundred square yards. As soon as anyone dares put up his head, he gets it blown off.'

'Hold yer water, Sutherland, hold yer water,' Hobbs said soothingly. 'I'll fix it. The Division's got a release on the Ninth TAC Air Force. I'll have the mediums up there within the hour.'

'You'd better, General,' Sutherland answered shortly. 'Because if you don't, there won't be much of the 119th left soon. Over.'

'Over and out,' Hobbs said perfunctorily and told himself once again that the guys in the line never saw the big picture – that's why they invariably panicked when something went wrong. He talked to his G.I. 'Get me Air will you – and make it snappy!'

The twin-engined Mitchells came in at 300 mph. Flak screamed up at them. A bomber exploded in mid-air. When the black smoke cleared, all that was left was a single wing floating down like a broken leaf. Still they came on until they were over the front line. The deadly black eggs started to tumble out of their silver bellies. The American soldiers stared upwards happily, careless of the Kraut fire now.

'Go on, boys,' they yelled. 'Give em hell!' But their enthusiastic cries died on their lips when they saw the direction the bombs were taking.

1. Armoured tracked vehicles mounting 4.20-mm flak cannons.

71

'Hit the dirt, guys!' a young officer up front cried urgently, choked with sudden fear.

He was too late, for the whole weight of the bombing had descended upon the American section of the front. They were submerged in a screaming inferno. The whole of the lead battalion was dead or dying. Frantic officers rose to their feet, bracing themselves against the trembling earth, unconcerned by the flying shrapnel, firing signal flares high into the air. The Germans at the flak wagons, a matter of two hundred yards away, reacted immediately. They fired the same colour flares, assuming – correctly – that the Ami pilots above them would think that the first set of flares was a trick to put them off their target. Then the battlefield was covered in thick yellow explosive fumes and nothing could save the 119th.

By dusk, Hobbs's advance had stalled completely and the survivors of the 119th, shocked and bitter called the Ninth TAC Air Force, the 'American Luftwaffe'. Hobbs ordered an inquiry.

In Aachen, a nervous von Dodenburg did not know of the failure of Hobbs's attack till much later. All that long afternoon with the rumble of the Ami artillery getting closer and closer, and the alarming reports of further Ami advances flooding into Donner's HQ, he wondered whether he had made the right decision. Twice he contacted the look-out post on Hill 239 which overlooked the Big Red One's positions and asked for news. But the observer's report was laconic and disappointing.

'Nothing to report from up here, sir. Unless you want to know about the Ami over there who's got the shits and is always using the latrine.'

Colonel von Dodenburg did not want to know.

It started to get dark. Still nothing from the First Division's front. He began to wonder if he had not made a major tactical mistake. Donner did not say anything, but his glassy stare indicated that he thought von Dodenburg certainly had. At five-thirty, at the start of another Ami bombardment of the old city, he put his panzer grenadiers on red alert. They were to stand by their half-tracks, ready to be thrown into the battle on the 30th Infantry's front. Still a voice within him warned him to hold them back. He hung on.

At six, he decided he must make some sort of attempt to find out what the Big Red One's intention was. He called Schwarz to his office.

'Schwarz, I'm going to take out a patrol to Height 239. One can cover the whole Ami front up there. Even though it's dark, I think I should be able to spot any large-scale concentration.'

The one-armed major, who knew how his CO had sweated out the afternoon, nodded his agreement. 'I think you are right, sir, but just one thing. I'd like to go with you sir. I'm getting sick of sitting on my arse here in the HQ.'

Von Dodenburg made his mind up quickly. 'All right, I'll take you, Matz as driver and Schulze as muscle. By the way, where is Schulze?'

But the ex-docker was nowhere to be found. He wasn't even in the kitchen with the kitchen bulls, indulging in his second favourite activity – scrounging food.

In the end Matz volunteered to find him. 'I think I know where he is, sir,' he told von Dodenburg with a knowing look.

The CO smiled thinly. 'Don't tell me – I can guess, Matz. But tell him if he isn't back here in battle equipment ready to go within thirty minutes, he's going to be the unhappiest *private* soldier in Battle Group Wotan.'

'So this is where you are, you randy ox,' Matz gasped, as he pushed aside the little SA man with one careless sweep of his hand. 'I've been looking for you everywhere.'

'Piss off,' Schulze said without rancour. 'Can't you see I'm busy, you horrible garden dwarf!'

He was naked save for his dice-beakers and pistol-belt. He always maintained that 'a good soldier's ready for battle – or bed – at any time!' And Matz could see that the big sergeant-major was ready for both. Putting his hand on the blonde's pudding-like breast, he gave it a hard squeeze and stuck his tongue in her left ear, ignoring the red-faced, panting Matz.

'Schulze,' he pleaded. 'Come on, get your duds on. You're needed.'

'Didin't I tell you piss off?' Schulze breathed, his voice muffled. 'I don't fancy a threesome tonight. Go away into the corner and tackle the five-fingered widow, or have you hurt your wrist again?'

Matz ignored the insult. 'Schulze, the CO is going up the walls. You're wanted on patrol. We're off up to Height 239 – wherever the hell that is – you, me, the CO and that crazy man Schwarz. Now come on!'

Schulze took his hand from the whore's breast. 'Oh, you piss Henry, Matz, why didn't you tell me before?'

'I did, you horn-ox. But you wouldn't listen. Now in heaven's name, get on your hind legs and let's get the hell out of here before the CO has the eggs off us.'

Clamping his helmet firmly on his big head, Schulze turned to the whore and bowed gravely over her hard calloused hand, as if he were a hero in one of those Viennese operetta films that were so popular that autumn in the Reich, and she were some society heroine.

'Madam,' he declared, 'I'm afraid I must leave. The trumpets are sounding and the drums of war are beating. My duty is at the front where I shall ride at the head of my men. Till then I beg you to wait loyally for me. Hark, the cannon are beginning to roar.' He raised his left leg and gave vent to one of his celebrated farts.

His voice back to normal, he added. 'And mind you keep those knees of yours crossed till I get back. I don't want that dirty old rear-echelon stallion getting it up.' He indicated the SA man.

Laughing uproariously, Schulze rushed out into the street, naked as he was, his clothes in a careless bundle beneath his arm, with Matz limping after him as best he could.

The SA man waited till the sound of their boots on the cobbles had died away completely. Then he raised himself. 'I'm going out,' he announced.

The girls did not react.

'I said I'm going out,' he repeated.

'All right, all right,' said the blowsy blonde whore, busy pulling on her black panties again. 'Take off! Don't give me a shitty heart attack about it. Piss off!' She turned round, ignoring him as if he were less than the cockroaches which crawled up the dirty concrete walls of the cellar.

The SA man clenched his fists. 'Sow,' he cursed under his breath. 'Just you wait. One day soon you'll be singing a different shitting tune.'

But he controlled himself in time. Thrusting up his collar, he pushed aside the blackout curtain and stepped into the pink-tinged night. The Jewboys would be very grateful for the information he had about SS Colonel Kuno von Dodenburg – very grateful indeed.

74

FIVE

The little VW jeep, driven by Matz, ground by the straggling rows of houses that lined the country road, with Schulze eyeing the apparently deserted street suspiciously, finger on the trigger of his Schmeisser. At the least sign of movement, he would fire. Although they were still within the German lines, the big NCO had an uneasy feeling that everything was not well.

'What's the matter with you, Schulze?' von Dodenburg sitting beside him asked. 'Wind up?'

'Of course not, sir,' Schulze answered firmly. 'But you can't be too careful — and I wouldn't want to drive right into the Ami lines.'

'What? And miss that real coffee and real cigarettes they keep promising us in their leaflets?' von Dodenburg said.

'They can stick their real coffee and real cigarettes right up their fat Ami arses,' Schulze growled.

The little VW left the hamlet. A heavy, unnatural silence, broken only by the persistent rumble of the heavies in the distance, hung over the rough, winding road leading up to Height 239. They passed what had once been a thick pine wood. Now the trees were flattened and the German convoy which had been sheltering in its cover was scattered everywhere – overturned Opel trucks, burnt-out VW jeeps, a shattered armoured car, still glowing a dull-red with the heat, and dead bodies everywhere.

'Oh, my aching back,' Matz groaned at the wheel, 'there's enough roasted meat in that wood to feed half the Wehrmacht for a whole week!'

'Knock it off,' von Dodenburg snapped, appalled by the sight of half a dozen bodies lying in the nearside ditch, charred black by the intense heat and shrunken to the size of small children. 'Those poor bastards over there were once your comrades.'

They drove on in an embarrassed silence towards the height, outlined menacingly against the pink-tinged battlefield sky. Schulze swallowed and licked his dry lips, trying in vain to fight off a sense of foreboding and apprehension. He knew that something was going to happen – that something was wrong. But he could not put his finger on it.

Lieutenant Wertheim had planned the ambush on the narrow country road leading up to Crucifixion Hill very carefully. He had spread the bulk of his men along both sides of the road in the ditches to a depth of twenty yards. Once the Kraut colonel came driving up, forced to slow down by the hairpin bend site he had selected, one of his men would slip out of the trees and lay a daisy chain of Hawkins grenades to the rear. Even if the Kraut escaped the ambush and tried to back out, his vehicle would run into the grenades. His own guess was that if the Kraut became suspicious and tried to make a run for it, he would bug out to one side of the road, and as he told Fein, 'The boys will give the bastard what he deserves – a bellyfull of good old American lead!'

All the same he knew he had to make sure that he had gotten the right man. The success of the Big Red One's push depended upon their killing the SS colonel. According to Porter, von Dodenburg's SS Battle Group was the only real fighting force in Aachen. Without him, the defence would fold up and Huebner's boys would be able to take the city with their eyes closed and one hand tied behind their backs.

'So what do we do, Fein?' he had asked the burly unshaven Top Kick after they had picked the site of their ambush. 'You and me have got to check the bastard out. We'll stop him with this,' he had indicated the red light and the rough-and-ready German traffic signal he had fashioned during the night in the deserted farmhouse. 'Once we know we've got the right guy, we shout to the men and hit the dirt fast! My guess is that the Kraut will try to break left or right and you know what will happen then?'

Fein had nodded sagely. 'Yeah, Lieutenant, it'll be curtains for the Kraut.'

'You ain't shitting, soldier.'

But Lieutenant David Wertheim did not know the men of Wotan.

Time passed leadenly. Twice there were false alarms. Once a column of ancient nags bearing supplies for the men on the height came plodding by, the steel-helmeted German drivers clearly silhouetted against the night sky. For Wertheim it was a strange feeling to be crouching so close to them, while they passed in weary file unaware that they were being watched by men whom they had once driven out of their country so cruelly that now their greatest desire was to kill so many of their comrades as possible. Half an hour later a motor-cycle combination rattled past, the dispatch-rider's fat leather pouch clearly outlined against his greatcoated belly. Thereafter silence.

At about eight, as the Big Red One's artillery fire started to intensify, he heard the faint but definite sound of a motor grinding up the slope in second gear. Wertheim dug Fein in the ribs urgently.

'It could be them,' he snapped. 'Warn the guys.'

Fein slipped his two fingers in his mouth and gave a shrill whistle. Concealed by the bushes, the waiting men crawled into their positions, weapons held at the ready. To the rear, the man with the daisy chain crouched behind a tree ready to slip out and cut the road off, once the unsuspecting enemy had passed. Wertheim clutched the traffic disc in his sweaty palm.

'Stand by with that signal light, Fein,' he hissed, his throat strangely constricted.

'Wilco, Lieutenant!'

The roar of the motor came closer and closer. Wertheim felt his heart thumping violently. He swallowed hard and told himself to calm down. For a moment it worked. Then his heart was thumping so loudly again that he thought Fein, crouched next to him, could not help but hear it. Suddenly a little VW jeep swept round the corner and he found himself illuminated in the blue glare of its headlights.

'The signal, Fein,' he yelled and in the same instant, holding up the traffic disc, added loudly: 'HALT!'

Matz hit the brakes. There was a rusty squeal and the VW jeep slowed down rapidly. Wertheim pressed the trigger of his grease gun. Nothing! It had jammed.

'Fein,' he screamed, 'hit the bastards – *quick!*'

Fein dropped to one knee and levelled his carbine. Too late! Matz, bleeding from a shoulder wound, was reacting as the Wotan men always did, trained by the bloody partisan warfare in Russia where every secondary road behind the line was always liable to be ambushed. Cursing like a lunatic, he crashed home first gear, crouching low over the wheel. Next to him Schwarz let go a wild burst of Schmeisser fire. Behind him von Dodenburg and Schulze, carrying out the anti-partisan techniques automatically, fired into the trees on both sides. Then contrary to Wertheim's expectations, Matz drove his jeep straight forward. Wertheim flung his useless grease-gun at the roaring jeep. It clattered against the side purposelessly. At the last moment, he sprang to one side. The burly Top Kick was not so quick. He screamed piteously as the corrugated pointed nose of the jeep struck him squarely in the chest. Then he fell under it and the one-and-a-half-ton weight rolled over his body, the left wheel crunching his bearded face to a pulp.

'You sadistic bastards,' Wertheim screamed, tears of rage streaming down his cheeks. He fumbled frantically for the grenade attached to his belt. From the right a bazooka fired, but the aim was too wild. The projectile struck the cobbles a couple of yards away from the jeep. A shower of fiery sparks. The bomb ricocheted upwards and caught the vehicle in the rear axle.

The jeep skidded to one side as a tyre exploded. It slewed round in a crazy semi-circle, flinging the occupants of the jeep on to the road in a crazy heap.

But the veterans of the Wotan reacted quicker than their ambushers in the ditch. They scrambled hurriedly to their feet, firing as they did so. A heavy-set man charged Schulze. He side-stepped and gave him a swift chop across the throat. Another ran at Matz, tommy-gun clasped tightly to his hip. Matz, angry at being wounded for the fourth time and yelping with pain, lowered his hard head and butted him in the guts like an enraged billy goat. The man dropped, gasping hard. Matz bent, seized him by both ears and bashed his bare head against an upturned cobble.

'Over here – for Christ's sake, *over here!*' Wertheim yelled desperately, as the four SS men started to back up the hill firing in short, concentrated bursts. It was a foolish thing to do.

'*Get that bastard, Schulze,*' von Dodenburg ordered above the rattle of their Schmeissers.

Schulze doubled forward, while the other three covered him, swinging their crouched bodies from left to right systematically, as they swept the trees with tracer, keeping their ambushers at bay.

Wertheim flung his stick grenade. It exploded harmlessly, a good dozen yards behind the big man doubling towards him. All it served to do was to illuminate him momentarily in its blinding red-white light. Wertheim grabbed at his boot. He had his trench-knife stuck down inside. But his trembling frantic fingers never found it. Two hundred pounds of trained muscle crashed into him. He went down with a stifled gasp as a heavy nailed boot smashed into his jaw. Red lights danced before his eyes.

Just before he lost consciousness, he felt himself being lifted unceremoniously and flung over the big man's shoulder. Then Lieutenant David Wertheim blacked out, knowing that Operation Black Guard had failed.

SIX

'You filthy Hebrew swine – wake up, will you?' the metallic voice thundered. 'Come on, you heap of shit, open your eyes!'

The voice seemed to come from a long, long way away, but there was no mistaking its fervent hatred nor the fact that he was a prisoner in Kraut hands.

Slowly Wertheim shook his head. It felt twice its normal size. He wiped his hand across his face. He felt something warm and wet. He opened his eyes and stared down at his palm. It was smeared red with blood – his blood. He raised his head. A blurred picture of Adolf Hitler came into view. Then a face – a terrible, mutilated face, one half of which looked as if it had been chewed away by a wild animal. He closed his eyes again, wanting to blot it out.

'Schwarz,' rasped the voice which had awakened him, 'make him open his eyes.'

A small pause. Then a fist that seemed to be made of steel smashed into his unsuspecting face. Wertheim flew against the wall, his chair careening after him. A boot splintered his ribs. He cried out with pain. He let himself go limp to try to minimize the effect of the kicking. It seemed to go on for ever. He felt himself beginning to bleed inside.

'Thank you, Schwarz,' the voice said, 'that is sufficient.'

The man who was kicking him, his breath coming in thick pleasurable gasps, did not respond at once and the metallic voice had to repeat the order before the kicking finally stopped. Wertheim lay there weakly, allowing the warm blood to trickle down his side.

'All right, put him back in the chair, again, will you.'

Big hands seized him, as if he were an infant and placed him back in the chair. The horrible mutilated face came close to his. The stench of faeces was overpowering. He gagged. But the face did not move away. The one immobile glassy eye bored into his.

'Now, you shitty Yid,' the cold voice said without any emotion, 'I am going to ask you some questions and I want the answers to those questions – quickly!' To emphasise his point, the German grabbed Wertheim's cropped hair and pulled up his battered face to within inches of his own. 'Do you understand?'

'I'm an American officer – that's all I can say,' Wertheim gasped painfully, his tear-filled eyes screwed up with the pressure exerted on his scalp.

'You are a Yid, born in the East Mark[1] – and you have absolutely no protection. We can do with you exactly what we want. Then you were dressed in German uniform when we captured you. Even the shitty Swiss Red Cross can do nothing about that.'

Wertheim said nothing. His mind was racing, trying to find a way out. But he knew his position was hopeless, no better than that of a spy.

The mutilated questioner seemed able to read his mind. 'You understand, don't you Jew? You are a non-person now. A dead man who is still walking around. All that is left to you is to decide the manner of your death.'

'What do you mean?' Wertheim croaked through blood-caked lips.

Donners relaxed his grip on the prisoner's dark crew cut. 'Whether you will die as a human being or whether you are tortured to death like a base animal, Jew.'

Wertheim understood all too well. But his hatred was greater than his fear. He thought of Rosie and how beautiful she had once looked before she had disappeared into the maws of the concentration camp with its mocking sign above the gate, WORK MAKES FREE. 'Of course I understand, what you mean, you cripple,' he yelled angrily. Then his burning rage and fear ran away with him, 'CRIPPLE . . . CRIPPLE . . . CRIPPLE . . .' he shouted over and over again.

In the end Donner had had enough. Trying to control himself, feeling the faeces dribbling out of his ruined body as anger overwhelmed him, he thundered, 'Schwarz – Schulze, stop the Yiddish bastard, will you!'

Schulze rolled up his sleeves. 'All right, Lieutenant, this is where you started collecting your teeth in your cap!' He doubled his ham of a fist. But before he could bring it crashing into Wertheim's tortured face, Schwarz, his mouth contorted with rage, smashed his wooden fist down like a club on the nape of Wertheim's neck.

1. National Socialist name for Austria after its incorporation in the Reich after 1938.

The lieutenant screamed shrilly. Like two boxers working out in some dirty backroom gym, beating a punchbag with routine precision, the two SS men began to beat up the American officer, the silence broken only by their heavy breathing and the thud of their fists on his flesh.

It seemed to go on for ever, but finally a distant voice said: 'All right, he's had enough for the time being.'

The two SS men stepped back, panting. The one who spoke with a Hamburg accent spat on his knuckles as if they hurt. The other one – the officer – stood there motionless, his crazy black eyes full of hate.

The horrible face loomed up through the haze again. Once more the stench of faeces was overpowering. 'Listen Jew,' the metallic voice rasped. 'I am a professional police officer. I have been all my life. For thirty years I have been used to asking people like you questions and getting the answers to those questions. In the old days in Weimar we had to work more slowly. Now, our methods are a little more streamlined.' He doubled his fist to indicate what he meant. 'But in both cases, I always got my answers – even from much tougher people than you, Jew. Do you understand?'

Wertheim said nothing. His mouth was still full of blood from the gaps where his teeth had once been. Donner paused for a moment, considering how he should phrase the all-important questions. Behind him at the window, Colonel von Dodenburg frowned. He knew how vital it was to elicit the information from the skinny Jewish officer, but he didn't like methods of this kind. 'For God's sake answer and let's get it over with, Jew,' he told himself, angry at the Jew's stubbornness.

'Now, this is what I want to know,' Donner continued. 'Firstly when and where is your First Division going to attack. Secondly, who was your informant about Colonel von Dodenburg within the city?' He thrust his face close to Wertheim's, puffed up now to the size of a balloon. 'Now then, Jew, what do you say?'

With the last of his strength, knowing already what the results of his action would be, Wertheim hawked and spat directly into that terrible face.

Donner sprang back, pale with shock. With the spittle dripping down his cheek, he cried: 'Schwarz – Schwarz, hit the filthy bastard!'

A flood of icy water hit him in the face. Wertheim came to, spluttering with shock. He blinked rapidly several times. But the mist would not clear and for some reason that he could not establish, his eyes would not open properly. His vision was limited to a blurred slit. Then a pair of highly polished boots stepped into his line of vision. They halted. One of them thudded into his side as he lay in the puddle of water. He gasped with pain.

'You're awake, Jew, are you?' the metallic voice said. 'Good, well you've had your little sleep. Now we're going to get the answer to our questions without wasting any more time. Schulze, fill it up.'

'Must we?' a worried voice asked a long way away.

'There is no time to be squeamish, von Dodenburg,' the metallic voice answered. 'The fate of Aachen depends upon this. If you don't like it, you can go away till it's all over.'

'No, I'll stay.'

There was a long silence, broken only by the sound of rushing water. Wertheim tried to raise his head to ascertain what it was. But he simply did not have the strength.

Finally the rushing sound stopped. 'It's full now, sir,' snapped the Hamburg voice of one of his torturers.

'Thank you, Schulze. All right, you can begin.'

The man with the Hamburg voice must have hesitated, for the command was repeated: 'All right, Schulze, I said you can begin, man! Don't you understand German?'

'Yes, sir. Sorry sir.'

The next instant, a big hand seized Wertheim by the scruff of the neck. His head was forced down. Through the puffed slits that were his eyes, he stared down at a sheet of water. With sudden terror, he realised what they were going to do to him and he kicked out desperately. The man holding him had been expecting the move. He dodged the blow easily. The next moment his head was forced into the bath. His mouth opened. Water poured in. Frantically he tried to breathe. The water filled his lungs. He squirmed and struggled like a madman. But he could not escape that vice-like grip. A roaring blackness swamped him. Just when he felt he must drown, the pressure decreased and he was allowed to flop face-downwards on the tiled floor retching agonisingly and vomiting blood and water, his heart beating like a trip-hammer.

'Do you want to answer my questions now, Jew?' The boot thudded into his broken ribs once again. But now he no longer felt the pain, just an overwhelming sense of relief at being able to breathe again.

'It's no use, General,' the Prussian voice said, its horror apparent even to the man lying in the pool of bloody vomit on the floor. 'He won't crack and time's running out. Leave him.'

'He'll crack, von Dodenburg, don't worry. They always crack in the end. Schulze, once more please – this time a little longer.'

This time someone grabbed his feet and he was flung bodily into the bath. The side of his head struck the bottom. Blood-red stars exploded before his eyes. The bubbles of air shot from his mouth and his lungs started to fill with water. He writhed crazily and fought to escape that terrible hold. He evacuated his bowels with fear. He knew he was drowning. It was a matter of seconds now. A red roar filled his ears. In a second he would be dead.

They pulled him out just in time, vomiting pink-tinged water and screaming between his frantic hungry gasps for air, 'I'll talk ... I'll talk ... please let me talk ...'

And leaning cynically against the wall of the bathroom, staring down at the helpless pathetic wretch of a prisoner, Donner laughed.

'The First kicks off its attack at zero five hours tomorrow morning,' Wertheim whispered in a husky voice, his eyes fixed on the floor.

'Where?' Donner rasped.

Wertheim did not answer immediately. Von Dodenburg leaned forward anxiously.

'*Where?*' the SS General persisted.

Wertheim swallowed hard. 'Verlautenheide,' he whispered, so low that his silent listeners had to strain to understand. 'It's near—'

'Yes, we know,' Donner snapped irritably, 'we know. But what is the First's objective?'

The Jewish officer, his sorely beaten face already beginning to turn a hideous green and black, licked his bloody lips as if he were reluctant to answer. Donner thrust forward his hideous mutilated face aggressively, an unspoken threat in his one eye.

Wertheim whispered. 'Crucifixion Hill.'

'Where?' von Dodenburg broke in.

'Height 239 – where you took me prisoner.'

Von Dodenburg looked at Donner triumphantly. 'Of course,' he cried, 'the height. It dominates the whole area. If they link up there, with the other Ami division coming up from Rimburg, they've got us cut off from our supplies. Then they can reduce the city at their leisure.' He turned to Schwarz, who seemed unable to take his eyes off the broken prisoner's face, 'Major Schwarz, alert the panzer grenadiers. They can beef up the men on the height. We'll keep the tank companies in reserve lest the Amis throw a feint at the city itself.'

Schwarz shook himself out of his reverie. 'Yessir,' he snapped, clicking his heels together like the excellent soldier he was.

'Schulze, can Matz drive?' he swung round on the big NCO. 'Or is that shoulder of his too bad?'

'The only thing that'll stop Matz, sir,' Schulze said, relieved now that the nasty business of torture was over, 'is a big burst of HE in his eggs!'

Von Dodenburg had no time for humour. 'Good. Bring up the command tank. We're going out to the height with the panzer grenadiers. And check that the smoke launcher is armed. I don't want to be caught up there by Ami infantry with no smoke grenades, in case we've got to take off smartly. You saw what that Ami bazooka did to the jeep.'

'You don't need to draw me a picture, sir,' Schulze said, taking a last look at the man whose face he had helped to beat to a pulp. 'Mrs Schulze's boy is awfully anxious to come out of this war with his skin intact.' He saluted and disappeared through the open door followed by Schwarz a moment later.

Von Dodenburg bit his lip thoughtfully, while from below the first sounds of the emergency move – whistles, commands, angry shouts – start to float up. 'General, I'll need more muscle in case that feint develops into something serious. Can you release one of your stomach battalions for transfer to the Big Red One front?'

Donner shook his head. 'No, von Dodenburg. You'll have to make do with what you've got.'

'Can I go and clean myself up?' Wertheim interrupted.

The two SS officers turned. They'd forgotten about their prisoner. His head was hanging low so that they could not see the sudden determination in his pain-filled, bloodshot eyes. Wertheim weakly indicated his soiled pants.

Donner shook his head. 'We have no time for that now, Jew,' he said firmly. 'Besides, what the devil does it matter what you look like? You will die within the hour as soon as we have finished our work here.'

Von Dodenburg looked at the pathetic wreck of a man, swaying slightly as he stood there before them, the water dripping from his torn uniform. 'There is a latrine at the end of the corridor.' He slapped a hand against his revolver holster. 'You can go in there and clean up, but don't try anything foolish.'

'Thank you,' Wertheim croaked, still not raising his face, afraid that the look in his eyes would give him away.

He started to stagger down the corridor, trailing water after him. The two SS officers watched him, amazed that he could still walk after his terrible punishment. Von Dodenburg was the first to realise what the Jew was going to do.

'HALT!' he roared.

Wertheim broke into a shambling run. The window he had spotted from the room where the black bastards had tortured him was only ten yards away now.

'HALT – OR I FIRE!' von Dodenburg yelled, fumbling with the flap of his holster.

Wertheim drew on his last reserves of energy. Sucking in a deep breath and feeling the pain sear through his broken ribs into his torn lung, he flung himself towards the window just as von Dodenburg fired.

The slug slammed into the wall of the corridor a yard from his head. Plaster and brick showered his face. He shook his head angrily and, a split second later, dived forward. He hit the window headfirst, shattering the glass. The high-pitched scream of agony was ripped from his mouth by the wind as he hurtled to the ground. He struck the cobble yard four storeys below at nearly 60 mph. The fall broke every bone in his body, which bounced high into the air like a rubber ball, before flopping down once more. He twitched convulsively in his death throes then lay still, arms flung out dramatically, staring unseeingly at the dark German sky, dead at last.

High above, the two black-clad officers stared in reluctant respect at the body illuminated in the thin icy-blue beam of the command Tiger's headlights. Blood seeped everywhere, outlining Wertheim in a star of red. Then, mercifully, Schulze turned off the headlights and all was silent save for the steady purr of the Royal Tiger's diesels.

THREE: THE BIG PUSH

'We're the SS, Schulze, hated and feared wherever we go and one day those people who hate and fear us will attempt to take their revenge for these last five years. What else can we do but to fight on?' *Colonel von Dodenburg to Sergeant-Major Schulze, October 1944.*

ONE

The great 155-mm shell tore the dawn stillness apart.

'Arseholes up – three cheers, America!' Schulze yelled next to Colonel von Dodenburg and ducked.

The shell exploded with a hellish crash two hundred metres beyond Crucifixion Hill. Flame spurted high into the air, and the men crouched on top of the Royal Tiger were showered with dirt and pebbles.

'The symphony concert has begun,' von Dodenburg cried sardonically.

The Ami 'Long Tom'[1] spoke again. Automatically the observers underneath the towering cross sucked in their heads. Another shell threw up a great plume of smoke and dirt a hundred metres ahead of them.

'They're ranging in, sir,' Matz, his shoulder heavily bandaged, yelled, as the full weight of the Ami barrage descended upon the panzer grenadiers dug in at the crest of the hill. 'Here comes number three.' Von Dodenburg's answer was drowned in the roar of fire. Their Royal Tiger shuddered violently, as if it were a child's tin toy and not sixty tons of Krupp steel.

Now the whole front beyond the Ami start-line near Verlautenheide was deluged in a wave of fire from Huebner's eleven artillery battalions, supported by 4.2-inch chemical mortar batteries, borrowed from 'Lightning Joe's' corps artillery. The world became a screaming, red-roaring hell, as the earth beneath the panzer grenadiers rocked violently.

Above them the little L-5 spotter plane buzzed round in slow mocking circles, directing the softening-up barrage on to the German positions. Once a shell-crazed soldier sprang up on to the top of his foxhole and, legs braced apart, wild meaningless phrases tumbling from his slack, foam-tinged lips, fired an enraged burst at the Ami plane. It missed by a good hundred metres and a red-hot piece of shrapnel tore his arm off.

The trenches of the inexperienced stomach battalion, dug in a thousand metres below in the direction of Verlautenheide, were full of soaked, scared men, or silent, bloodied messes of

1. Nickname given to the 155-mm cannon in the US Army in World War II.

pulped flesh and crushed bone. And then everything was uncannily silent. It seemed even more sinister than the terrible barrage which had gone before. As the Ami infantry started to come out of their trenches to the attack, it began to rain.

'By the great whore of Buxtehude, 'Schulze cursed, 'and now even the angels are pissing on us!'

The GIs of the Big Red One's 18th Regiment slithered up the muddy, sodden bank behind which they had been crouching and lurched forward, helmeted heads bent against the bitter rain. Before them the Shermans had formed up into a ragged line. They doubled forward with mud-heavy boots to take cover behind their earth-churning wake. For they knew what to expect.

As the daylight crept across the desolate countryside from the east, the Kraut mortars opened up. The pillars of smoke rose swiftly towards the black-bellied low rainclouds. A crippled Sherman heeled to a stop and started to burn fiercely. Its infantry tail doubled heavily to the cover of the next one. Another tank stopped a mortar bomb and exploded almost immediately. White and red tracer ammunition zig-zagged wildly into the dripping sky.

Still the GIs plodded on, apparently ignoring the din of war around them. It seemed to them as if it was nature they were fighting, not human beings: the cold rain that dripped from their helmets into their collars, the mud that clung in heavy, clotted masses to their rubber boots, the slippery ground over which they stumbled. Soaked, sick, stunned by the roar of the Shermans and the din of the mortars, they trudged on across the bitter fields.

Colonel Smith, the regimental commander, looked back at his men. They were plodding in slow thoughtful groups, rifles and grease-guns at their hips. The attack was going okay. Then without warning he heard the familiar high-pitched burr of a Spandau. The morning air was suddenly filled with the hiss of lead. Men were crashing heavily to the mud almost before Smith heard the rattle of the German machine-guns. Here and there the replacements dropped hesitantly to one knee. In a second and they would be lying there full length, their attack paralysed.

Smith jumped on to a slight rise in full view of his men and the enemy. He waved his swagger stick with the silver head, his

89

only weapon. 'All right, boys,' he cried above the rattle of small arms. 'We can't stay here all day. Only the stiffs'll be doing that.' He smiled. 'All I'm asking you to do is move up to that next hedgerow over there. That ain't much to ask, is it?' He looked down at an eighteen-year-old replacement with glasses whose ashen lips were trembling violently.

'That ain't much to ask, is it son?' his face sad and un-soldierly.

'No, sir,' the boy gulped and got to his feet.

'That's the ticket!' Smith said enthusiastically. He turned, waved his silver-headed stick, and started to plod forward again.

The machine-guns chattered violently. Still they advanced, filled with the infantryman's unreasoning hope that it would be easy this one time, drawing steadily closer to the hedgerow in which the stomach battalion had dug themselves. Thin violet lights crackled along it. The bullets cut swathes in their ranks. The fire intensified until a concentrated hail of lead hit them from the right flank too. Each man suddenly found himself alone, engulfed in smoke and death, a lone gambler with fate.

Smith blew his whistle. '*At the double*,' he yelled. '*Keep moving, boys!*' Clumsy in his mud-heavy boots, he began to double towards the right flank.

His men followed, wild obscene curses flung from their wet lips, their eyes wild, white and staring. The mg nests on the flank opened up with all they had, but they stumbled on in the face of the fire. Man after man toppled over, faces upturned and contorted, hands clawing the air in agony. Within seconds the first line had vanished, and the ground in front of the mg nests was piled high with American dead.

Smith dropped into a shell-hole, gasping violently. All around him the survivors of the second line did the same, their hands trembling like leaves, their chests heaving, eyes blurred so that they could not even aim their weapons. He grabbed the walkie-talkie and called for mortar cover.

For what seemed an age, the survivors of the 18th Regiment clung to the hollow while wave after wave of machine-gun fire swept their ranks, washing them away like shipwrecked sailors clinging to the dèbris of a sinking ship. Then the fire of the massive 4.2-inch mortars descended on the German positions and the hail of lead ceased.

Smith did not waste his opportunity. He sprang to his feet, his once immaculate uniform smeared with mud from top to bottom. He wiped his mouth free and blew his whistle. 'All right, let's move it!' he yelled above the roar of the barrage.

The men crouching among the dead of the shell-holes hesitated.

'I said – move it,' he snarled.

Still they did not move.

A buck sergeant poked his head up hesitantly. 'What's your name, Sergeant?' Smith yelled.

'Kowalski, sir.'

'All right, Kowalski, you're acting top kick of this outfit. Now get your guys moving – *fast*!'

Polack Kowalski, whose ambition had never extended beyond the rank of sergeant, jumped out of his hole. 'All right, youse guys,' he yelled in his heavily accented English, 'get ya asses out of dem holes! Come on!' He lent urgency to his command by grabbing the nearest soldier and dragging him physically out of his hole.

Led by Colonel Smith and the new Master Sergeant Polack Kowalski, the GIs stumbled forward. Now at last they saw the camouflaged German helmets crouched over the thin quivering barrels of their Spandaus. All their pent-up fury and bitterness at the war, the CO, Kowalski, the rain, transferred itself to the Krauts. Yelling wildly, all fear gone, they launched themselves forward at the enemy. Kowalski was shot through the head in the first minute and the soldier he had kicked out of his hole heedlessly stamped over his dead body, forcing it deeper into the gory mud. Then they were in and among the Krauts.

The enemy tried to surrender. They dropped their smoking weapons. Raising their hands high, they cried, '*no shoot . . . no shoot . . . comrade . . . comrade!*'

But the enraged GIs were not their comrades. Bayonets plunged in defenceless stomachs, magazines emptied into ashen, terrified faces, ripping them apart, heavy, mud-encrusted boots crashed into crotches, sending their owners reeling back, mouths full of hot vomit. The survivors, screaming with terror, were kicked out of their holes and ordered to double to the rear towards the cages. Suddenly numb with fatigue, the men of the 18th Infantry Regiment – what was left of them – flopped down into the mud, eyes vacant, their trembling fingers the only indication of what they had just been through.

'*Hot damn*,' General Collins cursed. 'We've broken through!' He punched the upper arm of the aide who had brought the good news happily. 'I knew old Clarence's Big Red One would do it! Casualties?'

The young aide with the Social Register accent nodded. 'Yes, sir. General Huebner reports that—'

Collins held up his hand imperiously to stop him. 'For God's sake, Jones, if they're bad, don't tell me.'

'They're bad, sir.'

'Okay, I don't want to know – not just now anyway.' He swung round at his waiting staff, heavy portly men who looked a good ten years older than their energetic chief. 'All right, gentlemen, what's the situation with Hobbs's Thirtieth?'

A grey-haired staff officer with the red, white and blue ribbon of the Distinguished Service Cross of the old war on his fat chest licked his lips. 'Eighteen hundred casualties already and about three hundred missing—'

'Get on with it, Ben,' Lightning Joe interrupted impatiently. 'Give me the dirt.'

'Well, General, quite frankly, the steam's gone out of the 30th's attack. They took a bad beating at Rimburg yesterday. My guess is that Hobbs's is stalled for twenty-four hours at least.'

'The Air Corps?'

'No deal, sir. General Hobbs's doughs got plastered yesterday by the Ninth TAC. He's already screaming for an inquiry.'

'Sod it!' Lightning Joe cursed. 'He would.'

He ran his hand through his thick hair and wondered whether he should relieve Hobbs or not. He knew he'd have the support of the Army Commander, General Hodges, if he did. Only the day before Hodges, an infantry man who, like himself, had served on the Western Front in France in 1918, had told him that Hobbs was always 'either bragging or goddam complaining'. Still who would he put in the 30th Division Commander's place? No, he would leave that problem till after Aachen had been captured.

'All right, gentlemen,' he snapped to his staff. 'We're gonna give the Big Red One all the muscle we've got spare. They'll carry the main weight of the attack, seeing that the 30th is apparently stalled for the time being.' Pausing for breath so that his staff could get out their notebooks, he began to issue his orders in a staccato bark. 'Two battalions of tank destroyers from the Corps reserve . . . fighter bombers from the Ninth TAC . . .

siege artillery from 12th Army Group . . . extra beef from the 29th Infantry . . . replace them in the line with the 1104th Engineering Combat Group . . . Gentlemen,' he proclaimed sternly, his eyes flashing round their pudgy unsoldierly faces, 'I want that height – what did Clarence call it at the conference, Ben?'

'Crucifixion Hill, General.'

'Thank you. Okay, gentlemen, I want that goddam Crucifixion Hill within the next twenty-four hours, regardless of the cost, do you understand?'

'Okay, gentlemen, let's pop to!' And with an airy wave of his hand, he dismissed them to their wall maps with the acetate overlays and their red and black crayon markings. Stage two of the battle for Crucifixion Hill was under way.

'Fasten down the hatch,' von Dodenburg ordered. 'Turret two o'clock. Range seven hundred. Ami Shermans.'

A sweating Schulze spun his dials rapidly. Graduated lines, blurred and hectic, spun past his right eye.

'Got it yet?' Von Dodenburg followed the progress of the line of enemy tanks anxiously through his own periscope. Their lone Tiger had to stop the Ami Shermans before they got within firing range of the first line of panzer grenadiers dug in half way up the hill. The panzer grenadiers could take care of the Ami stubble-hopper by themselves.

'On target,' Schulze rapped, as four black shapes crawled into the bright circle of glass.

There was a sudden hush as if a giant were drawing in a breath. A 75-mm AP shell, solid-white and slow, tumbled through the air awkwardly towards them. Schulze closed his eyes instinctively. The next instant it had struck the earth fifty metres behind them. The Tiger shook like a leaf in gale.

'Shit in my hat,' Matz breathed over the intercom, 'that nearly cut my toenails for me!'

Furiously Schulze set to work spinning the dials again. The range figures leapt before his eyes. 'Six hundred and fifty. Six hundred. Five hundred and fifty.'

'Holy straw sack, Schulze!' von Dodenburg cried. 'Aren't you on yet?'

'On, sir!' he gasped.

'Fire!'

He jerked the lever. The blast hit him in the face like a fist.

He opened his mouth automatically so that the pressure would not burst his eardrums. The gleaming, red-hot cartridge tumbled to the metal deck. Von Dodenburg pressed the fume-clearing apparatus button. The fans started to whirl. A sound of clicking and the great hanging 88 was ready again. Down below the Sherman had come to a sudden stop and was burning furiously. Tiny black figures were racing from it, angry machine-gun fire kicking up spurts of dust at their heels.

'Target one o'clock – range four hundred. FIRE!'

The turret swung round. Schulze spotted the target at once. An Ami self-propelled gun, heavy with its 105-mm cannon, the only gun the Amis had which could tackle a Tiger. Once they had knocked it out there was a good chance that the rest of the Shermans covering the infantry attack would break off the fight and make a run for it. The long cannon leapt at his side. A metre-long spurt of violet flame shot from the muzzle brake. The shell struck the SP just above the boogies. Von Dodenburg could see the red-hot glow of its impact. The SP rocked wildly from side to side. A man was flung from his position on the side of the armoured vehicle. For a moment it seemed as if the steel giant would overturn. Then suddenly the target disintegrated completely and a whirling mass of metal hurtled skywards.

The remaining Shermans stopped in panic and attempted to retreat to the cover of the woods beyond. It was a fatal mistake, and Schulze did not waste the opportunity offered him by the inexperience of the Second Armoured Division's tankers. The 88-mm shell ripped swiftly and surely through the afternoon sky towards the nearest Sherman. It struck it squarely on the glacis plate. Von Dodenburg could see the glow of impact, but nothing happened.

'What the hell—' von Dodenburg began.

Suddenly a thin white spiral of smoke started to rise from the Sherman's turret. Dark figures flung themselves out of the escape hatches, retching and gasping for breath while the flames leapt up greedily in search of anything combustible.

'Oh, my aching cheeks,' Matz chortled, 'look at those banana suckers hoofing it!'

But Schulze saw that there were still two Shermans to be dealt with. Swiftly he swung the turret round, his big hand whirling the dials. The first tank loomed up into the shining circle of glass. He fired. A Sherman disappeared in a sheet of flame. He fired again, bringing the last Sherman to a halt, its

94

left track flapping uselessly in front of it. Schulze sat back, his right eye ringed a deep purple from the lens, the sweat pouring down his brow, his breath coming in great gasps.

'Wow,' he breathed, 'that was shitty nip and tuck!'

'It'll get you another piece of tin, Schulze,' von Dodenburg said hoarsely, thrusting back his helmet from a brow beaded in a sweat of apprehension.

'Shit on the tin, sir,' Schulze said thickly. 'I'd rather have an immediate transfer to the paymaster's branch!'

Crucifixion Hill quaked. Thousands of tons of steel thundered from the enormous blast furnaces to the west and deluged the height. Dugouts collapsed and the panzer grenadiers fought desperately to free themselves, clawing at the smoking earth with bloody fingers. A one-and-a-half ton VW jeep soared high into the air and burst apart thirty metres high. A machine-gun section was caught running across open ground and torn apart as they ran. When the smoke disappeared, all that was left was one lone boot, containing the bloody stump of a leg. The whole place was a bloody inferno of flying metal. The remnants of the 18th Infantry sprang up from their hiding places in the valley below. Screaming hysterically, they surged forward, confident now that all opposition must be dead. Von Dodenburg's panzer grenadiers waited in their shell-holes and half-destroyed fox-holes and let them come on. The veterans of Russia and Monte Cassino[1] shammed dead as the first wave rolled over them, so confident that they did not take the elementary precaution of bayoneting the supposed dead. Through their half-closed eyes they could see the mud-encrusted buckled Ami combat boots and hear their hectic breathing. They waited, knowing that the second wave would be at least a hundred metres behind. Then, when they were sure that the stragglers had run by, they sprang to their feet, shouting in wild triumph. Tracer slammed into the backs of the men in olive drab. They turned in horror, realising too late that they had been tricked.

Behind them the second wave came to a ragged halt. A few raised their weapons to fire into the SS men. Their officers yelled at them urgently, 'You'll hit your buddies!'

It was the opportunity that the panzer grenadiers had been waiting for. They raced forward, carrying sharp-edged en-trenching tools, combat knives, bayonets, anything which would

1. See Leo Kessler *Guns at Cassino*.

cut and slice. In an instant they were in among the trapped Ami stubble-hoppers. Slipping in the mud, they hacked, slashed, clove their enemies, while above them on the height in front of the great wooden cross, their commander watched the slaughter. An Ami staggered across the churned-up battleground, his hands held to his shattered stomach, intestines escaping from the ragged hole there. A panzer grenadier screamed like a wild man, slicing the face off an American sergeant, soaked in the vivid stream of blood that shot from his tortured mouth. A youth with the Red Cross armband on his sleeve knelt in the bloody mire, his arms limp at his side and allowed himself to be slaughtered like an animal by a great ox of a SS trooper armed with a razor-sharp entrenching tool.

It was a massacre, ended only by the flight of the handful of survivors and the crash of the Ami artillery recommencing its frustrated barrage. Again the western horizon erupted in flame. The first shell hit the twenty-metre-high wooden cross. It creaked like the mast of an old sailing ship in a gale. Von Dodenburg looked up anxiously. Jesus, suspended there in immobile wooden agony, trembled violently. But the cross still stood there.

'We'd better get on our hind legs, sir,' Schulze said, eyeing the cross trembling above them. 'That old boy up there won't be lasting much longer in my opinion.'

'Go on, Sergeant-Major,' Matz cried mockingly above the roar of the tremendous barrage. 'Don't you know that Jesus loves you? He'll protect and guard you.'

'Shut up, you carpet-slipper soldier,' Schulze roared. 'Or I'll shove your shitty wooden leg up yer lace-covered arse!'

Another shell struck the great cross and they began to run for the shelter of the Royal Tiger. Behind them the cross reeled from side to side. Von Dodenburg stopped instinctively and swung round. A jagged crack was running across the base of the crucifix. Jesus's head, surmounted by its crown of wooden thorns, dropped off and fell into the churned mud.

'*Sir*,' Schulze yelled urgently.

Von Dodenburg did not move. The crack reached the other side of the cross. A chunk of worm-eaten wood fell from Jesus's tortured chest. The whole structure teetered, dust pouring from the crack. Another shell slammed into its base. Slowly the headless figure began to disintegrate as the cross itself swayed and fell to the ground.

'Great crap on the Christmas Tree, sir,' Schulze screamed and grabbed the mesmerised officer by the arm, 'come on! . . . or you'll be looking at the potatoes from below in another second!'

As von Dodenburg pelted to cover with Schulze, followed by the Ami fire, it seemed to him as if the destruction of the great cross symbolised the destruction of their hopes.

TWO

As the battle for Crucifixion Hill raged back and forth, the shootings started in Aachen. In the second week of October, when it looked as if the bitter cold rain would never cease, Donner ordered a Gestapo detachment into the city from Cologne.

They descended upon the shattered city in their ankle-length green leather coats, mouths full of gold teeth, cheap ten-pfennig working-men's cigars stuck in their cold lips, and began their reign of terror.

'Defeatists, deserters, looters,' Donner had commanded, looking at the professional policemen's faces from which pity had long been absent, 'shoot the lot of them, without the slightest mercy.'

A fat granny who had 'organised' a bag of coal in one of the ruins; a pale-faced, skinny deserter from one of the stomach battalions; a child who had written 'surrender now while there's still time' on a wall in an immature chalk scrawl; a priest who had dared to ask the Lord's forgiveness in a cellar sermon for 'man's inhumanity to man' – they were all rounded up, heard the old routine statement beginning, 'In the name of the Führer and the German Folk, this specially convened court sentences you', and were quickly dispatched by a burst of machine-gun fire at the back of the Quellenhof.

But that wasn't enough for Donner – 'that godless Devil Donner', as the frightened inhabitants of the cellars and ruins called him behind his back. He took to shooting prisoners himself, maintaining that it was criminal to waste more than 'one bullet on such defeatist rabble at a time of crisis like this'.

He wandered the city, followed by his sinister guard of Gestapo men, selecting his victims at random, maintaining that, even if they were innocent, they would serve as a warning 'to the rest of these filthy Catholic traitors'. An army padre from one of the stomach battalions, with purple tabs and crosses on his collar instead of the usual Wehrmacht eagle and swastika. 'Come here, Pope! Why aren't you at the front with the rest of your battalion?'

The priest's face contorted with fear at the sight of Devil Donner and his leather-coated, squat henchmen with the machine-pistols cradled menacingly in their arms. 'But, General I have just brought a convoy of wounded from my battalion down here to the field hospital,' he pleaded. 'My commander specifically instructed me—'

'Shoot him!' Donner barked and, without another word, turned his back on the ashen-faced padre.

An ugly girl was sitting in the rubble of her shelled house staring vacantly at nothing, her legs spread apart so that passers-by could see the soft white flesh of her thighs above the shabby black stockings.

Donner and his men found her. 'What are you sitting there for, woman?' he snapped coldly. 'Have you no work to do at this time of crisis?'

The girl stared at him blankly.

Donner sneered. 'A complete idiot. Result of too much in-breeding in this area. Bad blood – the lot of them. *Shoot her*!'

As 'Pistol Paul,' the fattest of the Gestapo men, named because of his twin pistols, began to drag her away into the ruins to carry out the order, she started to cry. But she did not cry like young women normally do; her cries were those of an animal going to the slaughter. A single shot rang out from behind the cover of a shattered chimney stack. Pistol Paul ran his hand swiftly up her dress as she crumpled to the ground, licked his lips with pleasure at what he found there, then ran back to join the murder squad.

And so the slaughter of the civilians went on all throughout that terrible week of October. Yet even Donner could see that, despite his reign of terror, the physical and moral defences of the city he had sworn to hold were beginning to crumble. Both civilians and soldiers within the ruined city moved slowly and seemed indifferent to commands, even when those commands signified their own execution. Their faces had become pinched. Their glazed eyes sunk deep behind protruding cheek-bones, many of them just stared apathetically into space, dragging their feet leadenly behind them in the streets.

As the Big Red One cut off road after road leading into the city from the nearest railhead at Juelich, food became scarcer. By October 12th the daily ration of the men in the line became one can of 'Old Man' and half a loaf of canned pumpernickel per two men. The rear echelon stallions managed with half that. The civilians weren't fed at all.

But despite Devil Donner's heartless shootings, a hectic secret life went on among the ruins of the smoking city. When von Dodenburg came down to Aachen to report to Donner, Matz and Schulze seized the chance to visit the latter's private whorehouse. Their stomachs empty, they were drunk within minutes on the shot SA man's supply of cheap *Korn*.

'Off with the rags!' Schulze roared drunkenly, tearing off his own oil-stained black uniform until all that was left was his helmet, pistol belt and boots. 'And get those pearly gates ready! I've limped all the way here!'

'So I can see,' the big blonde said with mock coyness. 'Oh, put it way before I faint!'

'Go on,' laughed Matz, unstrapping his wooden leg and pausing momentarily to slap her heartily across her broad buttocks. 'You've seen more of those than I've had hot dinners!'

'Hands off,' Schulze threatened, swaying drunkenly. 'That's my bride.'

'Your bride,' Matz sneered good-humouredly, still fiddling with the straps of his wooden leg, attached to the stump of his knee. 'That Gerti of yours has been bride to half the shitty Wehrmacht!' Schulze hit him playfully.

Matz shot backwards over the couch, his wooden leg trailing behind him. The girls screamed and scattered, naked breasts quivering.

Matz pulled his leg free. 'Here, Heidi,' he ordered the girl he usually slept with. 'Get your big arse over here.' Then, supporting himself on her shoulder, Matz raised his wooden leg menacingly. 'All right, you big bastard — sergeant-major or no sergeant-major, I'm going to knock your stupid big turnip off for you.'

Urging Heidi forward, he advanced upon Schulze.

Schulze's ugly face was set in a broad grin. He smiled benevolently at the angry Matz. He farted leisurely. 'Let's have a little bit of green smoke first, shall we . . . We had pea soup at the HQ, Gertrude,' he explained to the blonde. 'Now, now, Matz, you're going to rupture yourself lifting that leg. If I were you, I'd save my strength to lift that pathetic little thing you've got down there!'

Matz lunged wildly at Schulze with his wooden leg. Schulze ducked easily. One big hand shot out and punched Heidi in her scarred, naked belly. She collapsed like a deflated balloon. Matz careened over the sofa and landed in the lap of a screaming redhead. Schulze threw himself forward. Matz rolled to one side. The two drunken NCOs rolled back and forth across the cellar floor, aiming wild punches at each other and laughing like two schoolboys. Thus engaged and cheered on by the shouting, naked whores, they did not hear the thin chill wailing of the air-raid siren until it was almost too late.

A kilometre away in another cellar, now shuddering violently under the impact of the bombs, Colonel von Dodenburg and the redhead stared at each other in silence, the flickering yellow candle throwing grotesque shadows across their pale young faces.

Von Dodenburg could see that she was reaching the end of her tether. Her green eyes shone hectically in her emaciated face. He had brought her two cans of Old Man but she had explained that she was 'too hungry to eat it', whatever that meant. Her hands trembled violently with every fresh explosion.

He leaned forward across the rough wooden table and clutched them tightly in his own. They were icy cold; they felt like the hands of someone already dead. 'Don't be scared,' he pleaded, trying to calm her. 'At the front we always say you never hear the one which kills you.'

'They're dying everywhere in the cellars now,' she said, her voice hardly audible. 'Old men, women, children – not soldiers. Just unarmed civilians. Dying everywhere.' Her voice trailed away and her green eyes filled with tears, as if she felt and bore the whole world's cares.

'We shall make them pay back our losses tenfold,' von Dodenburg snapped, iron in his voice.

Another 500-pound bomb dropped in the street overhead. The cellar swayed. The yellow flame of the candle guttered with the blast and almost went out.

'Pay them back?' she said listlessly. 'How can you pay for a life, Kuno?' her voice rose, 'they are dead. That's it.' She pulled her hand free from his grasp. 'Dead, finished, kaputt – nothing can bring them to life again! All that we must do now is save the lives of the few who are left before it is too late.' She stared at him, her beautiful green eyes hysterical. Like some front swine, von Dodenburg realised suddenly, she had seen too much and was preparing to escape into the blessed oblivion of voluntary madness.

He pulled her naked body close to his. She was lathered in sweat although the fat-bellied coal-stove in the corner was almost out. 'Don't talk,' he whispered urgently. 'Talk is for fools – *now*. All that counts is action – and love.'

Almost brutally, he thrust back on the hard wooden table. Her legs spread automatically. He forced the glistening triangle open. She shuddered – whether with pleasure or distaste he no longer knew nor cared. The frantic, panting, sweating act of love began, while all around them the world shuddered, trembled and died.

They scrambled naked against the banks of flame, wading out of the bomb-shattered, smoking cellar through a morass of dead bodies, their bare feet slipping in bloody, jellied flesh. Everywhere, now the bombers had gone, women's voices called in anguish for their missing children, children tottered aimlessly through the burning streets.

Schulze, who had rescued a bottle of *Korn*, raised it to his lips and took a mighty swig, not noticing that the fiery liquid was running down his unshaven chin. 'Where's Gerti?' he yelled.

Matz gave him his answer. He stumbled suddenly and would have fallen if he had not been supported by a weeping Heidi, still naked save for the one-legged NCO's issue pants, which reached to her plump knees.

'She's here, Sergeant-Major,' he yelled and tried in vain to stand to attention. 'May I respectfully report one casualty, Sergeant-Major? The whore Gertrude X, shot in the line of duty. Hero's death for Folk, Führer and Fatherland!'

Drunkenly Schulze staggered over to him and stared down at the naked body sprawled out grotesquely in the brick rubble, her face shaded a blood-red hue by the flames. He took another swig of the *Korn* and passed the bottle automatically to Matz, who was still trying to maintain the position of attention.

'She was a good whore, Matz,' he said numbly, while the other whores, shoulder bent, hands held protectively across their flabby breasts, sobbed steadily. 'Yellow card or not,[1] she put her heart into it, believe you me. I've had plenty of good workouts from that whore there! She knew her business.' He reached his big hand for the bottle, without taking his eyes off the dead woman. '*Korn*,' he commanded. He drained the rest in silence with a mighty gulp. He coughed and wiped the back of his big dirty hand across his mouth, then slowly bent down and closed the whore's legs. 'Better that way,' he said.

Matz grabbed him firmly by the big muscular arm. 'Come on, Schulze,' he said, 'Let's get back to HQ.'

Without a word, the two naked men, the one limping badly, slowly began to make their way through the burning streets, where the dust-white, frantic civilian police were beginning to lay the dead out in long lines ready for the flame-throwers. Already the big black rats and the half-wild city mongrels were gnawing the ones in the shadows, stealing off with chunks of dripping human flesh. They had almost reached the Quellenhof when the ruddy glare of the flames illuminated the faded white scrawl on a half-shattered wall. Schulze read it aloud in a dazed drunken voice, swaying from side to side as he did so: '*Give me five years and you will not recognise Germany again! Adolf Hitler.*'

With all his strength he hurled the empty *Korn* bottle at the fading notice. The bottle shattered loudly against the bricks. 'That you can say again, Adolf,' he groaned, 'that's for shitting sure!'

The two men staggered on.

THREE

On October 13th while Wotan's panzer grenadiers, aided by von Dodenburg's remaining fifteen Tigers, held the Big Red One half way down the embattled hillside, dominated now by the broken stump of the great cross, Hobbs's men finally managed to break through the Rimburg Line. The First Army Com-

1. Before 1945, prostitutes had to be registered with the police and inspected regularly by police doctors; hence the yellow card.

mander, Courtney Hodges, had personally been to see the situation on the 30th Division's front.

Afterwards he had told a troubled and apologetic Hobbs, 'All right, Leland, the chips are down. You either produce or you go. I hate to go over a corps commander's head to do this, but I want this goddam Aachen gap closed! After all, Ike's on my tail too with a big stick. He wants me to get my butt out of this Aachen mud and be on my way to the Rhine.' He had smiled thinly, but Hobbs had not been fooled. The writing was on the wall for him. He threw his last remaining strength into the battle, supervising the night attack personally; and it worked. By dawn the German positions around the onion-towered baroque Rimburg Castle were broken; by mid-morning the Krauts were streaming back towards Aachen in panic-stricken confusion.

Pandemonium reigned at Donner's HQ at the hotel. A young staff officer, his immaculate uniform now splattered with mud, 'monkey swing'[1] hanging loosely across his breast, blood streaming down the left side of his face, reported in a choking voice: 'Most of the lead companies have been wiped out, sir . . . position razed to the ground.'

'Artillery?' a frantic Donner yelled.

'Lost contact, sir,' a sweating fat staff major, crouched over the main command radio, yelled back. 'Everything's destroyed. The lines are down everywhere.'

'Heaven, arse and twine,' Donner cried angrily. 'How the devil can I defend a city when I've got nothing to defend it with? What do those rear-echelon stallions think they are playing at?' For one awful moment he remembered that terrible breakthrough of the Allies in France in September 1918 on that Black Sunday which had heralded the end of everything he had known and respected as a young officer in the old Imperial Army. Then he pulled himself together, aware of the young aide's shocked face and the fat staff major's gaping mouth. It wouldn't do to allow his staff see him go to pieces; they must have confidence in the leadership even if the world was damn well falling apart all around him.

Before he could act, however, the field telephone shrilled. He beat the aide to the instrument. 'Donner,' he barked.

Even his voice could not calm the hysterical officer at the other

1. SS nickname for the decorative lanyard worn by officer aides on the staff.

end. 'Large tank formations bearing down upon us from the east,' the officer cried, forgetting all wireless procedure. 'We've got no AT[1] left. No bazookas. All our mines have been used.' The officer sobbed hysterically. 'Sir, you've got to send reinforcements . . . !'

'Pull yourself together, man,' Donner snapped, sickened. 'Hold on – I make you personally responsible for the position. It's your head!'

'But, sir.'

Donner slammed down the phone. His spirit was restored. Full of energy, he started rapping out orders.

'Major, don't just sit there! Get your base stallions moving. I want reinforcements – I *demand* reinforcements! Turf anyone who can hold a rifle out of the dressing stations! Throw in the police – they're all trained to use weapons. Get the cooks – the clerks. Go through the hospitals. This is not the time to allow the malingerers to lie there farting between clean sheets while better men die. Well, come on, get moving!'

'You,' he turned to the bleeding aide. 'Get on that damned motor-cycle of yours and press on the tube. I want you to get through to Colonel von Dodenburg. At all costs, do you hear? I need big friends[2] – and I need them quick!'

The aide ran out, trampling over the useless maps with his dirty boots. The time for strategy was over. The naked struggle for the existence of Aachen had begun.

The retreat from the Rimburg Line was a shambles, governed by panic, powered by naked fear. While the whole horizon burned brick-red with the barrage from Hobbs's massed batteries and the very earth rocked with their insane hammering detonations, the survivors struggled back; an endless stream of Horch staff cars, eight-ton Opel trucks, looted tractors pulling farm-wagons piled high with groaning wounded, ambulances covered fearfully by Red Cross flags in the pathetic hope that the *Jabos* of the Ninth US TAC would respect them. And in the midst of the forlorn, frightened grey-coated stream, the two Tigers stood like steel fortresses, their long guns pointing menacingly the way the Amis must come.

Von Dodenburg had positioned well the only two tanks he could spare from the vital height. The half-track load of panzer

1. Anti-tank guns.
2. SS code for tanks.

grenadiers he had brought with him to cover the Tigers against Ami bazooka attacks had blasted the great oaks which had bordered the cobbled road for a distance of five hundred metres. Now they blocked it like huge fallen matchsticks, forcing both the retreating German infantry and their American pursuers into the fields on both side. Krause had taken up his position on one side of the road and his tank on other, both covered by their thin skin of infantry. Forced into the fields, the Shermans would lose the advantage of their superior speed and greater manoeuvrability, and be easy meat for the Tigers' 88s.

Thus while the survivors streamed shame-faced into the city where Donner's head-hunters were already waiting to reform them into new companies, at pistol-point if necessary, the two lone Tigers prepared for the uneven battle. Above them the huge crimson sun hung in an iron-grey sky heavy with menace.

'Do you know, Matz,' Schulze said as they draped the Royal Tiger with camouflaged netting and oak branches, 'that there are over two hundred million Ivans.'

'Someone ought to invent the Parisian[1] in Russia then,' Matz growled, aiming a fruitless kick at a soaked and hatless straggler who almost bumped into him.

'And there's nearly the same number of shitty Amis, not to mention the Tommies and all that nigger cannon-fodder they've got from India and Africa.'

'Well, all I can say, Sergeant-Major, is that I've been doing my best these last goddam five years to plant as many of them as I could in the soil.' He sniffed. 'But still I didn't realise that there were so many of 'em.'

Schulze nodded his head significantly. 'No, and a lot more people don't either. Five hundred million of the shits and all we've got on our side is a few greasy spaghetti-eaters and a lot of operatic tenors from Hungary and Rumania, who cream their knickers as soon as they hear a popgun go off.'

Matz finished his side of the big vehicle. Across on the other side of the road, Krause's crew was also finished. 'We've still got the V-weapons, Sergeant-Major. You can't overlook the Führer's V-weapons, you know.'[2]

Schulze made an obscene gesture with his middle finger. 'You know what you can do with the Führer's V-weapons, don't you, Matz.'

1. Slang for a contraceptive.
2. Vengeance weapons, such as the V1 and V2 rockets.

'But the rockets, they're giving the Tommy civvies a hard time in London, according to the papers.'

'You'll be telling me next you believe in Father Christmas and Grimm's Fairy Tales,' Schulze sneered, dropping the last of the netting on the gun into place.

'And if you'll forgive my German, Sergeant-Major, you're talking out of the back of your arse. We've got V-weapons that'll win the war yet for Germany. When I was in hospital in Heidelberg after Cassino getting this movable saucer fitted,' he tapped his wooden leg, 'I heard them talking about a new poison gas that would—'

'Poison gas!' Schulze interrupted scornfully. 'The only poison gas you'll see in this war is when those kitchen bulls serve shitty pea soup and those big farmboys of the heavy weapon company start farting. No, Matz, we've got half the fucking world against us.' He paused for breath. 'How come we're holding this road with only two Tigers. Explain that, will you, you sodding field marshal!'

'I can explain, sodding Field Marshal Schulze,' von Dodenburg's Prussian voice said behind them.

The two NCOs sprang to attention, but he waved to them to desist. 'Don't try to bullshit me,' he said with a faint smile. 'I know you like the back of my hand. The two of you have no respect for an officer and a gentleman.'

'Well, they do say that human beings begin with the rank of lientenant, sir,' Schulze said pleasantly, standing at ease.

'You see what I mean,' von Dodenburg said. His handsome young face hardened and the smile vanished. 'You asked, Schulze, why we're out here trying to defend that damned road there with only two tanks against what is virtually a whole Ami division? I'll tell you why. Because we wear this cursed black uniform and these damned stupid silver badges.' Angrily he tapped the gleaming SS runes on his collar. 'Because our cap badge is a death's head that makes half Europe tremble with fear. We're the SS, Schulze, hated and feared wherever we go and one day those people who hate and fear us will attempt to take their revenge for these last five years. What else can we do but fight on? Each day gained is another day of life for people like us, whether we achieve it with poison gas or with this beautiful monster here.' He slapped his gloved hand against the Tiger's metal side, his eyes glowing with a warm fanaticism. 'Because the day we stop fighting we'll be looking

at the potatoes from beneath within the hour. Understand?'
His blue eyes searched the big Hamburger's face.

Schulze nodded. 'Yessir,' he gulped.

'Good, I'm going over to check out Krause's camouflage. You carry on here.'

Matz waited till the lean colonel had crossed the road to Officer-Cadet Krause's Tiger; then he tapped his dirty finger significantly against his temple. 'Schulze,' he said slowly, 'I think the Old Man's going off.'

The big Hamburger did not reply, but his brown eyes set in their deep exhausted rings followed von Dodenburg anxiously.

'Loaded – safety catch released,' snapped Schulze, as the little red light began to glow.

Below, the big Maybach engines burst into life. 'Engines started – ready to go,' Matz reported over the intercom.

'Thank you,' von Dodenburg said, as cool and collected as ever now, searching the desolate horizon for the first sign of the Amis.

Schulze sighed and looked at the long line of shells lying in the bin. All sparkling new innocence. Soon they would become the harbingers of destruction, making men quake, scream in torment and terror, die.

'Here they come,' von Dodenburg reported, lowering his glasses for a moment to wipe the lenses clean with a dirty handkerchief.

Schulze thrust his right eye against the sight and adjusted it quickly. A line of slow black beetles had breasted the height, prevented from using the road because of the fallen oaks.

'Watch that armour car,' von Dodenburg barked. 'At two o'clock.'

Schulze spun the 14-ton turret round as effortlessly as if it had weighed 14 grammes. A six-wheel Ami Staghound was racing past the tanks, bouncing up and down across the bumpy fields. 'Recce, sir,' he said.

'Yes, give it six hundred metres and then we'll inform them that we are here. Just before they die, they'll learn they have carried out their mission successfully, eh?'

Nine hundred metres . . . eight hundred . . . seven hundred . . . The Staghound started to slow down, as if its commander sensed trouble was awaiting him somewhere ahead. Behind him the line of Shermans rumbled closer. The Staghound commander knew he had to go on. Schulze could almost sense the Ami's fear. He guessed he'd be sitting there in his dark, oil-stinking turret, the sweat pouring down under his leather helmet, eye glued to the periscope, one hand held ready on the trigger of the smoke-discharger, which would cover his flight once the trouble started. Carefully he adjusted his sight so that the first shell would hit the left side of the armoured car's turret where the three smoke-dischargers were located. He told himself it was a shitty thing to do – it meant the Staghound would be a sitting duck – but, as the CO had said, it might also mean one more day of precious life to them.

'Krause,' von Dodenburg snapped over the radio. 'We shall open up in a moment. Enemy armoured car to our front – two o'clock. See it?'

'Yessir.'

'As soon as we do, hit the Ami flank up there. We'll do the same to the right. Once we open up, move forward. Through that stream and right into them.'

In spite of being a veteran, Krause could not conceal his excitement. 'Christ, sir, this is going to be like Panzer[1] Meyer at Caen when he tackled a whole British tank brigade with one Tiger!'

Von Dodenburg sniffed. 'Well, he's a general and generals are allowed to do such things. Let's hope we're as lucky.' He pulled down the hatch and dropped into the leather seat next to Schulze. The lid slammed shut with the hollow ring of finality. 'All right, Schulze, fire at will!'

Schulze squeezed the firing bar carefully. The great gun reared at his shoulder. The Tiger shuddered as the flame blazed from the 88's muzzle.

'Right on, Schulze!' Matz yelled excitedly, as the Tiger moved forward, 'got him right up the arse!'

Five hundred metres away the Ami Staghound halted as if it had run into a brick wall. Sparks were showering along the length of its motor cowling. As it burst into flame, an Ami hurled himself out, his uniform ablaze. Twice he rolled over in the mud, arms threshing wildly. Then he was still.

'Exit the reconnaissance element,' von Dodenburg said. 'The first act is over. The second can begin.'

The first Sherman got off its shell quicker than Schulze. Its 75-mm belched orange flame. A shell ricocheted off the Tiger's

1. Famous tank general.

thick front armour. The turret was suddenly full of a burnt-cinder stench. Schulze ducked instinctively and cursed with surprise.

'What's up, Sergeant-Major?' Matz's voice came over the intercom mockingly. 'A bit of wind gone up yer drawers?'

'A bit of knuckle sandwich'll be finding its way into your big gob, if you risk another fat lip like that,' Schulze growled, fiddling frantically with his dials.

'Knock it off,' von Dodenburg broke in. 'Perhaps you gentlemen may recall we're fighting a war?'

The next moment Schulze's gun spoke again. 'Hit!' von Dodenburg roared.

A hundred metres away, Krause, keeping pace with the command tank, scored a hit too, bringing a Sherman to a stop, oily black smoke pouring from its shattered turret. The crew tried to escape. But the panzer grenadiers dug in at the side of the road showed no mercy. They mowed them down before they had run five metres. They fell like puppets, suddenly gone crazy, arms and legs flailing in their death agonies. A Sherman burst from the bushes to von Dodenburg's right. Another came down from the barred road.

'They're coming from the flanks, Schulze,' Matz screamed.

A 75-mm shell slammed into the Royal Tiger's side. From within they could see the metal glow a dull red for a moment, then the AP whined off with a deafening howl. Schulze fired. From somewhere an Ami machine-gun opened up. Slugs sprayed the hull. One penetrated a gun slit. The eighteen-year-old 'booty German' second-driver reeled back, clutching his face, the blood streaming from between his tightly clenched fingers. 'I can't see,' he screamed in his thick, accented German. 'I can't see ... I'm blinded!'

With surprising gentleness Matz pushed him to one side and continued driving. 'It's all right, sir,' he gasped into the intercom. 'Everything's under control ... everything's in butter.' As the great tank rattled towards the Shermans, the young driver began to die on the shaking blood-soaked seat.

Another AP shell slammed against the Tiger's thick armour. The sixty-ton monster rocked violently, but the big Maybachs kept running. Schulze fired once – twice in rapid succession. The Sherman on the left flank, stricken, its driver dead at the controls, his head shorn off, barrelled at 30 mph into the road embankment where it exploded a second later. A group of Ami infantry appeared from nowhere.

'*MGs*', von Dodenburg bellowed.

But the infantry did not want to fight. They raised their hands in surrender. Matz pushed aside the dying boy who kept sliding against his shoulder, and put his foot hard down on the gas pedal. The Amis began to scatter. The tank cut into them, remorselessly churning up their defenceless bodies under its broad metal tracks.

Ahead the line of Shermans had come to an uncertain halt beyond the stream. Von Dodenburg knew they would turn and flee if he pressed home his attack; the Ami tankers always did when they were faced by the superior Tiger.

'Advance – full speed!' he commanded excitedly, eyes sparkling with the bloodlust of the chase.

Matz crashed his way through the Tiger's thirty-odd gears. It gathered speed, engines roaring deafeningly. Krause drew parallel. The stream loomed up. Von Dodenburg sized it up swiftly. It didn't look too deep for the Tigers.

'Prepare to ford, Matz,' he ordered. 'Check watertight seals. Raise the stand-pipe.'

Matz slowed down and guarded the six-metre-long gun carefully over the deep bank. Ahead the Shermans still hesitated. With a thick grunt, it went over. Krause's Tiger followed suit. Its nose splashed into the water. It went under. The water came up to its deck. Deeper. Now the standpipe only showed above the surface. Von Dodenburg gulped. He always hated this moment. Was the Tiger really watertight? Would the Maybach keep functioning? Would an enemy shell catch them just when they were at their most vulnerable?

Then Matz's voice reported with complete calm: 'Everything all right, sir. Vision correct.'

Then the Maybach engine took the extra strain and they were waddling up the steep bank, shaking water everywhere like some amphibious monster ascending from the deep. Von Dodenburg flung back the hatch. Ahead the Shermans were obviously preparing to flee, unnerved by the appearance of the Tiger on their side of the stream. He looked behind him.

'Krause!' he gasped.

'What is it, sir?' Schulze cried.

'He's stuck half way across. I can just see the top of his stand-pipe. His engine must have flooded.'

'What are we going to do, sir? Officer-Cadet Krause's a good soldier – and he's only seventeen.'

Von Dodenburg hesitated only for a moment. He could imagine Krause's crew fighting off the water in their armoured coffin, screaming and struggling as the water rose higher in the green gloom. But he couldn't stop now. The whole front depended upon his breaking the Ami armoured thrust.

'Move out,' he rasped. 'There's nothing we can do for them now.'

Matz pushed the dead driver to one side and slammed home the start gear. The Tiger began to roll again.

By late afteroon, the lone Royal Tiger had broken the Ami attack and the Second Division's armour, covering Hobbs's 'Butchers', was streaming back the way it had come, followed by the panic-stricken doughboys.

Von Dodenburg, standing high in the turret of the Tiger, the metal gleaming brightly at a dozen points where it had been struck by Ami 75s, could hardly believe the success of his lone attacks. As they rolled deeper into enemy territory, he knew he should turn back, before Ami air spotted them. But something drove him on despite the risk. 'Big trap, with nothing behind it,' he recalled the phrase they had used to describe the typical Berlin big-mouth during his schooldays in the Reich capital. Now he, too, was a 'big mouth with nothing behind it': one lone Tiger pitted against an Ami division. Still, their boldness was paying off and every hour he gained for Donner would give the Police General a better chance of getting some sort of provisional front together behind him.

'Ami dump, sir – four o'clock,' Matz's voice came through the headphones, routine and emotionless. He swung round and saw a couple of hastily erected bell-tents, with naked men pouring out of them, towels clutched absurdly to their genitals.

'Ooh, sweetie, look at all those lovely bottoms,' Schulze simpered. 'Worth a fortune if you were a warm brother.' [1]

Von Dodenburg pressed the trigger of the turret mg. Tracer sprayed the muddy grass outside the shower tent. The Amis threw down their towels and galloped across the fields towards

1. German slang for homosexual.

the wood in the distance. Von Dodenburg took his finger off the trigger.

'Let them go,' he said, laughing. 'Seems wrong somehow to shoot a man without his clothes on.'

'I can see you'll end up in the Salvation Army after all, sir,' Schulze said. 'There's a heart of gold underneath that rough exterior, sir.'

'And you'll feel my rough boot up your golden arse, if you're not careful,' von Dodenburg said. 'All right, Matz, stop her. Let's see what we can inherit from our rich Ami friends.'

The 'inherited' a great deal. While Matz dragged out the dead driver and dumped him in a nearby ditch, Schulze looted the shower unit's kitchen, retrieving a steaming saucepan full of meatballs, corned beef, dried ham and eggs, sardines, tomatoes – the booty of a great pile of cans.

'Sir, would you like to indulge?' He pulled another hand from behind his back to reveal a bottle. 'Firewater – Ami firewater!'

While the dead driver lay in the ditch ten metres away, staring sightlessly into the darkening sky, they tore into the lukewarm food ravenously, washing it down with great swigs from the litre bottle of looted bourbon.

'Like shitting God in France,' Matz chortled, spearing a meatball with his combat knife. 'That's the way these Amis live! Why oh why wasn't I born an Ami – with such lovely fodder!' He touched his oil-stained dirty fingers to his greasy lips, and thrust the meatball into his mouth.

'Yeah, why? Why should the Reich suffer a bastard like you?' Schulze dipped his canteen cup into the revolting mixture. 'Let the Amis have you! Shitting foot and mouth disease you've got, Matz. You eat too much and wear out too many boots.'

'I've only got one fucking leg, Sergeant-Major,' Matz protested. 'And, by the way, how come you're using a shitty canteen cup instead of a spoon like the rest of us?'

'Because I'm a sergeant-major,' Schulze said majestically, dipping his cup into the mixture once again, 'and you're just a lowly sergeant. It's as simple as that, Matz.'

Von Dodenburg, feeling the fiery Ami spirits now, laughed, as he listened to the two veterans' banter. For a moment he was confident, but the time out of war was soon at an end.

'What's that racket?' Matz asked suddenly.

Von Dodenburg dropped his spoon. A black speck was roaring in at them at tree-top level. 'Get back to the tank!'

They dropped their canteen cups with a clatter. The black speck became a Mustang fighter-bomber barrelling in at 400 mph, its engine cowling painted like the snout of a shark. As they pelted for the Tiger, its engine howled, a monstrous black shadow preceding it across the desolate countryside. Violent purple lights crackled along the Ami plane's wings.

'Rockets!' von Dodenburg yelled, *down!*

As they flung themselves into the mud, crimson flame stabbed the sky. The rockets flew at them, trailing a tail of fiery sparks. Explosions mushroomed all around. As the Mustang flashed by above them, blackening out the sky momentarily, Schulze yelped out in agony.

'My shitty left wing!' he cursed. 'The bastard got me!'

'On your feet – quick,' von Dodenburg cried. 'No time for that now, Schulze.'

While the Mustang zoomed high into the leaden sky, preparing for another attack, they flung themselves into the battered Tiger.

'Let's go,' van Dodenburg ordered breathlessly, as Schulze slumped behind the cannon, his broad face pale.

As Matz crashed home the gears and the big tank started to rattle towards the railways embankment close by, von Dodenburg swung the turret mg round to face the Mustang. Howling hideously, the Ami plane came hurrying in once more. They heard the crackle of cannon-fire. Twenty-millimetre slugs started cutting the air all around them, gouging up earth in angry bursts behind the Tiger.

Von Dodenburg pressed the trigger of the mg. Tracer streamed towards the Mustang with its great silver stars. He had missed. The next instant the plane soared over his head, almost knocking him from his perch with its howling slipstream, before racing straight upwards into the sky. Desperately he changed the cartridge belt, cursing madly because the mg barrel was already red-hot and burned his fingers. While he did so, his eyes swept the horizon looking for better cover. Then he spotted it – a small opening beneath the railway, perhaps constructed by the engineers of the Reichbahn to allow the farmers easy access to their fields beyond.

'Matz,' he cried above the howl of the plane, coming in for the attack once more, 'head for that tunnel over there!'

'Our arse will stick out!'

'Damn you, Matz, do as you are told – I don't care if your eggs stick out! That's our only—'

The rest of his words were drowned by the Mustang's eight cannon. They drenched the whole area in their burning light. The Tiger reeled as one hit a nearside boogie. For one frightening moment, von Dodenburg thought she would throw a track. But Professor Porche's brainchild had been well constructed. The Tiger rumbled on towards the cover of the tunnel. And then the Ami pilot made a mistake. Confident of his kill, he broke right, instead of zooming upwards at 400 mph. To reduce speed even more, he lowered his undercarriage. Now, coming in round for the last attack, his speed was less than three hundred, and his fire-spewing exhaust was directly in von Dodenburg's sights. The SS colonel did not waste the opportunity offered him.

He pressed the trigger. A vicious stream of tracer hit the Mustang. Pieces of metal started to fly from its fuselage. The tail disappeared. Desperately the pilot tried to control the crippled plane as thick white glycol started to stream from the engine. Von Dodenburg did not relax his pressure on the trigger. He had no sympathy for these impersonal Ami and Tommy killers, who had murdered with impunity these last few months. The tracer struck the plane over and over again, tearing great lumps off, as the frantic pilot tried to ride it to the ground in one piece.

One wing hit the side of the railway embankment, crumpling like a banana skin. The Mustang somersaulted. Its blue-painted belly struck the line in a cloud of dust. It bounced up twenty metres into the air. Crashing down the next instant, just as Matz reached the safety of the tunnel, it burst into flame, silhouetting the trapped pilot against the blaze, a panic-stricken figure clawing frantically at a canopy-cover which would not open. But von Dodenburg's attention was already elsewhere. In his dying agony, the Ami had called for his running mates. Five black dots were silhouetted against the darkening sky, racing towards the burning Mustang, sensing blood, eager to finish off the tank trapped beneath the embankment for good.

'Heaven, arse and twine!' Schulze cursed weakly just before he passed out, hand clutched to the gory mess of his shoulder, 'the bastards have really got us by the short and curlies now, sir . . .'

FOUR

'Gentlemen,' the King said, raising his glass to the assembled American generals, 'm-m-may I give you a t-t-toast?'

Eisenhower, Bradley, Patton and the rest, now flushed with good food and wine, raised their glasses dutifully. They knew that the British King had come to Belgium specifically to boost Monty's[1] morale after the failure of his Arnhem drop; but still this visit to Hodges's First Army HQ was a nice gesture and as an ebullient Patton had commented a little earlier to Eisenhower, 'Hell, Ike, the guy did give me another medal, didn't he?'

'I-I-I would like to wish you s-s-success over the J-J-Jerries in Aachen in the next forty-eight h-h-hours!'

'I'll second that, sir,' Eisenhower said, his broad face split in a happy grin. He raised his glass.

The top brass followed suit, and settled down to an evening of military small talk, with the irrepressible Patton dominating the conversation, as usual, punctuating his stories with vicious stabs of his big cigar which he used as if it were a bayonet. 'Why,' he chuckled in his strangely high-pitched voice, speaking of the thievery of the Tunisian Arabs during the North African campaign, 'I must have shot a dozen Arabs myself.'

King George VI looked impressed. 'I say, is that s-s-so?' he stuttered.

Eisenhower, a little flushed now from his bourbon and branch water, winked at Bradley, Patton's superior, and asked: 'How many did you say, Georgie?'

Patton pulled at his expensive cigar. Then his thin tough face relaxed in a mischievous grin. 'Well, maybe it was only a half a dozen.'

'*How many?*' Eisenhower persisted. At the bottom of the table, running the length of the bare dining room in the commandeered Belgian château, the First Army Corps Commanders laughed at Patton's discomforture. It was good to see old 'Blood

1. Field-Marshal Montgomery's grandiose plan to 'bounce' his way into Germany had come to nothing when his First Airborne Division had failed to hold the vital bridge at Arnhem in September 1944.

and Guts', commander of the heartily disliked Third Army, taken down a peg or two.

The big general hunched his shoulders and laughed. Then he turned to the King, and said: 'Well, at any rate, sir, I did boot two of them squarely in the –ah, 'he caught himself just in time, 'street at Gafsa!'

The King laughed uproariously. 'I s-say,' he stuttered, 'that's weally wich, P-P-Patton!'

It was just at that moment that an anxious aide appeared at the door of the candle-lit dining room and crooked a hesitant finger at General Collins. 'Sir,' he whispered, cupping his hands around his mouth carefully. 'Urgent.'

Collins inclined his blond head towards the head of the table. No one seemed to notice. The top brass was engrossed in another of Patton's scurrilous stories. Hastily he slipped through the door.

Down the corridor, some cook or other was singing: '*The officers they give us can stand up to the worst. You find 'em every weekend, shacked up with a nurse!*' in a low monotone.

'What is it, Jones?' he asked swiftly.

The aide's eyes gleamed. 'Good news, sir! The Big Red One's just reported they've taken Crucifixion Hill. Thirty minutes ago. Colonel Cox's Second Battalion report they're only one thousand yards from the nearest foxholes of Hobbs's 18th Infantry.' He stopped expectantly.

'Goddam!' Collins yelled and punched his fist into he palm of his other hand, his eyes gleaming wildly, 'that's the best goddam news I've had in the whole goddam campaign! Now we can really root hog!'

In the kitchen, the cook sang: '*The coffee that they give us, they say is mighty fine. It's good for cuts and bruises, in place of iodine.*'

But Lightning Joe did not hear the dirge, not the muted laughter of the top brass, nor the persistent rumble of the heavies, the background music of war. All he heard were the magic words – *one thousand yards*. One thousand yards more and the Aachen gap was closed for good!

The bunker was heavy with the stink of sweaty feet. But nobody seemed to notice. The men of Cox's Second Battalion no longer had the sensitive noses of civilians. In these last two years they had smelled too much explosive, too much blood, too much death. Packed close together on the straw they slept or talked in low whispers, while the guns pounded away outside. A few just lay there, wide awake, not talking, but smoking cigarette after cigarette as they stared into the darkness.

In a couple of hours, they would be the point of the final attack to close the gap; and those who were awake knew what that would entail in the way of casualties. Every one of them had written his last letter home, which had been collected personally by the company commanders lest they revealed anything about the forthcoming attack. The only magazine they possessed, a tattered copy of *Yank*, had done the rounds earlier, read from cover to cover by every GI until it had been finally consigned to the big can which held the scanty supply of latrine paper.

Someone laughed suddenly. It was an uncanny sound in the middle of the night in that tense stinking bunker.

'What the hell you laughing for?' a sergeant cried angrily and the sleeping men stirred uneasily.

'Because if I didn't laugh, Sarge,' one of the smoking men said softly, not turning his head in the direction of the angry NCO, 'I'd go nuts!'

The hours passed leadenly. Outside the roar of the artillery grew steadily louder. Now Cox's men could no longer sleep. Grumbling sleepily at the 'God awful racket', they sat up and yawned, shivering the next instant with cold – and fear.

The sergeant who had complained started a game of poker. But it petered out quickly. The sergeant tucked away the money in his olive drab shirt pocket.

'Listen, fellers,' he announced, 'I've got forty dollars in this roll. If I buy it in this push, split the dough between you and play one goddam hot game of poker in my memory, willya?'

The men laughed too loudly, even the man who had protested he would go nuts. They were all wide awake. The artillery barrage was reaching a crescendo. It wouldn't be long now. A thin sliver of grey light, heralding the dawn, slipped in under the bunker's great steel door.

'Looks like a great day for the Purple Heart,' someone said gloomily.

'I wouldn't mind a Purple Heart,' another soldier commented.[1]

'Depends where you get it,' a third said. 'In the leg okay. In the guts, no thank you, brother!'

1. American award for being wounded in action.

'Trench foot is the best,' a bespectacled corporal said scornfully. 'I thought even you dumb oxes knew that. It's pretty lousy at first when the medics take your shoes off. It's like as if you was walking on needles or some wise guy was giving you a hot foot. But brother it got me ninety days in hospital back in North Africa with real white women nurses. Brother!' He rolled his eyes expressively.

'What about false teeth?' a pale-faced rifleman with freckles said. 'I heard if you lost your choppers they took you out of the goddam line and sent you back to the rear to get new ones made.'

'You heard wrong, soldier,' the sergeant said. 'What the hell do you think you're here for – to shoot the Krauts with your Garand or bite the bastards to death?'

'Oh, what the hell you guys running off at the mouth for?' grunted a burly older staff sergeant, cigar at the corner of his tough mouth. 'Purple Heart, trench foot, goddam false teeth!' He spat on the straw. 'Hell, the Krauts ain't got nothing in front except a lot of old guys with glass eyes and wooden legs! Don't you guys know that they're scraping the bottom of the barrel on the Aachen front?'

'I don't care if the guy behind that gun is a syphilitic prick who's a goddam hundred years old, Sarge,' the pale-faced rifleman said. 'He's still sitting behind eight feet of concrete and he's still got enough goddam fingers to press triggers and shoot bullets.'

'Now, see here, soldier,' the staff sergeant began, but he never finished.

Outside, the whistles started to blow and the same old coarse voices commenced calling the same old orders: 'All right, youse guys – get ya arses out here. Don't ya know there's a goddam war on?'

At the Quellenhof, Donner raged. 'In the name of God,' he yelled at a mud-covered Schwarz who had just managed to pull the couple of hundred panzer grenadiers still alive off Crucifixion Hill, 'Where is Colonel von Dodenburg?'

Schwarz, swaying with fatigue and hunger, licked his blood-scummed lips. 'He carried out your orders, sir,' he said hoarsely. 'Went off to stop the Ami drive on the Rimburg front. There was the CO and Officer-Cadet Krause.'

In his agitation, Donner thrust out his glass eye and ran it through his blood-tipped fingers. 'So this is what the premier regiment of the Armed SS has come to, Schwarz – the CO and a seventeen-year-old boy trying to stop a whole enemy division?' Suddenly he buried his ruined face in his hands. 'My God,' he sobbed, 'where is von Dodenburg?'

The Ami fighters had gone. The whole countryside, still covered in the grey-white of the false dawn, was alive with enemy troops. Throughout the night they had heard the persistent rumble of their tanks and trucks and once they had seen a long line of lights heading towards Aachen as a confident Ami convoy drove by. Soon von Dodenburg knew they would have to make a bolt for it before they were trapped completely. But how?

Schulze, slumped in the seat next to him, groaned. Von Dodenburg opened his eyes. Schulze was badly hit, he realised that. The big NCO had tossed and turned the whole night long, while he and Matz had taken turns as sentry.

'Let me have a look at that shoulder, Schulze. Matz, flash your torch over here, but keep it shaded.'

Von Dodenburg ripped away the burnt, bloody shirt from the wounded NCO's heavily muscled shoulder. The wound was thick with black caked blood, congealed around the jagged silver fragment of a twenty-millimetre shell. In the thin blue light, he could just make out the faint red line of blood poisoning running into the matted hair of the ex-docker's powerful chest.

'The body beautiful,' Schulze said weakly, his half-closed eyelids flickering. 'Takes anybody's breath away . . . so exciting.'

Von Dodenburg looked at Matz. Outside another Ami convoy rumbled across the fields. The one-legged NCO licked his cracked lips.

'Don't look so pretty, sir,' he voiced von Dodenburg's unspoken fear. 'And that pong too.' He hesitated. 'I hope it's just the old sergeant-major's natural stink – and not gas gangrene.' He tapped his wooden leg. 'That's the bastard that did for me.'

Von Dodenburg knew what Matz meant. If some of the dirty cloth from Schulze's shirt had been forced into the wound, he was in for bad trouble. Even Diedenhofen, as much as he loved his SS men, would have no compunction about whipping off Schulze's arm, rather than leave it and risk the big NCO's life.

'What do you think, Matz?'

Matz flicked off the torch. Schulze's eyes closed and he relapsed into unconsciousness again, his breath sharp and shallow. Matz did not speak for a moment. 'The best thing, sir, is to get him back to the bone-menders as quick as possible. But—' he hesitated.

'Go on.'

'Well, sir, I think we ought to get that lump of lead out of him. God knows how long it's going to take us to get back to our own lines and by then the damage might be done, if we leave that in his shoulder.'

Matz flicked on his torch again. With his free hand, he reached down into his dice-beaker and whipped out a long sheath-knife, decorated with the diamond-shaped swastika of the Hitler Youth. 'Got it when I was a youth leader before the war. Kept it ever since.' He ran a horny thumb over its blade. 'Sharp as a razor. The tip's like a needle.'

Von Dodenburg looked at the knife. 'We've nothing to deaden the pain,' he said. 'And hygiene.'

'Leave it to me, sir. It won't be the first time. In Russia in '43, I whipped two toes off a corporal with frostbite in two seconds flat. As for hygiene.' He ripped open his flies and standing upright on the turret aimed a hot stream of yellow urine at the knife's blade. 'They say my urine'll kill anything, ever since I had the Spaghetti clap this spring.' As the liquid dribbled down the side of the Tiger, he turned and bent over the unconscious Schulze.

'Sir, you'd better get a good grip on the big bastard. He's strong as a bull. And as soon as he feels this inside him, he's going to kick up something horrible.'

Von Dodenburg nodded his agreement. He sat with his whole weight on the wounded man's good shoulder, twisting him sideways so that he could grab his elbows, pull his arm back and expose the wound to its full extent. Matz clamped the torch between his teeth, took a firm hold of the dripping knife and plunged the razor-sharp blade into the side of the wound.

Schulze screamed. His great body heaved like a tied-down stallion. Von Dodenburg exerted all his strength. He heard the knife scrape sickeningly against the shoulder bone. Schulze screamed again, his spine arching sharply with agony. Von Dodenburg freed one hand hurriedly and stuffed his dirty handkerchief into Schulze's wide-open gasping mouth.

Matz worked rapidly, the sweat standing out in dull pearls on his forehead, the knife digging deep into the flesh around the wound as he eased the shell fragment out. What Schulze felt neither man knew; the dirty handkerchief gagged whatever cries he made. But a sweat-lathered von Dodenburg, fighting desperately to keep him still, could well imagine that Matz's knife must feel like a red-hot poker, stabbing and gouging in the wound.

And then Matz spat the torch out of his mouth. He took a deep breath. 'Sorry, you big bastard!' he gasped and heaved. He turned the knife with a swift flick of his wrist. There was a soft sucking noise. Next instant the 20-mm shell fragment clattered on to the Tiger's deck, and Matz was squatting on his haunches, fingers red with fresh blood, panting with exertion. As a suddenly exhausted von Dodenburg removed the gag, Schulze relapsed into a merciful unconsciousness. Outside the guns had stopped. Von Dodenburg knew what that meant: the Amis were going to attack.

'Come on, you lucky bastards,' the older staff sergeant cried, 'earn a day's pay, will you!' He waved his carbine and slogged on down the hill into the grey cloud of artillery smoke.

Cox's entire Second Battalion was sweeping down the far side of Crucifixion Hill in an unbroken line. An abrupt blast of 88 fire directly overhead illuminated the card-playing sergeant on his right knee pumping shot after shot from his Garand into the Kraut positions. Another horrifying blast swooshed through the air. Darkness. Then the brilliant bluish flash of the shell exploding revealed the sergeant, still on his right knee, but without his head.

As he fell, the freckled-faced young PFC ran forward and began searching the headless body's pockets for the forty dollars poker money. The First's artillery crashed into action and silenced the 88. Cox's Second Battalion pushed on again, squelching over squashed bodies, slithering on squirming entrails. A sudden potato masher grenade threw the man who couldn't sleep into a deep foxhole. He found himself wedged face to face with a Kraut. The German was as surprised as the American. For a long moment the two of them stood there transfixed. The American had a rifle; the German none, but the trench was too narrow to use it. The American grabbed his commando knife. He thrust the brass-knuckled grip into the

German's mouth, who reeled back spitting teeth and blood. With all his remaining strength, the man who couldn't sleep stabbed the knife into the German's stomach. The Kraut gasped, '*Oh, holy Mother . . . holy Mother!*' The American felt the hot blood spurt up his right arm. He pulled the knife out and rammed it home again. Again and again. The Kraut's body sagged. His knees gave way beneath him. The man who couldn't sleep reeled and vomited.

Behind him a coarse official voice shouted. 'Jesus H. Christ, man, don't kill 'em all – we need some cruddy prisoners!'

Cox's artillery officer looked at the smoking hole filled with dead and dying men, which a moment before had been one of his 75s. Little bits of human anatomy were strewn from one end of the pit to the other. The maimed bodies of his artillerymen had poured blood and guts over the earth so that the ground had first turned purple and was now beginning to go black. Their extremities seemed to be wriggling still, as if they were trying to rejoin the bodies from which they had come.

The artillery officer had seen it all many times before. He tried to reassure his shocked men. 'The Kraut 88,' he lectured them as if he were back at the Point and not in the middle of a battlefield, 'is no wonder weapon. It is merely a dual-purpose gun with a jacketed barrel, an easily detachable set of breech rings, a supported interchangeable A-tube, a carriage consisting of an upper carriage with a protective armour shield, a buffer fitted into the barrel cradle, a hydro-pneumatic recuperator fitted above the barrel and a special trailer which is fitted with pneumatic tyres and is drawn by a half-track.' He smiled at them, confident that he had his men under control again, while they, faces white with shock, stared back at him as if he had suddenly gone crazy. 'In other words, the 88 is a gun like any other gun. There is no need to suffer from 88 fever, men. No need at all.' He peered at them through his gold-rimmed pince-nez. 'A gun like any other gun,' he repeated.

The rest of his words were drowned by the great hurrying rush of another 88 shell. A booming explosion sent shrapnel flying everywhere in the thick acrid yellow cloud of smoke of impact. When it cleared, the survivors saw that the artillery officer had succumbed to the '88 fever' himself. His headless body was crumpled in an untidy mess at the edge of the fresh brown shellhole. And still the advance went on.

Behind the crumbling German line, forced steadily backwards by the pressure of the two US divisions – Roosevelt's Butchers and the Big Red One – the rear echelon stallions started to retreat. 'Destroy, burn, leave nothing,' Donner's order had stated. And they carried it out to the letter. Every thirty seconds a vehicle laden with anything worth transporting rumbled off in the direction of Aachen, accompanied by the crump of another dump exploding. Speed, frenzy, horror were the order of the day behind the German front, as the Amis pressed home their attack. The gap between the two divisions was only a matter of yards now.

Another Sherman was hit. The gunner's hair and uniform caught fire at once. He had been wounded in the leg by the panzerfaust rocket. All the same he dived through the open turret hatch. Pulling himself out, he grabbed the metal with both hands. The hot steel ate into the flesh as if it were butter, tearing it away in livid strips. He struck the ground, screaming, face first. He sat up in the swirling smoke and tore off his combat jacket. It came away in flaming shreds. All the strength had gone from his lower limbs, but he found that by digging his elbows into the ground and pulling, he could move about ten feet every five minutes. He started to crawl. As he gasped to the medics just before he died in agony: 'Brother, I'm not about to kick off just yet ...'

And the veterans of the Big Red One who had been in North Africa went into the attack humming the words of their own divisional song:

> 'Dirty Gertie from Bizerte
> Had a mousetrap 'neath her skirtie,
> Strapped it on her kneecap purty,
> Baited it with Fleur de Flirte,
> Made her boy friends most alerty,
> She was voted in Bizerte,
> Miss Latrine for nineteen thirty.'

That was until the last German machine-guns opened and the song died on their lips as the lead struck their leading rank.

The men of the Big Red One could see their comrades of the 30th quite clearly now, and Colonel Cox began to grow anxious lest his boys start hitting Hobbs's fellows by mistake. Staff officers made their cautious way into the firing line to ensure that no unfortunate accidents took place. The two divisions were only five hundred yards apart.

'Lots of guys pass out,' the burly truck driver was saying to the two stragglers from one of the 30th Division's infantry outfits, as the three dug their spoons into cans of cold hash, 'The gas fumes get you after a while,' he indicated the back of his truck with his spoon, and the heaped rows of petrol jerricans, 'Sometimes you just keel over and sometimes you get real sick. You get lead poisoning. Looks like poison ivy. On a real hot day, you can see the fumes. Looks like heat coming off a railroad yard.'

Von Dodenburg, crouched in the bushes fifteen metres away, looked up the dirt road. No sign of any other Amis. He nodded to Matz, gripping Schulze's Schmeisser and held up his right hand, fingers outspread. Matz indicated his understanding. Five seconds and they would move in. Behind them a semi-conscious Schulze groaned.

'I remember our trucking company was billeted in this apple orchard in Normandy with the little apples just coming out and fuck me if the whole lot didn't go and die in a week from the gas fumes.' He flung away the empty can of hash. 'Now what do you guys say to that?'

'Yeah, it must be tough,' the younger of the two infantrymen said, the blue of the combat soldier badge decorating his dirty khaki, 'pretty damn tough in the Service of Supply. You ought to get a transfer to the infantry, soldier.'

'Aw you guys are pissing me,' the driver said smiling slowly.

'No,' the other soldier began, 'we know you guys are—'

He never finished the sentence. Matz stuck his machine pistol into his back Then von Dodenburg was standing in front of them, Walther pistol levelled at their bellies.

'Hands up!' he snapped in his heavily accented English.

The three Amis standing around the parked 'deuce and a half' truck shot up their hands, their eyes suddenly fearful as they recognised the silver SS runes worn by the black-clad, hard-faced officer with the pistol. Von Dodenburg ran his swift gaze over them. The two infantrymen had dumped their rifles, and they were only armed with bayonets. The truck driver was unarmed.

Von Dodenburg nodded to Matz. 'All right, Sergeant, take those two heroes,' he indicated the pale-faced infantrymen, 'and get Schulze – and watch how they treat that shoulder of his. I don't want the bastard bleeding again!'

'Yessir.' Matz pushed the two infantrymen forward. 'Move,' he ordered. The soldier with the combat infantry badge bit his lower lip fearfully. 'You can't shoot us, sir,' he stammered. 'Not in cold blood.'

'I can,' von Dodenburg answered with a chill smile on his haggard unshaven face. 'But I won't – just yet. Now move.'

A few minutes later Schulze was stowed in the back of the truck, bedded down on the driver's blankets, with Matz and von Dodenburg crouched beside him, their weapons levelled at the terrified Amis' heads through the slit at the back of the cab.

'Now listen,' von Dodenburg said carefully after the burly driver had switched on the truck's engine. 'Your lives depend upon our getting to Aachen safely. If you make a mistake,' he clicked his tongue significantly, 'you are dead.'

'But the MPs, sir,' the driver protested. 'They might stop us.'

'Your problem,' von Dodenburg answered coldly, though his mind was racing, trying to imagine what problems might arise in their five-kilometre journey to the city. But he knew this was the only way to get through. The kilometre they had struggled across the fields since they had abandoned the Tiger in the tunnel had been a nightmare. Both he and Matz was exhausted. They had been unable to carry the wounded delirious sergeant-major any further. There was no other course open to them.

'All right,' he snapped, 'let us get started.'

The driver crashed home first gear and slowly the two-and-a-half ton petrol truck started to drive away.

Everything went smoothly until they reached the outskirts of Aachen itself. Now the steady stream of vehicles heading for the front started to congest. Twice they had to get off the muddy, pitted roads to let long ambulance convoys hurry by with their sirens howling and signs in their windscreens announcing in blood-red letters CARRYING CASUALTIES. The traffic still moving forward was mostly armoured now. They crawled by rear defence units, dug in grimly on both sides of the road, gripping their weapons in sweaty palms, as if the enemy might come storming out of the smoking rubble of the suburbs at any moment. They passed a road sign reading: 'RAISE DUST AND YOU'RE DEAD, BROTHER! THIS ROAD IS UNDER ENEMY FIRE!'

But they didn't need to be told that. The sledgehammer of sound was beating down regularly. Peering out of the sides of the truck, von Dodenburg could see the terror reflected in the faces of the infantry trudging towards the front. Their eyes shone hotly as if tears were close, their flesh was ashen and their mouths trembled every time another shell struck the quaking ground ahead. All other vehicles had vanished from the littered, cratered road by now. They were alone with the infantry.

'Sir,' the truck driver gasped, muscles rippling as he swung the vehicle around another crater, 'Somebody's gonna stop us soon ... What we gonna do then?'

'Leave that to me,' von Dodenburg said hoarsely. 'You keep on driving.' He looked at Matz and then at Schulze, lying on the dirty floor of the shaking truck, his breath coming in shallow gasps. He put his hand on the sergeant-major's burning hot forehead. He told himself fiercely that he was going to get the rogue through. Germany would need men like the loud-mouthed, cocky ex-docker in the terrible days to come. 'Don't worry, Matz,' he urged. 'We'll get through.'

Matz, the veteran, pursed his lips scornfully. 'I'm not worried, sir. I'm a regular, you know, sir. Not like this asphalt soldier here.' He jerked a dirty thumb at his companion of many a drinking and whoring session. 'I was wondering whether you'd recommend me for acting sergeant-major when that gold-bricker goes into hospital. I mean while he's having a good time getting a fly feel at the nurses' tits, lying between clean sheets, I might as well get a bit of the glory. It'll look good on my records. Might get me a bigger pension.'

Von Dodenburg shook his head. 'Shit on Sunday,' he cursed, using the soldier's expression, 'you're even a worse rascal than Schulze, Matz. Yes, you'll get your temporary promotion. That is if we ever get out of this mess.'

'Stop,' shouted the bareheaded lieutenant, leaping up out of the rubble to their right, carbine at the ready. 'Jesus wept, are you guys sick of life? This is the goddam line!'

The burly driver hit the brakes. Helmeted heads raised themselves cautiously from the brick rubble on both sides of the road. Von Dodenburg, his heart beating wildly with shock, recognised the high-pitched burr of a Spandau somewhere ahead in the smoke-shrouded scene. The German front, he told himself.

'Well?' the lieutenant demanded, when the driver did not speak. 'What the hell are you doing so far forward with a gas truck? I thought you guys from the Red Ball Express didn't get this far up the front.'[1] Still the driver didn't speak. Somewhere behind them a mortar started to howl obscenely. The red-faced lieutenant did not even jump. It was clear he was a veteran. Suddenly he noticed the three soldiers' strange silence.

'Hey, you guys,' he commanded, raising his carbine. 'Let me have a dekko at your ID.' He turned to his platoon sergeant. 'Joe, come on over here—'

Matz fired. The men in the cab ducked too late. The two infantrymen's heads were blasted apart. Blood and bone flew everywhere. The windscreen shattered into a sudden spiderweb. The lieutenant standing in front of the truck flew backwards.

'Drive on!' von Dodenburg yelled frantically.

The driver, the side of his face and shoulder soaked in blood, crashed home the gear. The truck shot forward. Zig-zagging crazily, it roared down the street in first gear, followed by the wild angry fire of the GIs. Blinded by the shattered windscreen, the driver careened into a lamp post. He wrenched desperately at the wheel. Th truck skidded to the right with a wild howl of protesting tyres.

'Hold the bastard!' Matz screamed in German. 'Hold it, man!'

Too late. The truck crashed into a heap of rubble. The driver shot over his wheel, smashed through the shattered windscreen and lay still, his head twisted at an unnatural angle, his neck broken.

'Here!' von Dodenburg grabbed Matz's machine-pistol and fired a wild burst towards the Ami's lines. Answering slugs pattered against the Americans. 'Grab a hold of Schulze – quick!' he gasped and fired another long burst at the GIs trying to edge their way in the cover of the shattered building towards them. The answering fire stopped momentarily.

Matz slapped Schulze hard across the face. 'Come on – wake up,' he yelled. 'We've got to make a run for it.'

Schulze groaned, but his eyes remained obstinately closed. Matz slapped his shoulder. Schulze screamed. His eyes opened.

1. Red Ball Express. Supply route reaching from the Normandy beach-head to the front.

'What?' he gasped.

Matz grabbed his good arm and tugged. 'Get to your feet,' he hissed. 'The Amis are only twenty metres away!'

Weakly the big NCO allowed himself to be hauled up and led, swaying wildly, to the edge of the truck. Matz dropped first and cursed with pain as his wooden leg thrust itself into the socket. Schulze followed and collapsed on his knees. Matz hit him again. A thin trickle of blood flowed from his nose. Slugs were hitting the ground all around them now.

'For Christ sake – move!' von Dodenburg cried. 'I'll cover you – MOVE!'

Like crippled caricatures of soldiers, the NCOs began to stagger towards the German lines, while their CO knelt and tried to hold the Amis off.

'Hold your fire,' a voice ahead commanded. 'It's two of our lads – from the Wotan!'

Sobbing like an athlete at the end of his tether, weaving from side to side with the strain, Matz supported the half-conscious bulk of the big NCO in the direction of the voice. Together they stumbled through the fallen masonry, tripping over the tangle of fallen wire, eyes narrowed against the thick acrid smoke; while behind them von Dodenburg swept the street from side to side keeping the Amis back. And then they tumbled into a hole, and helping hands were grabbing at them, and figures dressed in the black of the SS Wotan were shouting with joy: 'It's Matz and big Schulze . . . Matz and big Schulze!'

'The CO,' the sergeant-major gasped just before he passed out. 'The CO.'

They needed no further urging. In one crazy rush the panzer grenadiers were out of their holes and charging down the street, firing from the hip as they ran. 'WOTAN . . . WOTAN . . . WOTAN!' their battle-cry was flung from their open mouths with fanatical, new-found energy. And von Dodenburg, crouched in the doorway of a destroyed butcher's, trying to fit his last magazine among the long-abandoned hooks and wooden chopping boards, let his Schmeisser drop into the rubble, relief overwhelming him. His men were coming to rescue him.

At almost that very same instant on that October 16th afternoon, a patrol from Colonel Cox's infantry, led by Staff Sergeant Frank A. Karswell, set off to make the first physical contact with the men of the 30th Infantry. The Big Red One veteran did not get far. The patrol had just reached the main Aachen-Wuerselen highway when the enemy artillery barrage descended upon them. The patrol dropped as one and let the blast and heat sweep over them. Someone screamed and there was the smell of burning flesh. The burning houses to left and right swayed like gigantic loose back-drops in the theatre. When the survivors scattered for cover in the lull between the salvoes, Staff Sergeant Karwell was not with them.

His men had lost heart, all save the two skinny scouts, Privates Krauss and Whitis. 'I'm for going on,' Ed Krauss yelled above the roar of the barrage. 'What about you, Evan?'

Whitis nodded. Leaving the rest behind, the two of them continued, creeping cautiously through the burning, smoking moonlandscape, their bodies tense, waiting for the burst of mg fire which surely must come and cut them down at any moment.

A hundred yards. A hundred and fifty. Still they had not been halted. Suddenly Krauss stopped. 'Look – GI uniforms!' he gasped.

Even Whitis narrowed his eyes against the smoke. 'Hot damn,' he breathed, 'you're right, Ed.'

Almost at that same moment, the strange GIs spotted them. 'Hey,' they yelled joyfully, 'We're from K-Company. Come on up!'

'And we're from F Company,' Whitis and Krauss cried back. 'Come on down!' Obediently the other infantrymen started to file down the battle-littered, smoke-shrouded hillside to shake the hands and slap the backs of the two lone scouts.

It was 16.15 hours and Roosevelt's Butchers had finally linked up with the Big Red One. The Aachen Gap was closed at last; Germany's Holy City was cut off from the Reich.

FOUR: THE END

'There was an Austrian – a Jew to boot, if I am not mistaken –
who wrote a long time ago, "In the time of the sinking sun,
dwarfs cast shadows like giants". The sun is going down, von
Dodenburg, and I do not want to live in the time of the dwarfs.'
SS General Donner to Colonel von Dodenburg.

ONE

There was no sound save the harsh stamp of the young lieutenant's highly polished jackboots on the concrete of the hotel drive. Next to him the three Ami officers moved noiselessly in their rubber-soled combat boots. From the windows the curious, hollow-eyed staff officers stared down at the scene, while the HQ's battleworn defence platoon fingered their weapons uneasily.

At the regulation ten paces from the Battle Commandant who was waiting with von Dodenburg at his side, the young lieutenant halted, clicked his heels together and flung up his arm in the German greeting.

'Heil Hitler,' he shouted smartly.

'Heil Hitler!' Donner returned the greeting.

The grey-haired Ami colonel, flanked by the two officers carrying the white flags, looked startled by the greeting. But Donner ignored them.

'What are these men doing here?' he rasped, although he knew quite well what the Americans wanted.

'Beg to report, General,' the young lieutenant said formally, 'that these officers are enemy parliamentaires. They wish to speak to you, sir.'

Donner nodded curtly and turned his terrible face fully to the Amis, noting with pleasure the look of horror on the face of the youngest of them. 'Does any one of you speak German?'

The grey-haired colonel said, 'Yes, General, I do.'

Donner wrinkled his nose and flashed a significant look at von Dodenburg. The SS colonel read his unspoken thought: the Ami officer must be a Jew. 'Well, then, what do you want?' he asked briskly.

The Ami colonel pulled a piece of paper from the pocket of his stained combat blouse and cleared his throat pompously: 'I have a message here from my Corps Commander, General Joseph Collins. He has asked me to read it to you, General. I shall read it first in the English original and then in German.'

'My good man,' Donner rasped, trying to control his temper, but raising his voice so that the spectators hanging out of hotel

132

windows could hear, 'you can read it in Chinese, if you wish. All I am interested in is the German version.'

The grey-haired colonel flushed. He bent his head over the paper and began to read: 'The city of Aachen is now completely surrounded by American forces. If the city is not promptly and completely surrendered unconditionally, the American Army Ground and Air Forces will proceed ruthlessly with air and artillery bombardment to reduce it to submission.'

The American looked at Donner significantly. Donner stared at some unknown object in the far distance, as if he were bored by the whole business. Behind him, von Dodenburg allowed himself a faint smile of admiration. The Police General was putting on a great show, for a commander who was completely cut off from the main force and whose total fighting strength was reduced to five thousand men, of whom Wotan's five hundred survivors were the only troops of any real fighting quality.

The Ami shrugged and began to translate. When he had finished he looked up at the German general standing on the bullet-chipped steps of the hotel and asked: 'Well?'

Donner fixed him with his glassy stare. 'Well, what?'

'Do you want to surrender to my Corps Commander?' He licked his dry lips. 'You know the consequences if you don't, General?'

Donner laughed scornfully. '*Consequences!* You can no longer bomb us without endangering your own troops. If your ground people attack, they will have to fight us from house to house, from street to street. Aachen will become another Stalingrad for your Army. Can you afford to pay that price?'

'Well, then, what message do you want me to take to General Collins?'

'Message? A very simple one. He can go to hell – and if you aren't out of my area within the next five minutes, you will precede him there forthwith!' He turned to the elegant Army lieutenant. 'Take these men back the way they came.'

The American colonel's mouth dropped open. Across from him, Major Schwarz, black eyes gleaming fanatically, dropped his hand on his pistol holster significantly. The Americans took the hint. Swiftly they turned and started moving back down the shell-littered road, carrying their white flags with them disconsolately.

Donner did not even bother to look at them. Instead he turned to the spectators.

133

'Listen, soldiers,' he rasped. 'Our position is not so desperate as some of you might think. We are dug in in an excellent position. We have food for two months. Reichsmarshal Goering has promised personally to keep us supplied with ammunition by air and already the Führer's planners are working out a scheme to break open the Ami ring around the city and relieve us. I expect, therefore, that each and every defender of the venerable Imperial City of Aachen to do his duty to the end, in fulfilment of our Oath to the Flag. I expect courage and determination to hold out.'

He flashed a hard look around their battleworn faces, knowing only too well how limited their staying power was. Snapping to attention, he thrust up his arm in that salute to a man who had brought new hope to a ruined, chaotic Germany a mere eleven years before: 'Long live our Führer Adolf Hitler and our beloved Fatherland. *Sieg Heil!*' The courtyard echoed and re-echoed to the iron stamp of their heavy boots and the great answering cry of *Heil . . . Heil . . . Heil!* In the white-stripped trees, the black crows rose in alarm, croaking their hoarse protests.

Donner waited a moment or two for the sound to die away and then he said. 'Now we'll show the Ami bastards what we German soldiers are made of. Major Gehlen!'

'Sir,' the red-faced artillery major answered from a second-floor window. 'I want all guns to fire a five-round salvo at the enemy positions.'

'But that's our total ration for the day, sir,' the artillery commander protested.

'I don't give a damn. Fat Hermann[1] will provide us with more. I'm going to show the pompous, over-confident swine over there that they haven't won the battle for Aachen by a long chalk yet.'

As the first howl of the six-barrel electric mortars tore the still afternoon apart, von Dodenburg grinned and hurried back to his quarters to fetch his battle equipment. Donner had given a tremendous performance. Now he would have to be ready to withstand the Amis' answer.

'The arrogant, pig-headed Kraut bastard!' Lightning Joe raged in Huebner's cellar Command Post after the staff officer had

1. SS nickname for Goering.

departed who had brought the news. 'Doesn't he know that the chips are really down, Clarence?'

'Apparently not, sir,' Huebner answered, a little pleased to see Lightning Joe so rattled, as the first shells from the Kraut screaming meemie[1] began to explode all around outside. 'Just get a load of that!'

'Yeah, I hear it,' Lightning Joe said, pacing the cellar grimly, ignoring the white dust falling from the shaking ceiling on to his gleaming lacquered helmet, embellished with the polished yellow stars. 'The Kraut general must be absolutely nuts. Doesn't he know he's had it?' He pulled himself together, stopping in mid-stride and swinging round to face the old man. 'Okay, if that's kind of ball, he wants to play, I'm the guy who can give him it. And how! Okay, Clarence, what's the deal? What are you going to do now?'

General Huebner rose heavily and poked a fat forefinger at the map of Aachen. 'The Kraut is strapped for bodies, sir, as you know. Intelligence estimates that that crazy Kraut commander has got five to six thousand men at his disposal. But they're enough to give us a hard time, especially fighting as they are in an easily defensible built-up area.' He paused.

'Go on, Clarence,' Collins urged, as the sounds of the surprise barrage started to die away, to be replaced by the cries of the wounded shouting for the aidmen. He knew that Huebner wanted more men. But he knew too that Huebner wasn't getting them. He needed all the muscle he had for the drive to the Rhine; Huebner would have to take Aachen with what he could spare from the Big Red One.

'So, sir, I can't risk my doughs in all-out attack. The Krauts would slaughter them. What I intend to do,' he pointed to the map, 'is to slip Colonel Seitz's 26th Infantry into the city here and here. The left wing will cut its way right across the place from its jumping-off place on the Aachen-Cologne railroad.'

Lightning Joe nodded.

'At the same time, Seitz's right wing will strike out for these three hills – here. They dominate the city's northern fringes, in particular, the Lousberg – the troops call it "lousy mountain". It rises to a height of nine hundred feet and casts a shadow over almost the entire city.'

Collins held his hand up, 'Spare me the guidebook details, Clarence,' he said.

1. GI name for the six-barrelled mortar.

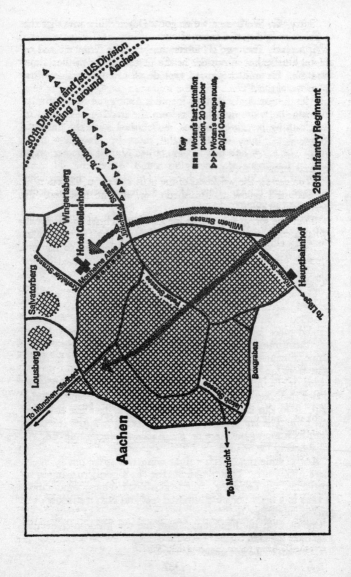

30th Division and 1st US Division
Ring 'around' Aachen

26th Infantry Regiment

Key
▦▦▦ Wotan's last battalion position, 20 October
▷▷▷ Wotan's escape route, 20/21 October

Lousberg
Salvatorberg
Wingertsberg
Hotel Quellenhof
Monheim Allee
Krefelder Strasse
Jülicher Strasse
To Düsseldorf

Wilhelm Strasse
Hauptbahnhof
To Liège
US 26th
Boxgraben

To München-Gladbach
Aachen
To Maastricht

'Sorry, sir. Well, once we've got the three hills, we've got the whole city laid out in front of our artillery, as if it were spread over a plate. Then we go in for the kill. The Kraut HQ at the Hotel Quellenhof. Once the head's gone, the body'll flop down and die.' He smiled, pleased with himself. 'I think it's the best plan to take the place with the minimum of loss. Hit the head and let the guts die of their own accord.'

Lightning Joe was silent as he considered Huebner's plan, glancing from time to time at the map of Aachen. The cellar shook as a convoy of self-propelled 155 cannon rumbled by on their way to the front. He waited till the last one had disappeared before he spoke.

'You can see the weakness of the plan, can't you, Clarence?'

Huebner's sallow face flushed. 'No, sir,' he hesitated. 'I'm sorry to say I can't.'

· 'Don't be sorry,' Lightning Joe said with a brief smile. 'That's what a corps commander gets paid for – to shaft over-confident divisional commanders. Your plan is excellent in so far as it doesn't get the main body of Seitz's infantry involved in goddam street fighting. Capture the heights and the town's yours. You can blast the place to all hell until the Krauts are begging you to be able to surrender. Excellent, as I've just said. But look at your flank – how exposed it is! Up where you've linked with Hobbs's 30th, your guys are pretty thin on the ground. One of those damn Kraut counter-attack artists could come barrelling in from the north one dawn and then you'd look kinda funny when they'd broken through the line and hit Seitz in the flank. They could be cut off just like that – and they'd have no built-up area to protect them or dig their toes into. Then it would be your turn to know what it's like when the head goes.' He looked challengingly at the older man. 'Do you read me, Clarence?'

'I read you, sir,' he answered unhappily. 'But what do you suggest as an alternative?'

'Nothing,' Collins answered a little maliciously, pleased to see Huebner caught on the hop for a change. 'I've no bodies to spare to beef up the 26th. Besides I don't want this Corps to do another Brest.[1] Aachen is not going to be another pyrrhic victory for the United States Army. You play it the way you've planned.'

1. The siege and capture of Brest, a useless port on the Breton coast, had cost the US Army 10,000 casualties that October.

He paused for breath, the smile vanishing from his handsome face.

'And?'

'And? Well, Clarence, you'd better keep one good eye cocked over your right shoulder all the time you're attacking those three hills. Otherwise,' he looked challengingly at the older man, 'the Krauts are gonna catch you with your drawers down. Good afternoon, Clarence.'

But for once, General 'Lightning Joe' Collins was mistaken in his estimate of the direction from which the German attack would come.

TWO

The stench of the tunnel when the ancient, wrinkled, civilian had finally prised open the sewer lid hit von Dodenburg in the face like a physical blow. It was a compound of human waste, the coppery stench of blood and disinfectant from the dressing station drains and the heavy cloying odour of creosote.

The civilian chuckled at the look of disgust on the officer's face. 'Nothing to worry about, sir,' he croaked in his Rhenish accent. 'Just the good old honest stink of human shit. I've lived and worked in it these last fifty years and it hasn't done me much harm.' He chuckled again and showed the yellow stumps of his crooked teeth.

'That's what you think, you dirty old shitehawk,' Matz growled. 'You stink worse than that place down there.' He indicated the dark sewer shaft below. Wrinkling his nose in disgust, he ordered. 'Get your shitty self to windward of me, will yer?'

'All right, that's enough, Sergeant-Major,' von Dodenburg snapped, instinctively keeping his voice low.

'Sorry, sir,' Acting Sergeant-Major Matz said and, kneeling stiffly on his good leg, joined the rest of the volunteers waiting crouched in the darkening courtyard of the city works office.

'All right, I'll repeat the drill,' von Dodenburg said softly. 'We go down in groups of four, each under an officer or NCO. We all follow the same route – at one-minute intervals to avoid confusion in the dark – until we reach what Mr Gerhardt here calls the main square. There we split up and spread out to our objectives. At eighteen hundred hours precisely, when Intelligence estimates the Amis will be standing down for the day,' he sniffed, 'they're real nine-to-five soldiers – we hit them – *and we hit them hard!*' His keen blue eyes, sunk in their dark circles of strain, flashed around the thirty volunteers from what was left of his tank crews who were prepared to tackle this dangerous mission. 'Five minutes to get inside their billets, five minutes to do the job, and then we beat it. I want bodies – a couple of prisoners will do – and one hell of a panic behind the Ami lines to put their generals off their stroke.'

'We'll scare the lace knickers off their lily-white arses,' Matz said confidently, rubbing a dirty hand over his unshaven chin.

'Let's hope so, Matz. Now, any questions?'

A gangling rawboned farmboy, whose red hands hung out of a tunic which was much too small for him, asked awkwardly. 'Don't think I've got the wind up, sir. But how do we get back when the shit starts flying?'

'The same way we went in.'

'But how do we get back to the – er – main square. I mean,' he added hurriedly, rather red in the face with embarrassment, 'it's dark down there and I wouldn't like to get lost in that shit pit.'

Von Dodenburg smiled. 'Don't worry, Trees. That problem's been taken care of. Every group leader has a piece of chalk of a different colour. I'm green, for example. Each group leader will mark his route from the main square to the sewer opening. On the way back, you simply play your torch on the markings which will lead you back to the main square assembly point. Major Schwarz or myself will be there then to guide you back into our own lines here.' He smiled at the embarrassed boy. 'Understand?'

'Yessir,' he answered, relieved. 'Understood. I didn't fancy getting lost down there in all that shit, that's all.'

'Go on,' Matz cracked. 'Shouldn't worry you. You farmers live in shit all your life. Probably have it on bread for breakfast instead of syrup for all I know.'

The volunteers laughed softly, including Trees. Von Dodenburg took a last look at the darkening October sky, lightened here and there by the pink of the Ami evening bombardment, the last of the day. He nodded to Schwarz who would bring up the rear. 'All right, old man,' he said to old Gerherdt. 'Let's get on with it.'

The civilian pulled at his thigh-high waders and without another word swung himself with practised ease over the top and began clambering down the dripping iron ladder into the nauseous, evil-smelling mess below.

Von Dodenburg took one last deep breath of the good air and steeled himself for the ordeal in front of him. 'All right, my section – follow me !'

'Christ,' Matz groaned as the stench hit him, 'the things I do for Folk, Fatherland and Führer. Now I've got to fight up to my eggs in shit.'

Stiffly he started to descend the ladder and in an instant the gloom had swallowed him up. The first section had moved off on the daring operation.

It had been Schwarz who had suggested the mission in the first place. Von Dodenburg had just returned from a visit to Schulze, who was now coming out of his coma after Diedenhofen had operated on his shoulder to clean up the mess made by Matz's knife. A panting runner had summoned him to Donner's HQ.

Donner and Schwarz were standing in his office, faces tense and set, watching two sweating staff officers as they drew in the red arrows on the acetate cover of the big map of Aachen.

'What is it, sir?' he asked, putting down his machine pistol on the littered table.

'It's started, von Dodenburg,' Donner rasped, not taking his eyes off the new arrows. 'They're coming up on both sides of the Wilhelmstrasse. There and there.' The telephone rang again, and one of the harassed staff officers took the call. 'Yes, yes, clear,' he said brusquely and slammed the receiver down. 'They've reached the crossroads at the Romerstrasse, sir,' he said to Donner, and began to pencil in another red arrow.

Donner groaned. 'Look at the strength they're putting in, von Dodenburg. I'm sure this is their main push.'

The hotel shook as one of the huge 155 cannon the Amis were now using in their attempt to reduce Aachen, opened up at less than six hundred metres range. Plaster dust streamed down from the cracked ornamental ceiling of the first-floor room. Donner did not notice it; his one eye was fixed on the map.

'But we can't be sure, sir,' von Dodenburg objected. 'It's clear that they're heading for the heights to the east of us. Once they've got those they can dominate all our positions if they can get artillery up there. But the Ami generals know as well as we do that we can burrow into the cellars and still hang on for a while

– at least as long as it takes the Führer Main Headquarters people to plan and launch their relief attack.'

Donner swung round on him and lowered his voice so that the two staff officers could not hear. 'There will be no relief attack, von Dodenburg.' His ruined face cracked into a parody of a grin. 'That was something I invented to raise the men's morale. We're on our own here, von Dodenburg. We stand or fall on our own merits and effort.'

'I see,' von Dodenburg said, mechanically registering the fact that Aachen would mean the end of Wotan. 'Well, sir, as I was saying – can we be sure that this is to be the only enemy attack? Won't they try to throw in another one – say up towards the Peterstrasse – and cut off this HQ from the bulk of the defenders? Cut us into little groups in other words and deal with us individually. I don't think I need tell you what the morale of the men would be, once they had lost contact with this HQ.'

'You don't,' Donner agreed. 'It would be piss-poor. They would cave in like vanilla pudding on a hot day.'

'There could always be exemplary measures,' Schwarz broke in forcefully, 'Their officers and NCOs could threaten—'

Donner held up his hand to stop him. 'My dear Schwarz,' he said slowly and patiently, 'let us not fool ourselves. This garrison only holds out because the bulk of my heroes are more afraid of me than they are of the enemy. Once they think they are beyond the reach of my long arm, they'll surrender quickly enough, believe me. But you were saying, von Dodenburg.'

'In my opinion, sir, we cannot afford to take men from elsewhere on the perimeter to help stop this new drive, that's all.'

Donner nodded. 'You are right, of course. Just as you were with that Rimburg business. But damn it all, von Dodenburg, I've got to do something! Am I supposed just to sit here and let the Amis walk through our defences until they capture the high country and then watch them pour hot steel down our throats?'

'I was just trying to approach the situation objectively, sir.'

'I shit on objectivity,' Donner snapped angrily. 'I don't want objectivity – I want goddam answers!'

'General,' it was Schwarz. 'I think I've got an answer.'

'*You*?' Donner said. Von Dodenburg knew Donner's opinion of the one-armed major: he thought him brave, fanatical, loyal, but deranged. 'The man hasn't got his cups in his cupboard,' he had once confided to von Dodenburg. 'Hasn't had them for years. He's as crazy as a wild steer.'

'Yes, sir. My panzer grenadiers have been having the Aachen torrents ever since they've gone over to eating that horsemeal goulash.'

'Aachen torrents?' Donner queried.

'The shits,' Schwarz answered. 'The whole sewerage system in my part of the line was getting blocked up and I was worried about infections—'

'Get on with it,' Donner snapped irritably. The phone was ringing again, and he knew that it could only bring further bad news.

'Well, sir, I contacted an old civilian from the works office to help me out. During my conversation with him I found out he knew the whole sewerage system like the back of his hand. He'd worked in it for fifty years.'

'My dear Schwarz,' Donner said, restraining himself with difficulty. 'All very interesting, I am sure. But for the life of me, I cannot see what the recollections of your ancient shit-shoveller has got to do with the present grave situation.'

Schwarz flushed. 'Very simple, sir. We cannot attack the Amis with any strength *above* ground. But a handful of determined men could give them a bad shock *below* ground.'

Von Dodenburg's eye gleamed. 'You mean through the sewers?'

'Yes, sir. We know from the civilians roughly where the Ami rear-echelon stallions are billeted behind the main station.'[1]

'Yes, I know, in those former hour hotels.'[2]

'Well, sir, if we hit their rear line there hard – destroying as much men and material as we could before the Amis could tumble to our way of getting there, I think we could give them a nasty shock – perhaps even throw their whole attack off there, at least, for a short while.'

Donner's single eye blazed with renewed hope and new life. 'By the great whore of Buxtehude, Schwarz,' he yelled, making the two sweating staff officers at the map swing round in alarm, 'I think you and your ancient shit-shoveller have got it!'

Now von Dodenburg, close behind the ancient civilian, waded through the stinking filth, moving at what seemed to him a terribly slow pace. But Gerhardt would not be hurried. He did not seem to notice the terrible stench. Swinging his flickering

1. See Hauptbahnhof on the map.
2. German term for hotels where prostitutes hired rooms by the hour.

142

carbide lantern from side to side on the white-caked dripping walls of the main sewer, he ploughed steadily on through the hot steaming human waste, as if he were taking a summer stroll in Aachen's Farwick Park.

Behind von Dodenburg, Matz with his Schmeisser held high above his head, gasped thickly. 'Can't you get that ancient sow to move a bit faster – I can't stand this much longer. If I puke one more time, I'm going to lose my ring for good.'

Gerhardt glanced at the one-legged sergeant-major. 'I shouldn't be so nasty if I were you, Sergeant-Major,' he croaked. 'I just might take it into my noddle to leave you down here – and then where would you be?' He chuckled throatily. 'Besides,' he added, running a filthy gnarled hand through the liquid, 'this stuff's liquid gold, if you would but know. Makes things grow better than all the horseshit in the world.'

'Why don't you rub it into your scalp then, you bald-headed old coot?' Matz growled. 'Might make yer shitty locks grow a bit more.'

Von Dodenburg grinned thinly and waded through the stinking mire. Time passed leadenly. Once they were startled by a gigantic shadow which blocked out the side of the sewer, flickering slightly in the white light of the old man's carbide lamp.

'What in the name of Jesus-Mary is that?' Trees, the Bavarian farmboy, asked fearfully.

The civilian clapped his dripping hands loudly together. The shadow slipped away with the soft patter of clawed feet. 'A rat,' he croaked, 'There's a lot of 'em down here. They were skinnier before the war though. But now there's plenty of grub for them down here. You'd be surprised at the kind of eats they can find in the sewers in wartime.' His worn old voice echoed hollowly along the length of the dark, stinking tunnel.

'Colonel,' Matz moaned. 'Can't you order the nutty old arsehole to knock it off, please? He gets on my tits with that laugh of his! Drives me up the wall.'

Von Dodenburg ignored the plea. He was too concerned with keeping his footing in the slippery mire. They plodded on. Then when it seemed that they would never escape the waist-high, hideously bubbling liquid, it started to give way to cold water which drove away the overpowering stench within a matter of seconds.

'We're getting there,' the old man informed them. 'The main square isn't much farther now.'

He wasn't wrong. Two minutes later they plodded round a bend, splashing hastily through the clear water in their mired boots to emerge into a large cavelike area, illuminated by the thin grey light falling from half-a-dozen gratings.

'The main square,' Gerhardt announced proudly, as if he were showing them Aachen's noble Cathedral Square. 'Over there exit to the Bahnhofstrasse. That one there is the Lagerhausstrasse. Before the war I used to spend many a happy hour looking up that one. The whores didn't use to wear any knickers in those days. Surprising what you saw if you looked long enough. I remember one time—'

'Shut up,' von Dodenburg hissed, 'and put that shitty lantern out, will you?'

They could hear the stumbling progress, interrupted by the whispered curses and grunts, of the other sections. In dripping silence, they waited till they emerged around the bend, gasping with relief as they breathed the fresher air coming through the gratings above their heads, the section leaders snapping off their flashlights automatically.

Von Dodenburg waited till the last section had recovered its breath, and the one man who had been unlucky enough to slip and fall full length in the mire had managed to get the worst of the mess off his face with the help of the underground stream. 'All right,' he said softly, 'we're all here now. Check your weapons first. But keep it quiet!'

There was the muted sound of the men drawing back their bolts carefully, checking whether the long trek through the mire of the tunnel had not affected their weapons. Here and there a man who had discovered a blockage of some sort worked his bolt a few times rapidly to ease it away. But finally they were all satisfied that their weapons would fire.

'Good,' von Dodenburg breathed, looking round their pale, tense faces. 'Everything seems all right. Take up your positions as the old man here calls out the street names.'

One by one the civilian, proud of his knowledge, called out the names of the individual streets, and the sections positioned themselves behind their leaders, chalk at the ready, eager to move off and leave the tunnel.

Von Dodenburg licked his dry lips. 'Happy landings, lads,' he called softly.

'Happy landings, sir,' they answered.

'All right, off we go – and give them hell!'

144

Splashing swiftly through the shallower water of the side drain, von Dodenburg led his little party, consisting of Matz, Trees and a young Hamburger named Frank, down towards the sewer opening behind the main station, drawing a broad green chalk line on the rough wall as he went. The light from the opening came closer and closer. He hissed a warning for them to be quieter. Behind him Matz gripped his Schmeisser more firmly. Then they were directly beneath the grating. Von Dodenburg stuck his pistol in his belt at the ready.

'Matz, bend down,' he whispered.

Von Dodenburg sprang lightly on his back. There was no sound from above. It was really getting dark outside now. He knew that the Amis had instituted a five o'clock curfew in their part of the city. The only people abroad now, therefore, would be enemy soldiers.

'All right, take the strain,' he ordered softly.

Matz tensed. With all his strength, von Dodenburg levered up the heavy iron grating. It came away with difficulty. He lowered it as gently as he could on to the cobbles and poked his head above the surface. *No one!* He heaved himself out and lay full length in the wet cold street, pistol in hand, surveying the ruins. There was no sign of the Americans, save for a burned-out White scout car at the corner next to a pile of dull brown C-ration cans. Ration cans, thrown away with their usual careless prodigality, were always a clue to the enemy's presence.

'Good, you can come up,' he called down, not taking his eyes off the end of the street.

'They would never have done this in the old Army,' Matz grumbled as Trees stepped forward and used his broad back to lever himself out into the open, 'using a senior NCO as a sodding doorstep. What flaming well next?'

Cautiously they moved down the deserted street. To their right, they could see the chaos of the main station's shunting yard, filled with useless locomotives mocking the proud boast that had been painted on their sides in the good days. 'THESE WHEELS ROLL FOR VICTORY!' Everywhere dirty white flags made from towels and torn sheets hung from the ruins, but there was no sign of any civilians. They came to a corner and halted.

Suddenly they heard the soft shuffle of what could only be an American combat boot. Von Dodenburg tensed. 'Trees – the knife!' he hissed.

The farmboy drew his combat knife and tensed, the gleaming blade gripped in his red-knuckled hand. The Ami came round the corner. A big Negro sergeant, pistol at his hip, a bag in his big fist.

'Hands up,' von Dodenburg hissed.

For what seemed an age, the black soldier did not react. Then he muttered: 'Aah, go and shit in ya hat!' and dived for his pistol with swift determination.

Trees was quicker. His hand shot out. The Ami's voice ended in a thick-blooded gurgle as the knife penetrated his neck. Trees stabbed him again. The blood gushed out and splashed his knuckles. The Negro's yellow eyes rolled upwards. Just as he was about to fall, Matz caught him.

'Come to mother, you black bastard,' he said.

'Lower him carefully,' von Dodenburg urged, as the Ami drowned in his own blood. 'Not a sound.'

But they were unlucky. In that very same instant the chatter of a Schmeisser started up close by, followed by angry shouts and the slower noise of an Ami machine-pistol. Matz let the Negro drop to the ground with the thud. 'They're on to us, sir!' he yelled and unslung his Schmeisser.

'You're right, Matz. Come on, lads.' Von Dodenburg started to run forward towards their objective. The operation, he told himself as the three men pelted after him, looked as if it might turn out to be a big ballsup after all.

THREE

Major Schwarz had been the first to spot the girl as his group doubled towards their objective. She was swaying back and forth on the kitchen table in a drunken parody of a dance; and her nubile teenage body was completely naked. He came to such an abrupt halt that the trooper behind him nearly crashed into him.

'Look,' he yelled hysterically, pointing at the window behind which the dark-haired naked girl danced to the delighted calls of the Ami soldiers and the music of a scratchy old gramophone record, 'a German girl dancing for those enemy pigs!'

'Sir,' the trooper protested, 'that's not our objective. If we open up—'

Schwarz had not let him finish. Face contorted with hate, he pressed the trigger of his machine-pistol. The glass shattered. A line of red holes appeared across the girl's breasts. Her mouth sagged open. Her knees began to buckle beneath her. Schwarz fired again. Her face became a welter of blood and bone. She dropped to the floor.

A moment later all was confusion and the Amis were firing wild bursts everywhere.

Panting heavily, von Dodenburg's section clattered past the shattered, bullet-pocked door into the hallway of the run-down hotel. Matz skidded on the stone-tiled floor and went full length with a wild curse. Somewhere beyond in the gloom, heavy boots clattered downstairs. An angry voice called something. Von Dodenburg lobbed his stick grenade upwards. There was a thick muffled crump, a flash of purple flame and an agonising scream. A door flung open. Von Dodenburg spun round. Von Dodenburg caught a glimpse of an Ami helmet.

Before he could react, Matz fired a burst from the floor. The Ami fell back screaming, his face a red pulpy mass without recognisable features. Trees sprang over the NCO and thrust open the door of the nearest room. It was filled with ashen-faced unarmed Amis sprawled out on makeshift beds on the floor in their khaki-coloured underwear. He tossed in the stick grenade and closed the door hurriedly. Hanging on to the handle tightly, his lips moved soundlessly as he counted the seconds.

Crump. The door jerked wildly in his grasp like a live thing. Thick smoke poured from beneath it.

'Open!' Matz yelled above the screams.

Tress flung it open and sprang back. From his position on the floor, Matz sprayed the room's interior from side to side. Black-faced, bloody men staggered blindly out of the yellow smoke and were flung aside by the murderous fire.

Von Dodenburg pelted up the stairs. A naked man, khaki-coloured towel over his shoulder, was standing in an enamel bowl, washing himself. Von Dodenburg fired once. A red hole tore his white stomach. The Ami fell to his knees in the bowl, clutching his belly. Von Dodenburg kicked him in the face and ran on. The bowl slid across the floor, scattering bloody soap suds everywhere.

A white face peered down at him from the stair-rail, eyes

wide with fear. Von Dodenburg reacted instinctively. Reaching up, he hooked his two front fingers in the man's nostrils, and heaved. The next moment Trees had plunged his knife into his throat and slit it as neatly as he might have done one of the pigs back on the farm.

An Ami grenade came rolling towards them from somewhere. Matz kicked it on down the stairs and yelled, '*Duck!*' The four of them dropped to the floor. Sharpnel and a hot blast that threatened to burst their lungs was zinging off the walls. Frank yelped as a piece tore off his little finger. They ran down the stairs again. Just as they reached the door, Matz flung a phosphorus grenade behind them into the hall. A soft plop. White steaming pellets of phosporus everywhere. The hallway bright with angry red flame. Somewhere a piteous voice called: 'Say, buddy, won't you help me? . . . I can't see . . . Say, buddy . . .'

But the von Dodenburg section had no time for blinded Amis. They doubled into the crazy confusion of the street. Everywhere there were cries of rage, anguish and fear. Someone opened up with .5 inch Ami machine-gun until a harsh voice cried: 'Will you stop that goddam firing, man! You're firing into our own guys!'

Screaming like wild men, the four SS soldiers clattered down both sides of the street, lobbing grenades into each house that looked occupied, lashing the façades with wild bursts of machine-pistol fire to keep the occupants down. A bare-headed soldier appeared at an upper window. Von Dodenburg shot him through the neck.

Suddenly an accurate burst of fire stitched a line of bullets across the road only five metres in front of them, blue sparks flying up as the lead struck the cobbles. They flopped to the ground, panting wildly. Sucking his bloody hand still, Frank lobbed a grenade in the direction of the pile of firewood from which the firing had come. It fell short. The next moment the machine-gunner opened up again. Lead struck the road all around them, as they hugged the wet cobbles, careening off with a dying whine.

'The pineapple-shitter's well placed,' Matz gasped. 'Do we go back, sir?'

Von Dodenburg flung a glance behind him. The darkening sky at the end of the road was lit up by the brilliant fireworks of small-arms fire. 'No, it's as bad there as here. We've got to get through the bastard!'

'Sir?' Trees yelled. 'There's a can of gas over there. We could burn him out.'

Von Dodenburg nodded. 'Get it,' he commanded. 'I'll get a bucket on the opposite side of the road. Matz and Frank cover us! *NOW!*' Madly the two of them doubled off in opposite directions, followed by an angry burst of fire, which switched from side to side, but just continued to miss them. Von Dodenburg clambered frantically through the chaotic rubble of the abandoned house, looking in vain for a bucket. Outside Matz and Frank kept up a desultory fire, breaking off every time the unseen Ami gunner sprayed the cobbles at their feet. In the end von Dodenburg compromised with an ancient enamel chamber pot, its bottom covered with a chipped and faded Imperial eagle.

'Here,' he yelled through the window. 'Matz, catch this.' With all his strength he flung it towards the NCO.

'Oh, my aching back,' Matz cried. 'Now we're down to fighting the flaming war with pisspots!'.

Trees had skidded across the road in a shower of sparks, followed by a frustrated burst of machine-gun fire. Von Dodenburg took the opportunity offered him. Body crouched low, he doubled back to the others. A slug tore off an epaulette. Another struck the heel of his boot. But he made it, chest heaving frantically.

'Put some of that gas . . . into the peepot,' he gasped. 'Quick.'

Fumbling frantically, Matz unscrewed the cap and poured the gas into the strange container.

'Trees, stand by with the grenades!'

The farmboy tugged the last two stick grenades out of his belt and curled his finger round the china ring of one of them. 'Ready, sir.'

'All right. When I throw this stuff, fling a grenade and drop – *quick!* Clear?'

'Clear!'

'Right then. NOW!'

Von Dodenburg sprang to his feet. The Ami reacted a little too late. With all his strength von Dodenburg flung the contents of the pot towards the pile of wood. It fell short. But that didn't matter. It was near enough. As he ducked, Trees' grenade exploded. There was a burst of flame. A piteous scream. A second later, the Ami came staggering towards them, hands clawing the air, his uniform alive with flames. Matz shot him neatly in the stomach. He dropped without a sound, his head in a puddle of burning gas.

'Come on,' von Dodenburg yelled. 'Let's get on!'

They needed no urging; the firing behind them was getting closer and closer.

In the next five minutes, they destroyed a line of Ami supply trucks with their remaining grenades, slaughtered a group of white-helmeted military policemen busy polishing their boots prior to going out on night patrol – 'well, that's one piece of bullshit they'll never have bothering them again', had been Matz's cynical comment – and shot up a large dormitory bedroom which, judging by the female underwear lying around, looked as if it had been used as an Ami brothel.

'I always said the Amis wore lace knickers,' Matz yelled, as they backed out, leaving the khaki-blanket-covered cots filled with dead and dying Amis and their whores.

But time was running out now. Von Dodenburg glanced hastily at his watch. They had been ten minutes above ground. 'Start moving back to the sewer,' he yelled above the confused snap and crackle of small-arms fire. Swiftly he pulled out his Very pistol and fired the violet flare, the signal for withdrawal. It soared high above the houses and bathed the chaotic scene of death and destruction below in its gaudy light.

They backed down the street, pausing and firing every few seconds, crouching close to the wall, spraying the street from side to side. A man loomed up from a doorway. His eyes were red-rimmed, his lips drawn back in a wolfish desire to kill. A speck of foam hung from the corners of his mouth. There was a gleam of metal. But Trees was quicker with his knife. In one and the same instant, his big boot kicked the Ami in the crotch and, as he doubled up, gasping in agony, his knife thrust home into the man's back.

The American fire was becoming more organised. Officers were shouting everywhere, trying to bring back order to their confused troops. NCOs were setting up block positions, cursing and kicking their men into the hastily erected barricades.

The escapers ran into one. Hastily they turned and doubled down an alley. A high wall blocked their way. Von Dodenburg ran at it madly, followed by a shower of lead, and sprang upwards. His eager fingers clutched the top and missed. He screamed as the rough brick ripped away his fingernails.

'They went down there, Sarge – I saw them!' a youthful voice cried behind them.

Von Dodenburg charged furiously at the wall once again. This time his bleeding fingers caught a projecting brick. It was enough. With all his strength he pulled himself upwards and swung himself on top. They heard boots running in their direction. 'Trees,' he cried, reaching down.

Trees caught his fingers. Red-hot pain shot up his arms. Von Dodenburg bit his lip till the blood came. 'Quick, you bastard,' he muttered through gritted teeth, his arms feeling as if they were being pulled out of their sockets. Trees swung himself on top of the wall just in time and fired a wild but effective burst at the advancing Amis. They came to a hurried stop.

'What the hell you guys waiting for?' a beery voice cried.

'You, Frank!' von Dodenburg ordered.

'Watch my finger, sir,' Frank protested.

'Shit on your finger – come on!'

Frank joined the two men on the wall. Von Dodenburg looked down at the one-legged sergeant-major. He crouched below, busy fumbling at the straps of his wooden leg.

'What the hell are you doing, Matz?'

'Never make it with this,' Matz yelled back, finally undoing the leg. 'Here, farmboy, get a hold of this.' He hopped forward and proffered the leg to Trees. 'And treat it kindly – it's the only one I've got.'

A bullet whanged into the leg as Trees hauled it upwards. Matz cursed. 'Marmalade-shitters – don't even have any respect for poor old cripples!' he yelled.

'Come on, you cripple, then,' von Dodenburg bellowed. With the help of Frank, who was yelping with the pain of his finger, he hauled up the struggling one-legged sergeant-major. Seconds later, covered by the wall and with Matz, hopping as he went, with his wooden leg under his arm, they were doubling towards the safety of the sewer. Seconds later, they had dropped inside and were swallowed up by its stinking gloom.

FOUR

Colonel Seitz, commander of the 26th Infantry, could not speak for a moment when he heard the news. His rage was too great.

'What the Sam Hill were you guys doing?' he roared at last at his pale-faced staff officers. 'Couldn't you figure that the Kraut might pull a trick like this?'

They remained silent. They knew Colonel Seitz's rages of old. It was better to say nothing.

Seitz pulled himself together. 'Okay, let's get on the stick. Tell the lead battalion to halt for the next two hours and dig in. I don't want them to be caught with their skivvies down by some Kraut counter-attack in the flank. Charley,' he swung round on a bespectacled staff officer, 'where's the nearest chemical warfare company? I want gas to smoke the bastards out of these sewers.'

The staff officers looked at the CO aghast. 'You can't mean that, sir?' Charley ventured. *'Gas?'*

'I would not have said it if I didn't damn well mean it. Where is the nearest company?'

'Verviers, sir.'

'Too far away. The bastards'll escape us by the time they get up here. Flame-throwers – that's the answer,' he said determinedly. 'Okay, what I need is a plan of those sewers. Then we block them somewhere on the north-south axis along the Wilhelmstrasse – that's obviously the way they're making off back to their own darn lines! Once we've blocked them, I want volunteers with flame-throwers down there to smoke them out like rats – *like rats*,' he emphasised. 'Do you understand? . . . Okay, what are you guys standing around for like spare pricks at a wedding? Let's get on the ball . . .'

The sudden burst of fire through the grating in the main square caught them completely off guard. Frank fell dead and Trees hit the water, clawing the air in pain. Matz and von Dodenburg ran towards him and pulled him out. He was chewing his tongue and the saliva which dribbled down his unshaven chin was pink with blood. His eyeballs were already beginning to slip upwards so that only a little of the white showed.

As the others scattered for cover and began trying to aim up-wards at their unseen assailants, Matz cried. 'We can't let the shitty hayseed die like this, sir . . . He's choking to death.'

Von Dodenburg nodded grimly and tried to prise open his tightly shut jaws and release his tongue. Desperately he looked round for something with which to force them open. 'Matz,' he cried, 'give me your knife.' Another burst crashed through the grating, splattering lead everywhere. Bullets whined off the walls.

'No, sir. If he falls on it or rolls over,' Matz protested, 'he'll cut his damn tongue off.'

'Don't argue. Give me the knife! No, better if you stick it in when I lever his jaws open.'

With all his strength von Dodenburg forced open the farm-boy's jaws and Matz slid the knife between his lips. Immediately Trees started to grind his teeth on the metal, twitching convul-sively. His breath became more normal and von Dodenburg sat back on his heels, cold with sweat, feeling he had saved the boy's life. But he was mistaken.

'Look at this, sir,' Matz said, removing his hand from below the boy. It was covered with blood.

Suddenly von Dodenburg was aware of a disgusting stench which didn't come from the sewer. He looked down at the boy's nether parts. His trousers were soaked wtih blood. He slid the knife out and slit open the trousers from the knee downwards. There was a cloying odour of rotting flesh.

'Turn him over,' he commanded.

Matz rolled the boy over. His buttocks were a mass of yellow-red blood. 'Haemorrhage,' Matz gulped. 'He's bleeding from behind. Shot in the gut.' Von Dodenburg parted the boy's legs and tried to stop the bleeding with his hand. The blood seeped through his fingers. He grabbed a handful of mud from the bottom of the stream and clapped it against the boy's behind. It was useless. The blood still streamed through, sweeping aside the mud poultice.

'Sir,' Schwarz cried from the other end of the underground chamber, 'I can hear tanks. They're bringing up reinforcements. We'd better move.' Von Dodenburg looked down at the dying farmboy. He would never see his dirt-poor Upper Bavarian farm home again, herd the cows up to the higher pastures in spring and slide the hay down in summer. He pulled out his pistol and placed it against the boy's right temple. The boy's eyes flickered open for a moment.

'Thank you, sir,' he breathed weakly. 'Sorry to have held you up.' He closed them again and von Dodenburg could see his pale lips moving to the words of some half-forgotten Catholic prayer. Von Dodenburg squeezed the trigger. The Walther erupted in his fist. The boy's spine curved like a bow. Then he fell back into the bloody dirt, mouth open, dead.

'Come on,' von Dodenburg yelled in the echoing silence, *'let's get the hell out of here!'*

With Schwarz's group bringing up the rear and the old civilian in the front, guiding them with his stinking carbide lamp, they waded into the main sewer again. Now the rats seemed to be everywhere. Whether it was due to the frantic activity overhead or because of the growing dark, von Dodenburg could not tell. All he knew was that the loathsome brown-grey creatures were everywhere, fleeing the first flickering light of the old man's carbide lamp, but slithering under their feet again as soon as the gloom had returned.

'Ugh,' said Matz, pushing on behind the CO, 'gives me the creeps to feel those long-tailed bastards nibbling – even on my wooden leg!'

'Keep it down,' von Dodenburg urged, 'all of you keep it down. And you, old man,' he ordered the civilian, 'shade that light. We don't want them tracking us along the main sewer.'

There was silence now save for the men's harsh breathing and the slithering of the rats. But despite the fact that they were progressing steadily towards the safety of their own lines, von Dodenburg had an uneasy feeling that, up above, the Amis were keeping pace with them, only waiting for a suitable opportunity to spring the trap.

Time passed. They squeezed their way carefully past a barrier thrown down a manhole by the Amis. One by one, hardly daring to breathe, they crawled through the mass of old chairs, ration crates, timbers hastily slung below by the enemy, knowing that at the first indication of their presence, the Americans would start firing with all they had. They marched on. Now they were up to their waists in the thick stinking mire. Their pace began to slow down.

One of Schwarz's wounded boys passed out and sank below the surface to be hauled out by his comrades, their faces contorted in disgust at his appearance. Schwarz ordered two of them to take off their belts and tie them round his arms. Thus they dragged the faeces-smeared boy on with them.

Von Dodenburg began to pray that they would reach their objective soon. He had had enough. His head started to spin with the fumes. 'How much longer, old man?' he asked thickly.

The civilian looked up at the dripping curved ceiling. 'Peterstrasse,' he announced after a moment. '*Horse piss corner!*'

'What?'

'Horse piss. Horse piss corner, we used to call it in the old days. There was a stable up here. On winter mornings, the horse piss used to come pouring in here by the litre, all hot and steaming like—'

'Oh for Christ's sake, shut up, old man,' von Dodenburg interrupted, his voice full of disgust. 'Can't you think of anything but shit and piss?'

'It makes the world go round, sir,' he answered, not the least offended. 'Without it, nothing would grow. No shit and piss and we wouldn't eat.'

Matz retched thickly. 'I'll never eat another goddam thing,' he croaked, pushing his way through the mire, Schmeisser held above his head. 'I swear I won't—'

He broke off suddenly. There was the clatter of a sewer lid being raised ahead and dropped on the cobbles of the road.

'*Freeze!*' von Dodenburg commanded.

A thin white torch beam cut into the green gloom ahead of them. They pressed themselves against the dripping walls, hardly daring to breathe.

'They're down there,' a hushed voice said. 'I'll bet my goddam bottom dollar they are ... Joe, are you ready?'

'Sir.'

'Okay, we're ready, Joe, when you are.'

Von Dodenburg raised his pistol. He could hear the metallic sound of someone fiddling with some sort of apparatus. His brow creased in a frown. What the devil were the Amis up to? Should they make a break for it and push on while they still had a chance? Or should they—

'Colonel!' It was Schwarz. His face was blanched with fear. 'What?'

'A flame-thrower ... they've got a flame-thrower up there!'

Now the young CO could hear the soft hiss. Schwarz was right.

'Quick – let's make a run for it!' he yelled.

They surged forward in a panic.

'*They're bolting!*' a voice yelled from up above, '*Joe, get that damn weapon of yours going!*'

A hush. A roar. An angry tongue of blue-red flame shot into the sewer, curled along the walls and sought them out greedily. A SS man screamed. He fell into the mire, hands thrown up frantically, consumed by flame.

'*Duck*,' von Dodenburg screamed. '*Duck into the shit!*'

They hesitated. The flame-thrower roared again. Once more the terrible hissing tongue flamed into the tunnel. The air trembled. The sour, choking stench of charring flesh and the copper odour of hot blood assailed their nostrils. The survivors flung themselves deep into the stinking mire and felt it drying hard above them. Then the horrifying fire was gone, and they were fighting their way out of the mud.

'Come on,' von Dodenburg croaked, wiping his face clean. 'As quick as you can!'

The survivors scrambled and waded through a morass of skinned, charred bodies, frozen into their last moment of desperate hysteria. Men screamed. Others flung away their weapons in their panic.

Von Dodenburg caught himself just in time. 'Schwarz,' he commanded. 'Stop!'

His helmet gone, his face blackened by smoke, Schwarz was self-controlled again. 'Sir?'

'I need you.' He spun round and faced the black-charred opening to the sewer. 'When I say fire, aim at that opposite wall. We must try to ricochet shots off it upwards. It's our one chance to try to stop them long enough for our people to round the next bend.'

Schwarz drew his Walther. Behind them the survivors panted and grunted while the mud sucked and gurgled at their boots, pulling them down like quicksand.

'FIRE!' von Dodenburg yelled.

Both men pressed their triggers simultaneously. The pistol shots echoed like cannon fire. The seven-millimetre slugs struck the wall just behind the grating. The stone chipped.

Up above a voice cried out in sudden alarm, 'Get the hell away from there, Joe! The Krauts are counter-attacking!'

They heard a heavy piece of apparatus being dropped on the cobbles. That was enough for von Dodenburg.

'Come on,' he shouted, tucking his empty pistol into his holster, 'Let's get the hell out of here, Schwarz!' Knowing that it was only a matter of seconds before the Amis overcame their surprise and reacted, they turned and began to wade through the mire and the jellied, bloody flesh of the dead.

The Amis pursued them all along their escape route. Time and time again the gratings ahead were flung open roughly and angry voices shouted to them to surrender before some new terror was launched at them. Phosphorus grenades which filled the tunnel with a burning white light and thick choking smoke; tear gas, which was harmless but which had them gasping and crying uncontrollably like children within seconds; satchel charges, containing twenty-five pounds of high explosive, which went off in the narrow confines of the tunnel with the impact of an exploding volcano. Still the procession of ghastly phantoms continued its progress, their heads swathed in their charred jackets, blindly ploughing their way forward behind Gerhardt.

The gas was affecting von Dodenburg's eyes more and more. He could only just see by narrowing them to slits. His eyeballs seemed as if they were bedded in thick sand and he had to keep blinking all the time. He noted automatically that his head was rolling from side to side like that of a drunkard. Time and time again he tried to control the rolling motion. But within seconds he had slipped back into it again. Now his legs began to lose all feeling; it was as if they were made of jelly. Around him, his men started to fall into the slush and were brought to the surface only by the determined efforts of their stronger comrades.

Time and time again, Matz rapped out that cruel reminder. 'MARCH OR CROAK.' And von Dodenburg, continually fighting off unconsciousness, realised in his odd moments of clarity, how true the phrase was. He held on to the thought with all his might. They *had* to reach the surface.

They edged their way carefully past the last Ami barricade – a rough, barbed-wire-covered hurdle festooned with hash cans, which the Amis presumably thought would serve to warn them of the enemy's presence. With Schwarz and Matz covering the grating up above, they slipped by and continued their stumbling nightmare progress.

The sewerage started to thin out again. The air became

clearer. Von Dodenburg shook his head violently. The thick sand at the back of his eyeballs seemed to vanish. Holding each other's hands like children in a nursery school, they pushed on in the gloom, following the ancient civilian. And then suddenly a shaft of light shone down upon them. They halted, hearts beating like trip-hammers.

'It's them,' a voice shouted. In German! Von Dodenburg felt his knees almost give way with relief.

Gasping, panting, sobbing, they started to climb up the makeshift wooden ladder lowered to them. They had reached the first German outpost. Filthy, exhausted, trembling with fatigue and shock, they emerged into the beam of the torch, to the cries of disgust of their rescuers.

'Ugh,' an unknown voice, called, 'give them room! . . . make way for the shit shovellers!'

Despite his exhaustion, von Dodenburg grinned. They had made it.

FIVE

Dawn came slowly, as if it were reluctant to throw its light on the stark, sobering tableau of the wrecked city. Once magnificent trees, stripped of their foliage by the ceaseless artillery fire, now looked like gaunt outsize toothpicks. Jagged chunks of brickwork and twisted steel rods that had once been fine houses. The mutilated carcass of an Opel truck that had struck a mine and had slumped to a dying stop like a live thing. And everywhere discarded equipment, American and German: gas masks, ripped overcoats, empty cans, helmet-liners, broken rifles. One of the GIs waiting to move out kicked a bloody shoe that lay among the mess of war and shuddered to see that it still contained a foot.

At seven-thirty, the big guns started to thunder. The mobile 155s fired their sixty-pound shells at point-blank range. The shattered buildings which made up the confused German front line shuddered like ships striking heavy seas every time the great shells hit them.

'Cigarettes out!' an officer ordered.

The infantry took a hurried last draw, then they stubbed out their cigarettes.

'Form up!'

They moved forward too slowly for the top kick, who had been a corporal the week before, and he snarled: 'Didn't you guys hear the major? Now get the goddam lead out of your tails! *Form up!'*

They scrambled into position.

At eight o'clock precisely the barrage stopped. The officers blew their whistles. Like an unruly accordion, the lead columns moved out, slithering, stumbling, falling one moment and picking themselves up the next, as they advanced into the chaos of the ruins. Ahead, the Spandaus commenced their old bitter song of death. Colonel Seitz's 26th Infantry were going in for the final assault.

Seitz was attacking on a different pattern. He had divided his regiment into small assault teams, each team covered by a Sherman or tank destroyer wherever possible. While the armoured vehicle covered the assault team, forcing the Kraut defenders into the cellar by its fire, they would rush the building and start clearing it out from the roof downwards.

Seitz realised that this meant it would be difficult to maintain contact between the assault teams – indeed the new pattern would make it very easy for the Krauts to infiltrate between them in the confused fighting among the ruins. To avoid this, his staff officers had worked out a series of check points based on street intersections and prominent buildings. No outfit could advance beyond these check points until it had established contact with its adjacent unit. Each rifle company was assigned a specific zone of advance to avoid confusion and each company commander, in his turn, assigned a street to each platoon. Thus the old city was divided into a series of interlinking squares which would have to be cleared out systematically before the next ones could be tackled.

But Seitz was still worried by the town's sewer system, especially after the surprise attack on his rear echelon had thrown his whole first push off its stride. He ordered that each sewer and cellar be located, however costly it was in time, and blocked off. But how? In the end one of his staff officers came up with a solution. Just across the border at the little Belgian town of St Vith he had discovered a factory turning out liquid cement. Immediately Seitz had General Collins order that its entire production be turned over to military use so that the cement could be poured down each new sewer opening and allowed to harden under armed guard until it presented an effective barrier against any Kraut trying to jump the advancing infantry from the rear.

As for the civilians crowding the cellars of the front-line area, they were not going to receive any kid glove treatment. Watching the first troops move out, one of Seitz's officers was approached by a hesitant private.

'Pardon me, sir, I can't find my officer,' the young GI said. 'And we've found some civvies in that house over there. We'd like to know what to do with them?'

The major stepped over the dead German, whose dusty boots were sticking into the street from the doorway in which he lay, and looked at the soldier. 'If you can spare a guard to send them back to the civilian cage, okay. If you can't, shoot them in the back! That's what we always did in my old outfit. Don't take no nonsense from them, boy.'

The 26th was taking no chances whatsoever this time, even if they had to commit mass murder to take the damn city.

By now Donner had transformed what was left of his command into a mass of barbed-wire entanglements, overturned tramcars and trucks, linked together with sandbags as barricades. The shattered houses had been joined together by interlinking tunnels, slits blown into their walls for machine-guns and heavy artillery. Disabled Tiger tanks had been buried into the rubble with only their heavy gun turrets visible. Mines had been strung across all the main approach roads and the rubble in front of the German positions was littered with deadly little butterfly anti-personnel mines.[1]

The city's remaining flak had been pressed into service as field guns and each major street was covered by 88 and 20-mm flak cannons, manned by sixteen-year-old volunteers from the Hitler Youth and grey-uniformed girl 'flak helpers'. And everywhere behind the line Gestapo man 'Pistol Paul' and his gang, plus a handful of middle-aged chain-dogs, kept watch lest there were any weakening in the troops' 'National Socialist fervour'.

That afternoon, the battle for Aachen became a battle for a shoe factory, the Technical University, a block of offices, the main police station. At the shoe factory, the 26th made a serious mistake. It attacked in the basement and started working its way

1. Named thus because of the many 'wings' protruding from them, which made them very difficult to defuse.

upwards. By the time the GIs had cleared the first floor, their enemy had burrowed back into the basement again. Once that force had been dealt with, the defenders of the second floor had destroyed the staircases leading upwards. Then they cut holes in the floor and started dropping grenades on the frustrated GIs below.

In the end two staff sergeants scaled the outside of the building, pursued by angry bullets from snipers in other buildings and reached the flat roof in safety. There they knocked a hole in it, poured in petrol and started a flash fire by dropping in white phosphorus hand grenades. The surviving defenders came streaming out, hands raised high, screaming 'comrade' to be mown down as soon as they appeared at the shattered door.

That afternoon, as Colonel Seitz reported gloomily to Huebner, 'Our gains have been measured from attic to attic and from sewer to sewer.'

Huebner remained firm. Before he slammed down the phone in poorly concealed anger, he snapped : 'John, I want those god-dam hills. You'd better get them for me – or you'd better not come back from this push l'

Donner was still worried by the strength and determination of the Ami attack. That evening he ordered von Dodenburg and the two hundred odd survivors of Battle Group Wotan to launch an all-out drive to stop the Americans' attack along the axis of the Wilhelmstrasse, drawing ever closer to the vital heights.

The German bombardment caught the Americans off guard just before their supper. It lasted only fifteen minutes, but the point-blank fire of the multiple 20-mm flak guns, manned by the boys and girls, shattered the GIs' nerves. Some broke down and cried. Others vomited the first bites of food and had to be ordered to eat by their officers. Some buried themselves at the bottoms of shellholes, hugging the mud. The battalion commander himself fled into his command post, ignoring the hectic activity all around him, sobbing softly, his haggard unshaven face in his hands.

For a while there was a heavy brooding silence. The officers and NCOs began to rally their nervous men. Here and there, the men finished their hasty meals and started to mount guard in the foxholes.

Suddenly there was a single burst of Schmeisser fire. Someone screamed. The GIs tensed. But no enemy infantry came scurrying out of the ruins, firing as they ran. Instead the mobile flak wagons moved up another fifty yards and with complete disregard for their own safety started plastering the American positions with a blistering hail of 20-mm shells from their air-cooled quadruple cannon. A sergeant tried to tackle one of the flak wagons with a bazooka. He didn't get ten yards. A blast of ten shells hit him immediately. The GIs could stand it no more. Panic-stricken, their faces white and ugly with fear, the lead company broke, throwing away their rifles and equipment, in their haste to escape that withering fire.

Behind them the commander of the rear company lost his nerve. Firing his carbine wildly into the air, he yelled, 'save yourselves . . . to the rear . . . *save yourselves!*'

The second company joined the rest in their fear-ridden rush to the rear. The battalion commander tried to stop them, as they came running down the Wilhelmstrasse, trying to outrace the 20-mm shells, pushing and shoving each other in their frantic efforts to escape. But it was no use. Stricken with terror they trampled over the seriously wounded men lying on the bloody cobbles screaming for help. They simply ran by him, thrusting aside his importuning hold. Even when he drew his forty-five and threatened to shoot, they took no notice.

'They're completely demoralised, sir,' he confessed, brokenhearted, over the phone to Colonel Seitz. 'I've never seen anything like it in fifteen years in the infantry. There's no sense in fooling ourselves, sir. Those men are not withdrawing – they're running away.'

At the other end of the line, Seitz turned to his pale staff officers, listening in awed silence. 'Charley?' he snapped, 'Get on to the goddam divisional reserve. I'm needing a new battalion commander. I'm sacking this guy – he's broken down completely.' But the shattered battalion commander never experienced the ignominy of being relieved of his command. At that same moment, von Dodenburg's mixed force of tankers and panzer grenadiers struck the retreating battalion's right flank with the dash of the great days of old. Screaming ferociously, the black-clad young fanatics crashed into the fleeing Amis. The battalion commander was shot where he sat sobbing at the phone. His staff were mown down around him. Pausing only to loot the dying bodies of their *Lucky Strikes* and Hershey chocolate bars, their killers swept up the cellar steps, firing and stuffing the precious chocolate in their mouths as they went.

Here and there, groups of Ami NCOs and officers tried unsuccessfully to stop the surprise German attack. Howling like wild animals, the men of Wotan simply swept them aside. Slashing, stabbing, gouging, firing, they broke up Seitz's lead battalion mercilessly, leaving behind them a trail of dead and dying Americans. It seemed that nothing could stop them. Two hundred metres, five hundred metres, seven hundred.

'Christ on a crutch,' Matz gasped, limping red-faced and panting at von Dodenburg's side, his belt full of stick grenades, 'if this goes on, we'll have the buggers running for the Channel soon!'

But Seitz reacted quicker than Donner had anticipated. He flung his mobile 155-mms into a stop line, risking the great guns without the protection of infantry. At the same time, he appealed to the Ninth TAC for help.

'God, General,' he pleaded with the Air Force Commander, 'I need air – and I need it now!'

'But what about your own doughs? I don't want another unfortunate incident, Colonel. You remember that business with Hobbs's Thirtieth?' The General cleared his throat. 'Can't risk that.'

'I don't give a twopenny damn about the doughs!' Seitz screamed into the phone. 'I must stop those goddam Krauts – whatever the cost. Now what about that air?'

He got it. The wild drive ran into the terrible fire of the 155s at two hundred metres range. Here and there small groups of crazied young men tried to tackle the self-propelled guns with their panzerfausts. But once the Ami Lightnings came barreling in at roof-top height, spraying the area with white-hot tracer, they too hit the ground and buried desperately into rubble, out of the murderous fire.

Von Dodenburg's sudden counter-attack had been an unqualified success. He had wiped out an entire Ami battalion and stopped the main enemy drive for yet another precious day. But the cost had been prohibitive, thanks to American domination of the air. Only one hundred of the desperate young men whom he had led into the attack limped back into the littered courtyard of the Hotel Quellenhof. His casualties had been fifty per cent. Battle Group Wotan would not attack again.

As the Americans continued their attack, morale inside the garrison started to sag. That same night, the Luftwaffe tried to supply the trapped men by parachute. But not one of the 'Auntie

Jus' reached their objective. A whole Ami anti-aircraft brigade had taken up positions around the city. They put up such a barrage with their 3·7-inch guns that the handful of ponderous three-engined planes which survived the fire turned and fled the way they had come.

Early next morning, the airfield at Cologne tried again. Just after dawn great black Do 242 gliders hissed silently over the American lines and came down to a crash-landing high on the Wilhelmstrasse, their skids bound with barbed wire to shorten their landing, flaps straight down. They crashed and braked to a halt in a cloud of dust, their wings ripped off here and there by the lamp posts. Their young pilots, the cream of Student's First Parachute Army, sprang triumphantly from their cockpits and crashed open the gliders' canvas doors to be met by a hail of machine-gun fire. They had landed in the midst of one of the Big Red One's recce outfits. A few minutes later the excited GIs were running over the pilots' bodies sprawled extravagantly in the dust to loot the stricken birds.

Another miserable day passed with Donner's perimeter shrinking more and more. Behind the line the rear-echelon stallions slouched around, bent-shouldered, filthy and louse-ridden, their sunken eyes staring out fixedly from grey unshaven faces. In the line, the defenders crouched in the rubble, blinking all the time to keep their weary, blood-shot eyes open, only firing when fired upon, too exhausted to shoot at the enemy even when he exposed himself carelessly.

The Amis made steady progress round behind the perimeter, eating their way ever closer to the first of the three vital heights. That afternoon the first of the hills surrendered (in spite of Donner's express command that the one-hundred-man garrison should fight to the 'last round and the last man'.) Pistol Paul, who had been sent up there to stiffen their morale, put one of his famed pistols carefully inside his gold-toothed mouth, gagged at the oily taste of the barrel and pressed the trigger. To the last, his aim was excellent. When the American intelligence team found him, with the help of some of their new prisoners, the back of his head had been blasted away and he bled to death on the ground in front of their boots, unable to answer any of their urgent questions.

Pistol Paul's suicide unnerved the rest of the Gestapo men. They went to plead with the Bishop of Aachen to save them, maintaining that they were non-combatants, civilian policemen at the most, whom he ought to give a certificate – any kind of certificate – to give the Amis when they captured the city.

The once despised Bishop looked at their craven faces in contempt. 'But I'm only a mere – pope, to use your old phrase,' he told them, between the ever new salvoes from the American 155s. 'What good would a certificate from me be?'

The heavy-set Gestapo men, who had reigned with club and thumbscrew these last eleven years, their faces shaking with fear, almost went down on their knees in the rubble of the Bishop's dining-room. But he remained firm and in the end they shuffled out in their ankle-length leather coats, defeated. One hour after Donner had been told of the incident by his own private information service the five Gestapo men had been sentenced and strung up as a warning to the rest by their former companions of the Field Gendarmerie.

Still the rot went on. During the night of the 19th, the garrison of the big bunker at the end of the Lousbergstrasse slipped out under their officers, after being battered by 155 cannon all day, and surrendered to the Amis. In Lousbergstrasse, the civilians came up from their cellars, blinking in the sudden light, and cheered the advancing Americans as if they were liberators, not conquerors.

More and more staggered into the smoke-filled street, as the GIs crept cautiously up each side, weapons gripped firmly in their hands. Ragged, filthy, sucking in the first fresh air they had breathed for days, they screamed: 'Why didn't you come earlier? Why did you wait so long to get rid of Devil Donner? He's killed our children, ruined our homes, starved us.'

'Aw,' a red-faced master-sergeant growled, pushing aside a distraught woman, who was screaming directly into his face, 'go and piss up yer sleeve, lady!'

His platoon commander, a weary young man in steel-rimmed GI glasses, who had the look of a school teacher about him, flashed a warning glance at the master-sergeant and said in poor German: 'We are glad to be here . . . to have freed you from the Nazis—'

He ducked rapidly, as a sniper's slug hit the brickwork a couple of feet from his head. *'Get that Kraut bastard!'* he yelled.

FIVE

Von Dodenburg's redhead opened the door of the cellar, knowing that the hammering with the rifle-butts would change to something more drastic if she didn't. Two Ami soldiers stood there: one tall and thin, unshaven and covered in mud, a carbine clasped in his hand; the other fat, undersized and Italian-looking, the spirit from the looted bottle of *Korn* stuck in his blouse dribbling down his dark chin.

For a long moment, the two of them gazed at her speechlessly. Even in her dust-covered shapeless dress, there was no denying the magnificence of her breasts, proud and upright despite months of near starvation.

The fat soldier whistled thinly through his teeth: 'Jeez, Al, get an eyeful of them tits. Wow, *is* she stacked!' He thrust a hairy hand into his pocket and brought out a bar of ration chocolate. 'You sleep with me,' he said in bad German, leering at her knowingly, his dark eyes flickering back and forth from her breasts to her deathly pale face, 'I give chocolate – one, perhaps two.' He held the bar under her nose in what he imagined was a tempting manner.

'What about me?' the taller man asked, not taking his hard blue eyes off the redhead.

'Cos I'm more handsome, you get seconds,' the Italian-looking soldier said, his voice suddenly thick with lust. 'Come on, baby, let's make some beautiful music together. We ain't got all day, you know. There's a war on.' He edged closer to her, still holding the chocolate in front of her nose. She backed away fearfully. The two of them came after her. Al kicked the door closed with the back of his heel.

'What do you want?' she asked tremulously.

'What do you think, baby,' the smaller soldier asked scornfully. 'To jig-jig, you Kraut bitch!' He thrust out a hand to grab her breasts. She avoided his grasp and backed closer to the couch.

'Aw, quit the fooling, Benny,' the big soldier said, without taking his cold eyes off her face. 'Get on with it. What the hell are you waiting for?'

'I tell ya, she's got a hot body for me, Al,' he said and took a swig of the fiery schnapps. 'Okay, baby,' he gasped. 'You heard what my buddy Al said – we ain't got all the time in the world.'

Benny lunged at her. She felt his hand clutch the cloth of her dress. She pulled backwards. The cloth gave with a rip. Benny was left there, holding the front of her dress. Her hands flew up to protect her suddenly naked breasts. Al's hard eyes rested on them greedily for a moment.

'Get the hell out of my way, Benny!' he yelled and thrust the other soldier aside with one sweep of his big fist. With the other he grabbed at her dress and pulled with all his strength.

'Hot shit!' Benny breathed. 'She ain't got no drawers on!'

Al thrust out his big hand again. The redhead groaned with pain and tumbled over the back of the couch, her legs in the air. 'Grab her arms, you stupid little wop!' he ordered, breathing hoarsely, his hard face suddenly aflame. Benny dropped his bottle and grabbed the struggling redhead's arms.

'*No,*' she screamed, '*please – no!*'

The two soldiers ignored her. While Benny held her, Al grabbed frantically at his belt. He dropped his mud-stained slacks. Swiftly he ripped away his khaki-coloured undershorts. 'Okay, baby,' he gasped, 'I'm gonna get you now. Try this one on for size, you Kraut son-of-a-bitch ...'

Slowly and painfully she reached for her father's razor, feeling as if every bone in her body were broken. As she did so, she caught a glimpse of her bruised, swollen face in the little fly-blown mirror. She looked away and slumped back on the stained couch. A long time passed while she thought of what the two soldiers had done to her. She flicked open the old-fashioned cut-throat razor and gazed at it lovingly. Outside the guns had started again. But her whole attention was focused on the little blade which gleamed in the flickering light of the candle. After a while she tested it with the wetted tip of her thumb, the way she had seen her father do it as a child. It was all right. Very sharp.

The cellar began to rock under the barrage. Letting out her pent-up breath, she drew the gleaming blade across her left wrist. The pain was virtually non-existent. For a moment nothing happened. She gazed disappointedly down at her blue-veined wrist. Then there was a faint reddening of the cut. She licked her parched lips. Blood started to well up all along the line, slowly but surely. Thick bright red blood. She watched it fascinated. Suddenly the hollow of her hand was full of blood. She wiped it on the stained blanket and quickly slashed the other wrist. This time she whimpered with the pain. The blood spurted out, showering her bruised knees a bright red.

With a sigh of luxurious relief she sank back on the couch and closed her eyes. As the blood drained out of her, filled the couch and began to drip on the soaked Hershey bar beneath it, she felt happy. It was all over at long last.

Matz crunched his way across the broken glass of the hospital and flung open the door of Schulze's room. In the same instant, he lifted up his wooden leg and let loose an enormous fart of welcome.

'Hello, old horse,' he bellowed, ignoring the other two patients, crowded into the former broom cupboard, 'are you glad to see me?'

Schulze, his face pale and his wounded arm suspended above his head, made a mock gesture of choking. 'Great crap on the Christmas Tree, what do you want to do – gas me as well, you perverted banana-sucker?'

Matz ignored the comment. He plumped himself down on the cot. 'Where's the whores?' he asked, thrusting back his helmet, 'I fancy a bit of the other tonight. It's all right for you wounded blokes, lying here like broad-arsed sows, having a go at the five-fingered widow beneath the blankets, while us lot are fighting for you at the front.' He paused for breath and nodded at the two still figures crowded into the other cots in the tiny, airless room. 'Who're they?'

Schulze shrugged. 'Don't know. Lung and gut, I call 'em. The one on the right is lung-shot – the one on the left gut-shot. The bone-menders say they'll croak within the next twenty-four hours.'

'Tough tittie,' Matz sniffed and took his eyes off the still bandaged figures. 'What about you? Are they going to pension you off, or when do you start looking at the potatoes from below?'

'No such luck,' Schulze grumbled. 'That butcher Diedenhof said I'll be fit for light duties again in a couple of weeks. You ought to have done a better job with that shitty sabre of yours. I might have ended up as a one-armed doorman in the Herbert-strasse.'[1]

1. Hamburg's famous red-light district. See *Guns at Cassino* for details of Schulze's adventures there.

'Yeah,' Matz drawled, 'and you'd be more upstairs dancing the mattress polka than downstairs doing your duty.'

Lung moaned. 'Aw shut up, you stupid bastard,' Schulze cried unsympathetically. 'Hey, Matz, where's the sauce? Don't tell me you came to visit me without any sauce?'

'The sister told me you weren't to have any booze.'

Schulze stuck up a thick thumb. 'The sister can sit her fat arse on that for all I care – where's the sauce?'

Matz reached in his battle-stained black tunic, heavy with the decorations of five years of war, and pulled out a little medicine bottle of clear liquid. 'Potato schnapps, cost a can of Old Man from one of those arseholes of kitchen bulls at the Quellenhof. It's a good gargle though. They say it'll blow the back of yer head off.'

'Give it here,' Schulze said greedily, reaching out a big paw. 'I haven't wet my tonsils for months.' He pulled the cork out with his teeth, spat it on to Gut's bed and took a great swallow of the home-brewed spirit. 'Christ on a crutch!' he breathed, gasping for breath, 'that stuff'll take the lining off'n lead coffin! But it's good.'

He took another tremendous pull at the little bottle, before Matz pulled it way from him, crying: 'Go easy, Schulze. Don't down it all by yourself. That's the last bottle of shitting schnapps in the whole shitting Wotan!'

Schulze wiped the back of his free hand across his big generous mouth and looked hard at Matz. 'Things are bad, eh?' he queried. Matz nodded. 'Watch in the pisspot, syphilis in the heart,' he said gloomily, using the old soldiers' despondent phrase. 'Shitting awful, if you ask me. The line won't last another forty-eight hours.'

'Wotan? ... The Old Man?'

'We're down to about one hundred and fifty effectives who can hold a weapon, and most of them are in a pisspoor state. The CO – he's all right. But he's like the rest of us, out on his sodding feet.'

Matz breathed out wearily and Schulze could see, despite the banter, just how worn the one-legged NCO was. 'Thank God, old Devil Donner has pulled us out of the line as his last reserve. Otherwise we'd have had the chop yesterday.' He passed the bottle back to Schulze. 'Go on, mate, you'd better have the rest of the sauce – it's probably the last of the stuff that either of us will see.'

'You are a happy little ray of sunshine,' Schulze growled and took the bottle. He finished it in a gulp and flung the empty bottle on Lung's unprotesting lap.

'All right,' he said, 'get out that damn sabre of yours!'

'Eh?' Matz said incredulously.

'You heard! Or have you been eating big beans again. Get it out and cut me free.'

'*Cut you free?*'

'What's up with you, Matz? Getting long in the tooth or something? Cut me out of this shitting gadget before the nurses come in. I'm going back to the Wotan . . .'

'All right,' Schwarz cried, his voice cracked with exhaustion, 'this is the panzerfaust. All of you take it in your right hand and place it on your right shoulder.'

Obediently the Hitler Youth boys took up their bazookas, their childish faces set and determined.

'God in flaming heaven!' Schulze breathed as they passed through the Quellenhof's battle-littered courtyard, 'they're nothing else but shitting kids, still wet behind the ears.'

'That's all we've got left,' Matz explained, keeping pace with him, as Schwarz showed the handful of boys how to load the single-shot anti-tank weapon. 'There's a whole company of them holding the line in our place. Fifty casualties they had yesterday alone.'

Schulze shook his head, but said nothing. Together they trudged up the stairs, passed a group of clerks man-handling the pieces of a 20-mm flak cannon to the second floor. 'Mind you don't rupture yourselves,' Schulze said, contemptuous of the office workers confronted with the prospect of action at last. 'Hate to see you pen-pushers hurt yourselves.'

The frightened clerks, their shabby grey uniform jackets black with sweat under the armpits, did not answer.

'Unsociable buggers,' Schulze growled, biting his lip suddenly with the pain of his shoulder.

'You've got to excuse them, Schulze,' Matz explained. 'They're already creaming their knickers – and they've not even had a sniff of gunpowder yet.'

They marched the length of the second floor. Everywhere Donner's staff – officers and men – were preparing the place for the coming siege, smashing what glass was left in the windows, lugging sandbags back and forth, setting up machine-gun posts, placing fire-buckets of sand at strategic places, spraying the ceiling with water from stirrup pumps to lower the danger of fire and the choking dust, once the artillery bombardment started hitting the place from the newly captured hills.

Schulze pointed to a red-faced, gross paymaster in his shirt-sleeves, hauling cases of 20-mm ammunition into position. 'Does my heart good to see rear-line stallions like that working, especially those broad-arsed paymasters. Owe me a packet those bastards do.'

'Well, don't worry about trying to collect it now, Schulze,' Matz grunted. 'Because where we're going, once the balloon goes up, we won't be needing any Marie[1] – just bits of wood to keep the shitty fire going.'

Schulze laughed grimly. Together they limped on.

'Well, as I live and breathe,' Colonel von Dodenburg breathed, as they entered the weapon-littered room and snapped to attention as if they were back at Sennelager and not in the middle of a battlefield, 'Sergeant-Major Schulze!' His tired face broke into smile. 'Stand at ease, both of you.' He stretched out his hand. 'Good to see you again, you waterfront rascal!' They shook hands. 'How's the arm?'

Schulze shrugged then wished he hadn't. 'The wing, sir? A little fish. No problem whatsoever. But I doubt if I'll ever lift two hundredweight of flour at the docks again.'

'You probably never did anyway. But you'll get a pension from a grateful Fatherland in due course, never fear.'

'I'd rather have a one-way ticket to South America, sir, especially at this moment.'

Von Dodenburg sat down heavily and indicated they should seat themselves on the case of Schmeisser ammunition. 'I know what you mean, Schulze. I think we'd all like one of those tickets at the moment.'

'How is the situation, sir?' Schulze asked, examining the CO's pale, exhausted face.

'In a word, Schulze – shitty.'

'And the drill?'

'That's a question only the Gods can answer – and naturally, the supreme god of all – SS Police General Donner . . .'

On the afternoon of October 20th, Devil Donner answered that particular question. A runner, gasping with the strain of cover-

1. SS slang for money.

ing the terrible, shell-swept three hundred metres that now separated the Quellenhof from the front line, stumbled into von Dodenburg's CP in the cellar of a wrecked store and panted: 'Sir, you're wanted immediately at General Donner's HQ.' He sat down abruptly on the nearest ammunition crate and gasped: 'Watch how you go, sir – there's all hell loose up there.'

When von Dodenburg, followed by Matz and a red-faced gasping Schulze, had safely crossed the main road leading to the Quellenhof and were out of the direct fire of the Ami cannon located on the three heights, he saw what the young runner meant. A hysterical mob of dirty civilians and what were obviously deserters from the line filled the streets, screaming and gesticulating. Roughly they pushed their way through them and the mob gave way reluctantly. They turned a corner. Another crowd was dragging a fat naked man along on a wheelbarrow. His hands were tied behind his back and there was a large placard hung round his neck. On it, in crude black letters, was written: 'NAZI SWINE.' A fat-breasted woman in a dirty flowered apron came up from one of the cellars and threw the contents of a chamber pot in the former official's face.

'Fat brown bastard!'[1] the woman cried. 'Now we'll settle with you lot at last!'

Matz raised his machine-pistol angrily, but von Dodenburg knocked down the muzzle, and shook his head. A little farther on two ragged men with the yellow letters EAST painted on the backs of their jackets, indicating they were slave labourers recruited in the territories once occupied by the Germans there, were busy burrowing into the basement of a wrecked house, obviously looking for something to loot. Again Matz looked at the CO inquiringly, and again von Dodenburg shook his head.

He simply said, 'Too late now.'

And Schulze, bringing up the rear, knew what he meant. The defence of Aachen had virtually collapsed. Now it was every man for himself. As they turned into the entrance to the Quellenhof, avoiding the huge new shell-craters everywhere, the mob had begun burning swastika flags behind them.

Donner was standing looking out of the glassless window in exactly the same position as when von Dodenburg had first met him, in what seemed another age. Slowly, he turned, a cynical

1. Brown here means 'Nazi', because of the brownshirts worn by the first National Socialists.

smile on his ruined face. 'I believe they call it rats leaving the sinking ship, eh, von Dodenburg,' he said wearily and slumped in his chair, indicating that the young officer should sit too.

'You mean—'

'Yes, that mob out there.' He took out his eye and cleaned it. 'I've seen it all before. In 1918 when the civilians stabbed the fighting army in the back. Suddenly they were all democrats, had never wanted war, had been forced to fight.' He put back his eye absently. *'Canaille!'*

There was a sudden silence, broken only by the persistent thunder of the Ami guns and the rattle of the horse-drawn ambulances, bringing ever new casualties to the eleven surgeons working in the hotel's cellar, their rubber aprons and boots awash with blood.

Donner was finished, von Dodenburg could see that. His one eye was sunk deep in his skull, which was not unlike the silver death's head badge adorning his collar, and a nerve twitched uncontrollably on the good side of his ruined face. The seconds passed leadenly. Then suddenly, Donner pushed a piece of paper lying on his dust-covered desk towards von Dodenburg.

'A blitz,'[1] he said tonelessly. 'Came in from the Führer's Head-quarters thirty minutes ago.'

'Should I read it, sir?' von Dodenburg asked. A blitz was usually reserved for general officers only.

Donner nodded wearily. 'Yes, it concerns Wotan.'

Von Dodenburg picked it up and read:

'Immediate and urgent.
'By officer only!
To SS and Police General Degenhardt Donner.
Order immediate withdrawal of Battle Group SS Wotan, com-mander Col. von Dodenburg, from Aachen front. Rejoin 1st SS Division Adolf Hitler Bodyguard in Führer Reserve at once.

Signed Jodl (Col. General).'

Von Dodenburg felt a sudden surge of hope at this oppor-tunity to get out of the Aachen death trap, yet also an unpleasant sensation of running out on Donner, whom he had come to like and admire over these last terrible weeks.

He put the blitz down carefully and asked: 'What does it mean, sir?'

1. An army signal roughly equivalent to the British 'top priority'.

'I don't think one needs a lawyer to interpret it, von Dodenburg. Your ruffians of the Wotan are probably going to escape the Aachen débâcle with a whole skin. That sly bastard of a Colonel General Jodl obviously wants you for some glorious new venture – and Jodl is impatient of delay. You are to go – and go at once.'

'And Aachen, sir?'

Donner did not answer at once. Below, some boy or other – perhaps one of the Hitler Youth – was screaming for his mother as they carried him into the operating theatre. He shrugged. 'Aachen is a matter of history now. It will last a few hours at the most. Your Wotan won't make any difference.'

Vainly von Dodenburg tried to find the words to express his emotions. 'But we can't go just like that, General – why, I've lost nearly a thousand men from my Wotan here. I can't . . .' His voice trailed away, as he saw that the man opposite was not really listening to him any more.

Donner nodded, as if the young officer had just made some casual remark about the state of the weather. 'I shall be glad to stay here and die,' he said. 'All these years – the struggle for power in the twenties, the rebirth of Germany in the thirties, the war—' he flung out his blackened claw of a hand wearily – 'all to end like this, with the mob fighting in the streets of Germany's most holy city – a German mob.' He looked directly at von Dodenburg. 'It was all for nothing – all that effort, all that sacrifice, all that blood!'

'But we can't give up, sir!' von Dodenburg protested with what energy he had left.

'One can – one can,' Donner said, rising stiffly to his feet and walking over to the shattered window once more. With his back to von Dodenburg, his face hollowed out even more by the ruddy light of the flames below, he said slowly: 'There was an Austrian – a Jew to boot, if I am not mistaken – who wrote a long time ago, "In the time of the sinking sun, dwarfs cast shadows like giants." The sun is going down, von Dodenburg, and I do not want to live in the time of the dwarfs.' He turned and thrust out his good hand. 'My dear von Dodenburg, as one war criminal,' he chuckled throatily, 'to another, may I wish you the best of luck.'

Stiffly von Dodenburg took the hand. It was icy cold, as if its owner were already dead. 'Thank you, sir.' He hesitated. 'And what will you do, General?'

174

Donner clapped his crippled claw of a hand on his pistol holster. 'The soldier's way out, von Dodenburg.' He straightened up into the position of attention. 'Colonel von Dodenburg, goodbye and Heil Hitler!'

Von Dodenburg clicked his heels together and flung up his right arm in salute. 'Thank you, sir. Heil Hitler!'

Devil Donner's eye gleamed. Then he bent his head in his hands; von Dodenburg was forgotten already. It was all over now.

SEVEN

'There's no way out, sir,' the young officer said hopelessly and slumped on the ration case, his face and uniform white with dust from the rubble. With a sigh of relief, he let his machine-pistol clatter to the floor. Von Dodenburg could see he was exhausted from the reconnaissance mission.

'Bring him a cup of nigger sweat, Schulze,' he ordered.

The big NCO nodded and with his good hand poured the officer out a cup of ersatz coffee from the big enamel bucket kept permanently boiling in the corner. Lieutenant Kleinbier, who had carried out a personal recce to try to find an escape route to the north or east, cradled the red-hot canteen cup gratefully between his two hands and sipped at the bitter black fluid.

Von Dodenburg gave him a few minutes. Outside, only a hundred metres away from their cellar, an Ami 3-inch mortar opened up. The cellar shuddered. Plaster started to drift from the ceiling like snow. 'All right, Kleinbier,' von Dodenburg said firmly above the roar, 'let me have your report, please.'

The young officer pulled himself together. 'Naturally sir, the OPs[1] on the three heights have got the whole area to our front covered, except when the gunsmoke gives us some protection. During daylight hours, we haven't got a hope in hell of getting out unobserved. In addition, they're massing between the Wingertsberg and the Salvatorberg. I couldn't get too close, but I could hear the rattle of tracked vehicles and they're laying down a smoke screen. So it's pretty clear what they're up to there.'

'And the sewers?' von Dodenburg interjected harshly, wishing the young officer would get to the point, for time was running out.

1. Observation posts.

'Blocked and filled permanently with some sort of gas,' he said despondently, letting the empty canteen dangle down between his mud-stained knees. 'For what my opinion is worth, sir, I think we've had it – there's no way out.'

Schwarz looked as if he were going to protest. But von Dodenburg shook his head. Kleinbier was like most of his men – absolutely exhausted, out on his feet, kept going simply by the Wotan spirit, living off nervous energy. He bent over the blood-stained map of his position. His force had been crowded into an area of two hundred square metres of ruins and rubble set along a line of what had once been the Monheimsallee behind the Quellenhof. On both sides the Amis were crowding in on him down the Krefeld and Julich strassen. It was obvious that the Amis pushing up from the rear via the Peterstrasse would co-ordinate their attack, with the final push coming from between the two heights. It was obvious too that it would be only a matter of hours before that final push came. Probably at dawn, he told himself; the Ami generals were not very imaginative about the time of their attacks; they always seemed to stick to the old dawn routine.

He stared at the map while the others crowded in the tight, candlelit cellar, watched him tensely, wondering how their CO was going to get them out of the trap. There must be a way out, he told himself. There had to be – over one hundred and fifty men's lives depended upon it.

Suddenly he remembered what his old tactics teacher had told them at the SS Officer Academy at Bad Tolz before the war: 'When faced with an impossible situation, gentlemen, there is only one way out – to disappear up your own arsehole – somewhat smartly! You don't just wait on your fat bottoms for the enemy to attack. How do you do it? You attack into the centre of the enemy's attack force and, if you're lucky, disappear before he can recover. The disadvantage – you hit the full weight of the enemy. The advantage – you catch him with his knickers down.'

Thus the long-dead Major von Arnheim. But how did one apply his 'disappearing arsehole tactic', as he had called it to the present desperate situation? *How?* Von Dodenburg racked his brains, while the cellar rocked to the Ami fire.

'Kleinbier,' he broke his silence, 'come over here and look at the map. Here.' He pointed to the green shaded area to the right of the Wingertsberg near the Julichstrasse, which he estimated would be the extreme left flank of the coming Ami attack. 'What did you see there?'

The young officer's face, which had brightened when von Dodenburg had called him, fell again. 'No good, sir—'

'I'm not asking your opinion, Kleinbier,' von Dodenburg snapped angrily, 'just what you saw.'

'Sorry, sir, a minefield, sir, one of our own, which has fallen into the enemy's hands. It's covered by machine-gun nests – here, here and here.'

'Infantry?'

'Nothing to speak of. But the Amis don't need stubble-hoppers out there. They have the mines and the machine-guns on fixed lines of fire. They wouldn't expect . . .' Kleinbier's voice trailed away, for von Dodenburg was no longer listening. He had found the arsehole he had been looking for.

The final barrage was tremendous. It had been going on unceasingly since midnight. Now to their right, where the Quellenhof lay, the sky was a dull red so that everything to their front stood out starkly. Von Dodenburg looked at the dark outlines of the wounded who had volunteered to stay behind to man the machine-guns so that the Amis would not suspect that they were abandoning their positions.

'Thank you, lads,' he whispered, 'and the best of luck!'

'You, too, sir,' answered a corporal who had lost his right leg. 'Don't worry about us. We know that the Wotan'll come back.'

Von Dodenburg felt the hot tears blind him momentarily. 'Yes, yes,' he lied hastily, 'we'll be back, lads.'

A hand reached out and clasped his. Then they set off through the smoky gloom with the burnt grass brushing against their rag-muffled boots. To their right a slow Ami machine-gun opened up. White tracer stitched the darkness. But the slugs went off into a southerly direction, way off them. A hundred metres. Two hundred. Still no enemy reaction. Suddenly they heard the alarming chink of metal on metal. They dropped as one, hearts beating like trip-hammers, sweating forefingers curled round the triggers of their weapons. For a long time they crouched there, scarcely daring to breath. Then Matz, up front with a small patrol, crawled towards them.

'All right, sir,' he whispered softly, 'Ami mg dug in about twenty metres to your right. My lads have got it covered. Just take it nice and easy and we'll get by it without trouble. The

177

Amis look as if they've got their heads down for the night.'

The mg nest with its snoring Amis was behind them. They edged their way out of the grass into a shell-shattered wood, where the twigs cracked and snapped under the muffled boots like breakfast cereal and slapped at their faces viciously when the man in front forgot to keep hold. They passed a group of their own comrades, sprawled out in a heap, arms flung about in careless abandon, the white hush of the tracer painting their dead faces in a ghastly hue. The men filing by their comrades killed in the final counter-attack carefully looked away, as if they did not want to be reminded that the same fate could well overtake them soon.

Suddenly von Dodenburg stiffened and held up his arm. 'Halt!' he hissed. Matz was barring his way, standing next to the familiar skull-and-crossbones sign with the frightening words written beneath it: 'ATTENTION – MINES!'

'We're here, sir,' Matz said unnecessarily.

'And the Ami mg nests?'

'As far as we can make out, sir, there's one immediately ahead of us, perhaps a hundred and fifty metres off, and one to the right there. Look, there it is!' Matz pointed to the sudden red blaze of muzzlefire, followed an instant later by the white morse of tracer.

'Good. Thank you, Matz.' Von Dodenburg turned round. 'All right, take cover. The volunteers up here.'

As his men dropped gratefully into the brush, the six men who had volunteered to clear the mines pushed through their comrades, bayonets at the ready. Von Dodenburg stripped off his equipment and handed it with his Schmeisser to Schulze.

'Hang on to that.'

'Be careful, sir,' Schulze said anxiously. 'If they're magnetic—' helplessly, he shrugged. 'Then good-night, Marie!'

'Don't be an old woman, Schulze,' von Dodenburg answered, with more assurance than he felt, 'All right, the rest of you follow me.'

Von Dodenburg clambered carefully over the rusty, twisted barbed wire which marked the start of the minefield and put his right foot gingerly to the ground. He pressed down, feeling the sweat spring up unpleasantly all over his body. Nothing happened. He put his other foot down. Again nothing. Drawing a deep breath, he advanced six metres, counting them out carefully, so that the first two men clambering over the wire behind him could hear. He stopped. There were three of them on the wrong side of the wire now.

'All right,' he whispered, 'this is the drill. We'll advance with myself in the middle, prodding the ground at every half a metre. If you hit a P.2S, remember it could well be wired in relay. If it's a Teller,[1] leave it.'

'And if it's a magnetic?' Kleinbier, one of the two leading volunteers, asked the question von Dodenburg dreaded.

The CO licked his dry lips. 'Stop, move back and leave it to me. I'll have a go at it. I've got nothing metallic on me. I might have a chance of defusing it.' '*Might*', a cynical little voice echoed within him. He ignored it by a sheer effort of will. 'All right,' he ordered, 'let's move out.'

Behind them the other four men waited to cross the wire. They would act as reserves and check the verges of the path cleared, just in case a mine had been overlooked.

Sweating like frightened pigs, hardly daring to breathe, each fresh step made only after what seemed an age of deliberation, they advanced in a six-metre-broad line, testing out the soft ground, pace by pace. For what appeared to be a long time, nothing happened. Von Dodenburg's heart began to react normally again. The sweat started to dry on his tense body. Then the man to his right froze.

'*Mine*,' he gasped. Behind them the reserves froze in the footsteps of the leaders.

Cautiously the volunteer who had discovered the prong of the mine protruding out of the earth, bent and began to sweep away the surface soil with the side of his hand. There was no sound save his harsh gasps as he probed the earth, the sweat pouring from his brow in streams.

'*Teller*,' he breathed in relief.

'*Shit!*' someone cursed, his voice a mixture of anger and relief. They pressed on a little faster now. They found another Teller mine and another. Von Dodenburg could see that a pattern was emerging. Whoever had laid the mines facing towards the Ami position had apparently covered the last few metres with anti-tank mines. Would that mean they would soon bump into the anti-personnel ones? Five nerve-racking minutes later, Kleinbier stopped, whispered a hoarse warning and dropped to his knees. His hands moved rapidly.

'*S-mine*,' he whispered.

1. An anti-tank mine, harmless to a foot soldier.

Von Dodenburg breathed out. The S-mine was easier to deal with than the P.2S and all his men had been trained to lay them and pick them up again. Hastily Kleinbier cleared away the soil from the surface of the little anti-personnel mine, filled with deadly steel balls which sprang out to waist height and had gained the name of 'deballocker' from the troops. Very carefully he ran his hand round its sides. Nothing. Slowly he slid his fingers underneath it to check if there were a matchbox fuse[1] lying there or a wire leading to another mine a few metres away.

'Anything?' von Dodenburg asked hoarsely.

'No,' Kleinbier answered, his voice equally hoarse, 'thank God!'

Slowly they progressed through the minefield, with the reserves playing out white tapes behind them within which the rest of the Wotan followed, tense and expectant, knowing that if the Amis spotted them now they were finished: helpless sitting ducks, crowded together in the narrow, mine-free lane driven through an open field, devoid of cover.

They bumped into a line of P.2Ss, wired in relay. They spent fifteen terrible minutes, while the volunteers took the mines apart bit by agonising bit, until they came to the thin glass detonator, which seemed to slip about in their sweaty fingers, as if it were covered in fine grease.

Von Dodenburg and another couple of men took over the lead while the original two slipped to the rear, their hands trembling. Now the whole western sky was a blood red hue. What was left of Aachen in German hands was burning. From their own section of the front, the machine-gun fire had ceased now. But they had no time to reflect on the fate of their wounded comrades; their own situation was too desperate. Von Dodenburg stopped suddenly. A cold shudder of fear ran through him. His fingers had touched the glass dome of a magnetic mine! He opened his lips to utter a warning. No sound came. He licked them and swallowed hard.

'Magnetic,' he croaked, 'get back!'

The other two backed hurriedly. Behind them the advance came to a ragged halt.

'Take it easy, sir,' Schulze's voice floated forward urgently.

Praying that he had nothing metal on him still, von Dodenburg's fingers groped around the glass dome. 'As if you were up

1. A spring-loaded fuse shaped like a book of matches. Once the pressure is released, the spring activates the fuse.

your beloved's knickers,' their instructor at mine school had explained the technique coarsely. It came up. Slowly . . . slowly, he began to turn it to the left. One slip and the whole thing would go up in his face.

The sweat was dripping from his brow now, almost blinding him. Hardly daring to breathe, he held on to the glass dome with his right hand. Carefully he reached out his left hand, his fingers trembling wildly, feeling as clumsy and as thick as pork sausages, and ran it around the mine. Nothing! Still holding on to the dome, he tried to force his hand underneath the mine. He couldn't!

'Anything wrong, sir?' Kleinbier asked urgently.

'Ach, hold your water!' he snapped angrily, his nerves almost at breaking point now. He bent down so that his face touched the damp grass. With his teeth, he began to tear away tufts of it, pressing down on the edge of the mine with his chin. It started to move. The fingers of his left hand moved underneath it, seeking fearfully for other wires, booby traps, knowing now that if the mine went off it would blow his face apart. Millimetre by millimetre they crept forward, meeting no opposition – no wire, no fuse-plug, no book-match fuse. Nothing.

For a moment he lay there, all energy drained out of him. Then he deliberately pulled himself together. With agonising slowness, he drew the mine out to reveal it in all its man-made ugliness. For a moment he longed to give it a great kick and send it flying. But there was no time for such outbursts of emotional relief. Carefully, he placed it to one side, as far as his arms would reach.

Spitting out earth and grass, he called sharply, 'Get that marker tape up here on the double, will you!'

The volunteers moved forward quickly.

'Kleinbier, get that mine out of the way!'

'Sir!'

Their snail-like progress began again while Kleinbier picked up the mine and let the hushed troopers slip by him, their eyes averted from the deadly little instrument. The lieutenant laughed drily.

'Don't look like that, lads,' he said softly, 'It can't harm you now. It's just a ten-pound piece of useless scrap—'

Lieutenant Kleinbier, nineteen years of age, handsomely blond, with the body of a professional athlete who had never had a girl in all his life, suddenly erupted in a terrible violet burst of flame. The thick crump came a fraction of a section later. His face shattered and he disintegrated. Blood, bone and flesh flew everywhere.

'*Over there!*' a frantic voice screamed in English. 'In the cruddy minefield!'

An American machine-gun started to chatter. Tracer cut the night wildly. Lead sprayed the minefield. Another mg joined from the right, its fire more accurate. A soldier behind von Dodenburg clapped his hand to his shoulder suddenly and went down screaming. Von Dodenburg came to life.

'Damn the mines!' he roared. 'Run for it!'

Completely unarmed, he began to pelt towards the Ami positions. The men hesitated. Before them lay twenty metres or so of uncleared minefield.

'Come on,' Schulze yelled angrily, '*Move, you dogs, do you want to live for ever?*'

The cruel exhortation had its effect. They stumbled forward. Another mine exploded, scattering bodies everywhere. It didn't stop them. All around von Dodenburg, his men were stumbling, falling, sobbing with fear, as they pelted towards the flash of the mgs, which indicated both death and safety. A round Ami grenade hissed through the air towards him. He dodged like a startled horse. It went off behind him and flung him in a crater, lined with two of his men, heads hanging limp, their guts ripped open and spilled out. His hands were bathed to the wrists in the bloody mess. He sprang up, screaming, following his panic-stricken men.

An Ami helmet loomed up. Someone kicked the GI in the face. He reeled back screaming. The nearest mg swung round on them. A line of troopers were mown down.

'Don't leave me . . . please, don't leave me,' a frightened voice pleaded. 'PLEASE—' Then they were in the American line, kicking, slashing, stabbing, shooting in a crazed frenzy of fear and rage. It was all over in a matter of seconds. Nothing could stand up to that terrible attack. A minute later, the survivors had broken through and were running leaden-lunged towards the east and safety.

EIGHT

At four o'clock on the morning of October 21st while the survivors of the Wotan were fleeing eastwards behind the Ami lines, an event took place which indirectly saved them. A telephone call came from the Petit Trianon at Versailles, Eisenhower's new Supreme Headquarters, and it was from his Chief-of-Staff, redhaired, ulcer-ridden Bedell Smith.

'Listen, Courtney,' he told Hodges, who had been awakened at his Spa HQ to take the call, 'sorry to get you up like this, but we've just heard here that Congress is considering Ike for his fifth star.'

General Hodges was awake immediately. 'His fifth!' he exclaimed. 'He'll be the first since Black Jack!'[1]

'Yeah,' Beatle said shortly, feeling his ulcers begin to act up again. 'Well, it'd look good if your doughs took Aachen – *as of now.*'

'Of course, Beatle,' Hodges agreed. 'I understand. Will do – and say – give my regards to Ike.'

'Will do,' Beatle said drily, telling himself that even army commanders fought their battles these days with one eye over their shoulders looking at the publicity boys.

Hodges got on to Lightning Joe at once. 'I'm sorry to get you up, Joe', he apologised, as courteous as ever.

'You didn't, sir. I was up. We're attacking at dawn, sir in the Aachen sector.'

'That's what I'm calling you about, Joe. I want you to get Clarence to release another regiment to Seitz – at once. I want Aachen taken – and I want it taken this morning.'

'We could do it with Seitz's 26th.'

'I'm not so sure, Joe. At all events, I want to be certain. Remember that the folks back home must be getting a little tired of this Aachen business. It's been going on for nearly two months now.'

Lightning Joe told the 'folks back home' what they could do

1. The reference is to General Pershing, US commander in World War I, who was nicknamed Black Jack because he had once commanded Negro troops and became a 5-star general in 1919.

with their opinions. But to the Commander of the First Army, he said : 'I understand. I'll see to it, sir.'

'Thank you, Joe.'

Within five minutes Hodges was back in bed on the second floor of Spa's Hotel Britannique, where the Kaiser had once had his HQ in the old war when Hodges had been a humble infantry captain bogged down in the mud of France. In another five minutes he was fast asleep. But now the First Army's communications had started to hum. Hurried telephone calls were made. Dispatch riders sprang to their machines. Orders were rapped out. Tense, weary, frightened men were roused out of their billets. Trucks roared into life, filling the dawn with the stink of gasoline. Half-warmed hash cans were handed out hurriedly. The wheels began to roll.

And in the confusion caused by the move of a whole infantry regiment into the 26th's sector, Colonel von Dodenburg and his handful of gasping survivors, bent, coughing and choking like a bunch of asthmatic old men, slipped through the ring held by the Big Red One and their comrades of Roosevelt's Butchers. Half an hour later they were moving cautiously down a tree-lined country road when a thin child's voice cried : 'Halt – who goes there?' Without waiting for an answer, their challenger fired. Matz gasped sharply and went down on one knee.

'What's up?' Schulze cried.

'The silly bastard shot me in the leg – my wooden one,' Matz cried angrily and tugged off the remains of his shattered stump, as a kid of perhaps sixteen appeared from behind a tree. He was clad in Hitler Youth uniform and carried a huge Lebel French rifle, dating from the turn of the century.

'What the hell did you do that for?' von Dodenburg cried. 'You're supposed to wait for an answer to the challenge before you act !'

'The corporal didn't tell me, sir,' the boy said, looking hang-dog. 'And I thought you were the Amis.'

Von Dodenburg's anger gave way to relief. Playfully he clapped the boy about the neck and grinned. 'Remember it the next time – the Führer's short enough of soldiers as it is, without the Hitler Youth killing them. Now, where's your HQ?'

But before the Hitler Youth could reply, Schwarz said : 'Sir – listen !'

Von Dodenburg spun round. 'Listen to what . . . I can't hear anything?'

'That's just it,' the major said urgently. 'There's no sound coming from Aachen!'

Von Dodenburg caught his breath. Schwarz was right. To their rear, the sky was red with flames, but there was no sound from the place where his men had fought and died for so long. The Holy City of Aachen had fallen.

At dawn a curtain of silence fell on the burning city. All that the tense GIs pushing their way up the littered streets could hear was the steady crackle of the flames, interrupted now and again by the crash of falling masonry as yet another shell-shattered ruin collapsed. Their enemies for so long had vanished, save for their dead sprawled in the dirty gutters like bundles of abandoned rags. Al and Benny broke away from the rest of the company and slipped by the red-raw, burned-out hulk of one of Wotan's Tigers, from which hung the obscene travesty of rags and bones which had once been an SS lieutenant.

'Round the back,' Benny said urgently, 'before the greedy bastards of F company get their dirty paws on the loot.'

Al nodded. Slinging his carbine and wincing with the pain of his torn shoulder where the Kraut dame had ripped panic-stricken at his flesh, he pushed his way into the rear entrance of the Hotel Quellenhof. Benny followed, grease-gun at the ready.

The former HQ was a shambles. Dead German officers lay everywhere among the bullet-pocked gilt furniture, and not all of them had been killed by Seitz's infantry. In front of a shattered wall mirror, a fat major lay dead, a pistol clasped in his nerveless fingers, half the side of his face blown away. While Benny covered him, Al looted the body expertly, stuffing the man's German Cross in Gold and Iron in his pocket, thrusting his Walther in his belt.

'Fifty bucks' worth at least,' Benny chortled. 'Check his teeth, Al.'

The tall GI thrust open the man's stiffening jaws. Something at the back glinted. Swiftly he inserted the dental forceps he had looted in France and tugged. The gold tooth came out easily. He dropped it into the bagful of gold teeth which Benny held ready to his feet.

'Okay, let's check the upstairs.'

Outside the men of F Company were breaking down the main door of the hotel. Hastily they clambered up the littered stairs. The corridor was filled with empty champagne bottles. Benny idly kicked a couple of them, just in case they might be full. One was. But he didn't pick it up. They had been caught like that before – just outside Verviers – when the bottle turned out to be filled with the urine of some fleeing Kraut soldier who had greatly fancied himself as a comedian.

'Over here, Benny,' Al rapped. 'Cover me.' He hesitated at the door to Donner's office. 'NOW!' He smashed his foot against the door. It flew open. Benny raised his grease-gun. But there was no need to fire. The man in the black uniform, slumped back against the high chair, was dead.

'Jesus,' Benny said in disgust, 'will you get a load of that Kraut's kisser!'

'And will ya get a load of that Knight's Cross at his throat,' Al breathed, unmoved by the dead man's mutilated face. 'Worth all of sixty bucks in Pig Alley. Come on – quick!'

They pushed into the room, heavy with the bitter-almond smell of the cyanide capsule with which Donner had poisoned himself. Al snatched at the Knight's Cross. Donner's body began to slump to the floor, while Al stowed the precious decoration away.

'Check his choppers, Benny,' he ordered.

The private hesitated. 'I don't know, Al,' he said. 'That mug he's got turns my guts.'

'Then get the hell outa my way,' Al snorted and pushed him to one side. He pushed open Donner's jaw. 'Nix,' he announced. 'All false!' He ran his hands expertly over the black uniform. But he found nothing save a wallet which contained cards and a few grubby Reichmark notes. He dropped them in disgust. The boys were already using hundred-mark notes as latrine paper. For a moment he stared at Donner's mutilated face. Then he spotted the artificial eye. 'Hey, Benny,' he exclaimed, 'the Kraut's got a glass peeper!' He pressed his dirty fingers against the scarred cheek.

'What ya gonna to do?'

'What the hell do you think?' he grunted. 'He might have diamonds or something like that hidden behind it.' But the blood-red cavity was bare. 'Sonavabitch!' he cursed. 'All that fuss and feathers for goddam nothing!'

In a sudden fit of rage he tore open his flies while Benny stared at him open-mouthed.

'Jes-zus, Al, you're not gonna piss on him, are ya?'

'You betcha!'

186

Thus Devil Donner, whose soul was now undoubtedly on its way to hell, was subjected to the final indignity.

'Everybody out,' Schwarz croaked.

Obediently they stumbled from the big open Opel trucks which had brought them to the Führer's new HQ in the Hessian Hills, whence he would direct the last great offensive in the west.

They were utterly weary. Leather belts and equipment had bit deeply into their bare flesh under the fraying remains of their black tunics. Their feet, without socks or foot-rags, had been rubbed red-raw in their torn, rotting dice-beakers, during their long march through the Rhineland. Slowly they formed up with their battered weapons, the blood speeding through the paper bandages covering their wounds, while elegant staff officers, all monocles, gleaming, bespurred riding boots, immaculate cavalry breeches complete with the broad crimson stripe of the Greater General Staff, stared at them as if they were creatures from another world.

'Look at the pansy currant-crappers,' Schulze grunted wearily, 'popped up from their gold-plated bunkers to see what a front swine really looks like.'

Matz, supporting himself on a rifle, his wooden leg slung over his shoulder, spat drily on the cobbles. 'One wet fart,' he announced contemptuously, 'and yer'd kill the lot!'

Von Dodenburg, helmetless, his tunic, the buttons removed for the mine-clearing, tied with a safety pin, walked stiffly to the front of his men. Schwarz, a bandage round his head, stood to attention, the eager fanaticism gone from even his dark eyes.

'Parade – parade attention!' he commanded.

Wearily the veterans of Wotan came to a semblance of the attention position. Schwarz shuffled forward and touched his hand to his bandaged head. 'Two officers, seven NCOs and seventy men present, sir,' he said.

'Thank you, Schwarz,' von Dodenburg returned the salute. He was just about to command his men to stand at ease, when the two black Horchs swung into the courtyard of the Führer Headquarters.

'The Reich Heini,'[1] Schulze whispered hastily, 'complete with some real soldiers.' He nodded at the two-metre-tall giants of Himmler's bodyguard, who were springing out in their imma-

1. A contemptuous name given to Reichführer SS Heinrich Himmler.

187

culate black uniform, machine-pistols at the alert even before the Horchs had come to a stop.

Von Dodenburg presented the parade to Himmler, the former chicken-farmer who had become the most feared man in Europe. The Chief of the SS nodded casually, his sickly pale face buried in his upturned greatcoat collar, the tip of his nose red and dripping. Slowly he inspected the men, stopping here and there to ask a question, but not waiting to listen to the answer. For a moment he paused in front of Schulze's massive, bandaged bulk, looked at his Knight's Cross, and muttered something about, 'as long as we are biologically superior, we shall win', before passing on.

Out of the corner of his mouth, Schulze whispered to Matz: 'What the fuck does he think I am – a shitty bull or something?'

But Matz was unable to reply. For the great door leading to the main building was opening to reveal the unmistakable brown-booted figure of the Führer's 'grey eminence' Martin Bormann. The Führer was coming!

Von Dodenburg commanded 'eyes front'. Himmler got out of the way, hastening to meet the Führer, a cold smile on his thin face. The men of Wotan straightened up. It was nearly two years now since the veterans had been honoured by the presence of the Führer. Bormann turned, as if he were having actively to encourage the German Leader to emerge into the cold, grey October morning. Then the expectant SS men saw why.

In the two years that had passed since they had last seen the man who had once been master of Europe from the Urals to the Channel, he had changed dramatically. Now he was a stooped figure with a pale, puffy face, dragging one leg behind him, vainly trying to conceal the acute trembling of his hands.

'Jesus, Maria, Joseph!' Matz breathed, *'is that the Führer?'*

Shakily, he allowed himself to be lead by the squat figure of his secretary until he was facing Wotan, his sick, old man's face almost buried in his greatcoat collar. He ignored von Dodenburg's salute. His glazed rheumy eyes were fixed on his men's faces. Slowly a tear began to trickle down his face, as if he were overcome by the sight which revealed just how much his soldiers were suffering at the front.

Bormann, his fat chest bare of any decoration save that of the Blood Order,[1] wiped it away and whispered in his coarse Meck-

1. Awarded to those who had shed their blood or suffered imprisonment for the Nazi cause before Hitler's take-over of power in 1933.

lenburg accent, 'The speech, my Führer – the speech.'

Adolf Hitler nodded his head numbly and wet his lips. 'German soldiers! Front fighters! Comrades!' he began hoarsely, his voice pitched so low that the men of the rear rank had to strain their ears to understand. He hesitated abruptly, and looked at Bormann, as if he sought encouragement or advice from him. Bormann nodded and gave a faint smile. Hitler clasped his hands together as if perhaps to control their trembling. 'If Germany loses this war, comrades, it will have proved itself biologically inferior and will have forfeited its future existence. But . . . it is the West that is forcing us to fight to the end . . .'

His voice began to grow in strength, as he warmed to his theme and von Dodenburg felt a trace of the old magic, but only a trace.

'It is, therefore, fitting that the West should be punished for this dastardly crime. And you and I will ensure that they are punished. Since September every step has been taken to raise a strong western front. Countless new units have replaced our losses in France. Colossal artillery forces have been raised. New, secret and terrible weapons are in place.' His hoarse Upper Austrian voice rose suddenly to the mesmeric height it had once achieved in the heady, great days of the pre-war Nuremberg Rallies and von Dodenburg felt a cold thrill of recognition. 'Thanks to your heroic actions at Aachen, Great Germany is now in a position to pay the West back – those Judeo-plutocrats, whose hands are steeped in the blood of innocent German women and children. At this hour, the eyes of the German nation are upon you, my brave fighters of Wotan, relying on your steadfastness, your ardour, your arms and your heroism to smother the dastardly Anglo-Americans in a sea of blood!'

The Führer broke off suddenly, an almost guilty look on his face, now flecked pink with the effort of speaking.

A few moments later, von Dodenburg knew why. Just before the Führer went inside again, supported by Bormann, he clasped both von Dodenburg's hands in his, genuine tears of emotion in his faded eyes. 'Colonel, I thank you,' he whispered. 'Germany thanks you. You and your heroic soldiers have done the impossible. Aachen was not a defeat. You held the enemy long enough there for us to plan a new blow against him – a great new blow which will be the turning point of this bloody war. The new offensive in the west.' His faded eyes bored into von Dodenburg's face with a faint trace of their old hypnotism. 'Do you understand?'

'A new offensive in the west, my Führer?' von Dodenburg repeated.

'Yes.' Hitler lowered his voice, as if he were afraid of being overheard. 'Yes, von Dodenburg. Before the year is out we shall strike again. You and your brave men, plus the many eager new recruits who will join their ranks soon, will have the honour of leading that great attack.'

He stopped abruptly and stared at the officer, as if he expected von Dodenburg to say something. But all the bemused young Colonel could ask was: 'Where, my Führer?'

Adolf Hitler's face cracked into the parody of a conspiratorial grin: 'Where? Why where those American gangsters least expect us – *the Ardennes!*'

And then he was gone, shuffling back to the warmth of his HQ guided by a solicitous Bormann, as if he were an old, old man, who had had his breath of fresh air for this day and who had now to be led back to the comforting atmosphere of his seat near the stove.

And in the officers' latrine, from which the two senior Wotan NCOs had hurriedly flushed out a group of elegant staff officers by means of two juicy farts and a massive discharge of what Schulze called 'green smoke', Schulze and Matz squatted in silence and stared at each other across the passage.

Outside, the rest of the Wotan men were wolfing down sausage and sauerkraut from Reich Leader Bormann's own kitchen. But Matz and Schulze were too weary even to be tempted by the best meal Wotan had eaten in many weeks.

'You know, Schulze, old horse,' Matz said, too exhausted to strain, content just to slump there on the scrubbed wooden boards and ruminate, 'a crap like this in a proper thunder-box, instead of balancing your arse on a pole between two ration crates, is one of the finest things in the world – even better than dipping yer wick sometimes.'

Schulze nodded morosely, only half listening. 'What we gonna do, Matz?' he asked.

'What do you mean, Schulze?'

'What do you think I mean, you cripple of a marmalade-shitter?' he snorted. 'How long are we gonna stand this? Getting slaughtered like this, reformed with a bunch of green beaks from the Hitler Youth, still wet behind the spoons, and then getting slaughtered again. It can't go on for ever, can it?'

Matz opened his mouth slowly. But he never answered the question, any more than anyone else did in the Third Reich during that fifth year of total war. There was no answer then to that question. Outside the same old whistles started to shrill. Schwarz rapped out orders. There was a rattle of mess-tins, followed by the survivors' groans of protest. Schulze rose wearily, pulling up his worn black trousers.

'Come on, Matz,' he said, his voice full of resignation. 'Get up, yer've had yer crap. Duty calls.'

Von Dodenburg, his thin handsome face grim and hard at the knowledge of what lay before him once his Battle Group had been reformed with the eager volunteers from the Hitler Youth, placed himself at the head of his ragged, bloody men.

'Battle Group Wotan,' he snapped: *'Battle Group Wotan – forward march!'*

Marching behind the CO, knowing that everything was hopeless, yet proud of the handful of weary young veterans who made up the Wotan, Sergeant-Major Schulze bellowed in that tremendous voice of his: *'A song!'*

'A song – one, two, three!' sang out the lead singer, a tall youth marching in the front rank, his arm in a bloody sling: *'Blow the bugle, beat the drum—'*

The survivors of the Battle for Aachen, their eyes sunk deep in their emaciated faces, marching off to new quarters and new tasks, burst into their brutal song as one:

> 'Blow the bugle, beat the drum!
> Clear the street, here comes the Wo-tan!
> Steel is our weapon
> To hew through bone.
> Blood our purpose,
> Wotan hold close.
> For Death is our Destiny.'

Then they were gone, leaving the silence echoing behind them.

GL 22/2/06